My Cousin, the Werewolf
From the found Zion Kennedy Journals

My Cousin, the Werewolf
From the found Zion Kennedy Journals

By *Mark T. Sneed*

Table of Content

DEDICATION

To my mother, family and friends who continue to inspire, encourage, and challenge me to be a better person, even when no one is around.

THANK YOU

To all the unsung dreamers, visionaries, believers, questioners, who possess the faith and belief in their convictions despite what others try to shout down. Know anything is impossible. Thank you for attempting to prove your beliefs, dreams, and ideas not to spite but to enlighten those of what a distinct perspective and trust can manifest in the world of possibilities.

My Cousin, the Werewolf
From the found Zion Kennedy Journals

My Cousin, the Werewolf
From the found Zion Kennedy Journals
By Mark T. Sneed

Preface.

Class had been dismissed for lunch and as the room cleared, I sat at my desk. I did not move. I did not want to leave the safety of the classroom. In the classroom, I was away from harm and bullying. Missus Fields, my teacher, had said that I could have lunch here anytime I wanted. I liked that.

Missus Fields sat at her desk at the front of the classroom and prepared to have her lunch. She was dressed in light blue sweater and her hair fell in loose curls below her ears. She looked like she had a lot on her mind. School was coming to a welcome end and Missus Fields was dating or dealing with someone she was dating. As she sat at her desk, she pulled out her cellphone and texted someone several times, waiting for a reply. I looked away from my teacher.

I bent down to grab my lunch from my backpack and noticed, just a desk away from me Sabrina Springer was still at her desk. She was one of the cute girls in class. That day she was dressed in a yellow top and a blue and white checked skirt. On her feet were Nikes. Sabrina was wearing her hair in two long braids that fell to her small shoulders.

As I sat up, with my lunchbox in hand, I noticed Sabrina biting her lower lip. She seemed upset.

Nicole Carlisle, her bug-eyed friend wearing jeans and basketball sneakers, seemed concerned as well. I sat at my desk and listened to the two girls talking in whispers, oblivious to my presence.

"I can't have lost it," Sabrina Springer said, clutching at her throat where her necklace had dangled earlier that day.

"Think," Nicole said, inches away from her friend. "Did you take it off during class?"

"No," Sabrina said, patting her blouse as if the necklace had fallen there.

"You sure?" Nicole asked, tilting her head with the question.

"I'm sure," Sabrina replied to Nicole.

I smiled at the conversation. I smiled, I guess because the two girls seemed genuinely concerned about each other. It was a nice moment, I thought.

Tina Miller, Sabrina's friend, pushed past my desk. She looked at me, scowled, and then concentrated on her friend.

"When was the last time you remember having it on?" Nicole asked.

"What's going on?"

"Think Sabrina lost her mother's necklace," Nicole replied.

"Should we tell Missus Fields?" Tina asked.

I shook my head. I could not help but smile.

"What is wrong with you silent Zion? Eat your lunch and stop ear hustling," Tina Miller fired back, annoyed. With Tina's raised voice Sabrina and Nicole turned and found me just a desk away from them.

"What is wrong with you silent boy?" Nicole Carlisle asked, annoyed.

"What's he doing?" Sabrina quizzed, concerned.

"You don't talk all year and suddenly you creeping on us?" Tina Miller accused.

"Creeping," Sabrina Springer said confused, her hand still at her neck.

"I know where your necklace is," I voiced aloud to Sabrina.

"You can talk?" Sabrina Springer said, puzzled.

I smiled weakly.

"You have it?" Nicole asked, menacingly.

I shook my head, no. I listened to the girls and tried to think what to say.

"I thought they said you were mute or something," Nicole said.

"Yeah, everyone calls you silent Zion," Tina Miller said, poking out her lower lip.

"I can't remember the last time you said more than a handful of words in a class," Nicole said, suddenly skeptical. "Is this some gag? You been playing possum?"

I shook my head, no, again. I raised a hand. "Sa--sa--selective mutism," I pronounced aloud, with a shake of my head. "I speak when I want to." I paused. "It's a phase." I took a breath. "They say I'll grow out of it."

The girls looked at me as if I was a lost puppy.

I frowned. The three girls were giving me too much attention.

"Damien Walker has your necklace. He either found it or took it before class ended. He was behind you a few minutes before the bell," I pronounced aloud as quickly and clearly as I could as the three girls listened, curious.

"You saw him?" Tina Miller asked.

"No," I voiced aloud. "I heard him tell his friends that he had a sure shot way to make you talk to him," I reported aloud. "Find Damien and you find your necklace." I smiled. "He likes you."

"He likes me?" Sabrina asked.

"That's why he is always bumping your desk and taking your pencils," I announced aloud, exhausted by the conversation. I stopped talking. I returned to my lunch box and lunch. Inside I found my bologna sandwich with cheese cut in two, an apple, cored and sliced, a punch box of juice and a small bag of pretzels.

Tina and Nicole looked at me and then Sabrina. I sat at my desk, having decided to forego lunch on the tarmac outside.

"Come on," Tina said, determined to get Sabrina's necklace back. "Let's see if that punk really has your necklace."

"If he does," Nicole began and suddenly she and Tina were at the classroom door and in the hallway. "We'll get it back."

Sabrina hesitated.

"Thanks, Zion," Sabrina Springer said, as she ran to catch up with her friends.

A few minutes later the three girls came bursting back in the classroom with Sabrina all smiles. Around her neck was the missing necklace.

"You were right," Nicole said, grudgingly.

"How did you do it?" Sabrina asked, with her necklace dangling from her neck. "I mean, you said you didn't see him take it."

I thought of all the mental exercises I had done in my head to conclude that Damien Walker had Sabrina's necklace. I had looked on the floor after hearing what was lost. I scanned the classroom. I replayed the moments before class let out. I recalled overhearing the dozens of conversations as the class was dismissed for lunch. More importantly, I recalled hearing Damien tell his friends he had a sure shot way to make Sabrina pay attention to him before he left for lunch. I had parsed the words and remembered how hard Damien tried to get Sabrina's attention. He sat on the far side of the classroom and was always on the opposite side of the class bumping into her desk, bothering her, or playing with her things. Before the bell for lunch rang Damien had gotten up from his seat and for some reason walked by my desk and stopped behind Sabrina's desk. I had put those varied and different elements together to eliminate all those things that could not be to come to a logical conclusion as to who might have Sabrina's necklace. It seemed reasonable in my head to boil all that information down to the only thing that it could be, but I didn't say any of that. Instead, I just shrugged my shoulders and ate my lunch at my desk.

"Thanks," Sabrina said.

"Yeah, thanks not so silent Zion," Tina Miller said, with a smile.

Chapter 1.

Effingham, Illinois. July.

Frankie was dressed in his werewolf costume, minus the strange cat-like head with yellow eyes, whiskers, and pointy cat-like ears. People, in and out of costume, were walking past at the Effingham Harvest Moon Festival. Some headed to the midway. Some heading to the bandstand. Others, I was sure, were heading to the corn maze. There were a lot of werewolves' costumes at the festival. It seemed an extremely popular costume choice.

"So, Michael Jackson wore this?" I asked, pointing to the cat-like head.

"No," Frankie answered. "It was a part of his Thriller video."

I shook my head. I had heard a few Michael Jackson songs, but I liked more edgy stuff like Drake and Little Weezy. I looked down at the bench and considered sitting down beside Frankie. I decided against sitting down.

"Can I talk to you?" I questioned.

"Sure," Frankie said. "About what?"

"Well, you know I found something in the field the other day where you were standing," I announced aloud.

"Okay," Frankie said after he pouted and bobbed his head.

I stood, not sure if I wanted to sit next to the sketchy brother of Paris Brooks.

"Well, I wanted to know what you know about what I found?"

"What you trying to say? You think I am mixed up in that?" Frankie asked, looking at me smugly. "If that is what you think then you got your wires crossed."

"Well," I began, cagily. I was watching Frankie. I was trying to figure if he was someone I could trust, like grandpa said. He was the wildcard in all of this. He was also the one that seemed to know the most about all of the disappearances. "What were you doing there that day?"

Frankie had his werewolf head by his side. I remained standing, watching him.

"Why?" Frankie asked, curious. He looked at me unsure. "Why you asking?"

"Well, it sort of makes sense that I would ask. Right?" I replied. "I mean I ain't saying you did or didn't do something, but I thought you might have a theory as to why that body was there."

"Well, it's funny you say it like that," Frankie said. "I do have a theory. Now, no one will hear me out, but I have a theory."

I smiled. I was not surprised by Frankie's belief that he knew something no one else might. Grandpa said that he was one of those martyrs.

"Okay, I was there because someone told me that something was in that field." Frankie paused. "But I didn't have anything to do with what you discovered. I went by to see if what I had been told was true or not."

"Who told you?" I asked curious.

Frankie did not answer. Instead, he continued on with his unexplained theory.

"So, if my theory is correct there is someone or someone's grabbing these people. Now, there could be a bunch of reasons, but I have to lean on the tried-and-true cause; jealousy."

"Who is jealous of these guys?" I asked.

"Or were these guys jealous of the someone picking them off?" Frankie asked. "And now he's getting his revenge.

I shook my head. Frankie's theory had too many holes to be believable.

"Okay, so you think it's jealousy?" I asked.

"Yes," Frankie said. "I think that's the reason there has been a missing person in Effingham every month all year," Frankie concluded.

"A flimsy reason," I replied.

"Hear me out," Frankie said. "At first, I thought the disappearances were just for publicity. You know? I mean we're in the armpit of Illinois and they are always trying to make it a place to visit. So, at first, I thought the whole werewolf thing was made up, for the thrill seekers. You know?"

I listened. I had learned not speaking much usually got more information than interrupting.

"Then, I started to think," Frankie said. "The mayor doesn't want bad publicity. He wants people to come down here and spend money." Frankie paused, thinking. "I think there's a reason, a pattern," Frankie said. "The men, most of them aren't the nicest."

"What do you mean?" I asked.

Frankie leaned forward. He almost climbed off the bench as he leaned forward.

"South-Central Illinois is not the most friendly place for people that are melanated," Frankie said, looking at me knowingly.

I frowned, uncertain.

"You know, no one wants to be labeled a racist nowadays," Frankie said. "So, they have traded in their white hoods for baseball caps and what aboutisms. They are still dangerous."

Just then there was a ruckus in the festival and Frankie stood up to see what was going on.

While I watched the people move from one side of the festival to the other Frankie slipped on his werewolf mask.

"Frankie?" I uttered aloud looking for him. He had disappeared in the surge of people. In his stead there were easily twenty people looking back frightened. Some of the people were costumed, some not in the midway. Behind them there were screams and shouts in the distance. A mummy ran by followed by a group of little green men. Two dozen people flooded into the festival midway.

"What 's going on?" I said to a girl in a costume.

"There was a fight," a girl dressed as the Black Panther said as she ran by looking for somewhere to hide.

"Someone had a gun," another person said wearing a Cardinals T-shirt and jeans.

I looked in the direction the crowd had run from. There were a handful of people, slower and older running to the Midway and looking over their shoulder as they did. I looked back where Frankie had been sitting before the crowd surge.

Three minions were standing where Frankie had been. Captain America, well someone dressed up as the first Avenger, stood on the bench behind the minions. Two Batman costumed kids ran past me, bumping me and nearly knocking me over.

There was a bunch of people suddenly in the midway. I looked for Frankie, Donny, Trey or anyone else, but everyone I knew at the festival had gone. I looked around and thought I should head back to the corn maze when Frankie appeared. Frankie, wearing his werewolf mask now, was at the head of the festival midway leading back to the darkened passage that led to the festival entrance.

I walked toward Frankie. He gestured and waved toward me. I grinned and closed the distance between Frankie and myself. Within arm's reach of the Michael Jackson inspired werewolf I stopped.

"Is everything okay?" I asked. "I mean, no gun or anything?"

Frankie bobbed his werewolf head.

I looked at my costumed cousin and frowned. Something seemed off with Frankie. I studied Frankie, confused.

"So, you think you have an idea of who's behind the disappearances?" I questioned, cautiously.

Frankie did not speak. Instead, he gestured and walked me away from the suddenly crowded Midway.

"Frankie? Where are we going?"

Frankie pushed me along a little roughly. I looked back and for the first time I felt that I was in danger.

"Frankie? What is wrong with you?" I questioned, trying to keep things light.

That was when Frankie lunged at me. He actually tried to grab me with those fake furry paws.

I dodged him and ran. I ran and thought that Frankie was trying to hurt me.

As I ran through the back of the festival with few people around that I knew I couldn't help but think that just two months before meeting Frankie my family, my mom, my sister, and I lived in Chicago.

* * * * *

Our lives changed when Mister Abraham Gilbert of Gilbert Gold and Silver Exchange went bankrupt. Mom, who worked for Abraham Gilbert for nearly two years, lost her job and her nonexistent reserves were drained instantly. Her losing her job meant as school ended for

12

summer, we lost our apartment. The first week of June, mom sat us down in our kitchen and told us the news.

"Things are going to be a little rocky this summer," Jessica Patricia Kennedy, our mom, said, sipping a freshly brewed cup of tea.

"What does that mean?" Bird, my sister, asked.

"It means that we are losing our apartment," Mom said, dressed in a sand-colored jumpsuit.

"Losing our apartment?" Bird repeated, her hands holding her egg-like head.

"Just for now," Mom said to Bird. "We're going down to my dad's and your grandpa's for the summer, so that I can figure things out," she said.

"What about if me and Zee stay with Aunt Lily or Uncle Benny?" Bird asked.

I didn't say anything knowing that Aunt Lily was trouble. She worked at a department store near downtown, but was a party girl, according to neighborhood kids. She liked to drink and go out. There was no way Mom was going to allow us to stay with her in her party apartment. Her brother, my uncle, was worse. He was a hustler. He was the black sheep of the family. Mom only allowed us to go over his house when our aunt was there.

"Not an option," Mom said, firmly. "I told you your father's side of the family and me don't get along. More importantly, neither one of them are someone I would rely on to take care of you or Zee over a weekend let alone for the summer. Besides, I want you where I am."

"This is so unfair," Bird said.

Mom agreed. She reached out to Bird. Bird pulled away. I watched silently.

"I know this seems so rushed, but for now, it's our only choice," Mom said.

"But mom," Bird said, in protest.

"No buts," Mom said. "Bird, I need you to be the big sister to Zion while I figure things out."

Bird jumped up from the kitchen table and seemed on the verge of screaming. She looked left and then right like she was lost. I watched as she turned. There were tears in her eyes.

Bo, our Chow, came padding into the kitchen curious from the raised voiced. Bo was our fluffy lion. He stood at the kitchen entrance trying to decide what to do next. He sat there watching the action. I smiled at Bo. Bo seeing me smile padded to my side and placed his big fluffy head on my lap.

I looked down and rubbed Bo's head. He kept his head there on my leg as my mom and Bird spoke.

"I'm sixteen and should have a choice," Bird said.

"I wish there was another option, baby, but there isn't, and we have to roll with the punches," Mom said.

Bird frustrated, and out of words, ran to her bedroom.

Mom stood at the kitchen table and she and I watched Bird disappear into her bedroom. Mom crossed her arms in front of her chest and then joggled her head. She placed her hands on her hips.

Me, I sat at the kitchen table thinking. Mom sat beside me and smiled lovingly.

"Zion, are you alright?" Mom asked.

"Yeah," I uttered aloud.

Mom smiled tenderly and placed a hand on mine. I looked at mom and chuckled nervously. She was, as always, this brown-skinned woman with short, curled hair that framed her big eyes and full lips. She was wearing a jumpsuit. In her ears hung dangling earrings.

"What are you thinking Zee?" Mom asked.

I wagged my head. I didn't know how to string together the words I wanted to say. So, I just wagged my head. I listened. I did not like that mom thought I was incapable of caring for myself or that she believed Bird needed to look after me. I did not argue. I simply listened.

I knew that most thought my reluctance to speak meant I couldn't speak. Some thought I was mentally challenged. Many wrote me off as being mute or having a very specific type of selective mutism. I did not. I just didn't feel the need to talk just to fill the silence.

In my head, things moved lightning quick. The words that I chose usually were not appropriate for the conversation people were having with me. My brain was always on and revving at eight thousand RPMs. I had all these thoughts in my head.

So, as Mom asked me what I was thinking I realized that opening my mouth and telling her all my thoughts was not what she wanted or needed to hear.

"It's okay. You don't have to say anything," Mom said. I liked that about mom. She didn't push. She wasn't one of those parents that had to know everything.

So, Saturday through Thursday we boxed up and packed up everything we had in the apartment. It took five days to pack up all we had in our little three-bedroom apartment and be ready to leave the city Friday.

In those few days I tried to think of someone to tell I was leaving Chicago for the summer, but no one came to mind. I tried to think of friends I had at Faraday that would care. I tried to also think of friends in the Garfield Park neighborhood that might miss me if I was gone for a few months. Again, I came up with no one.

"You know there's a real possibility that we will be going to school in Effingham if things don't improve by August," Bird said to me one day.

She was always saying things trying to trigger me. I listened and remained silent. She looked at me with her big eyes and waited for a reaction. I chose not to react.

School was school, I thought, but the thing that stung the most was the loss of our living in Chicago. I really liked living in Chicago. I was comfortable walking to my school from our apartment. I liked being close to Garfield Park. I liked the neighborhood. The people were friendly. They were always watching me whenever I was on the streets.

I tried to think if I didn't return to Faraday would I miss anyone. Fifth graders were still immature and weird. Sixth graders were even weirder. The seventh graders thought they were the coolest. The eighth graders acted like they were bored and ready for high school.

I looked at Bird and her Afro puffs. She was dressed in her summer outfit of T-shirt, jeans, and sneakers. If she wasn't dressed in that she was dressed in basketball shorts. I looked at my sister who was going to be a sophomore in high school. She had played basketball on the team and done pretty well. She wasn't Michael Jordan or Candace Parker but she was surprisingly good.

Bird averaged ten points a game. She also averaged six assists the whole season. The coach thought she was good for a first-year student. I knew. I sat behind the bench of her basketball games and overheard him say as much.

I smiled at Bird, thinking about how good she was as a basketball player.

"Zee? What are you doing?" Bird asked.

"Just thinking," I said to Bird with a grin.

"You're always in your head, Zee," Bird said.

I shrugged my shoulders.

"You need to find some friends," Bird said.

I laughed at the idea. I tried to think if I had friends. I knew the idea of friends. I knew the concept, but no one came to mind. In two years, I had not made any real friends at Faraday.

Unlike me, Bird had a bunch of friends at Westinghouse High School. Bird had seven close friends, all girls, that were her besties. She talked with her seven friends every day and told them that she was going to be out of the city for the summer. It was a big production. I didn't know them all. I knew three of the seven. Well, I had met three of Bird's friends.

There was Freddy, Sloan, and Marley. Freddy, AKA Fredericka Ramsey, lived at the end of the street we lived on. Sloan lived a block over. Marley lived just two blocks from us. The other girls Bird knew from school. Any time I showed up they looked at me like I was a growth or something.

Chapter 2.

When our last Friday in Chicago came that summer there was no big farewell. There was no send off. Instead, Bird and I walked down the stairs and out the front door of our apartment that June morning to the still quiet street. We walked to the sidewalk and stood waiting for our mom to arrive. Bird looked up and down the sidewalk expecting one of her friends to appear.

"It's too early for them to be up and out," I declared aloud.

"Shut up," Bird said. Her big brown eyes were wet with tears.

I grinned. Bird seeing me looking amused drew back a balled fist and tried to hit me. I ducked the punch and laughed at how silly Bird was that morning, dressed in a yellow T-shirt and blue jeans. On her feet were flip flops.

My sister, three years older than me, was a beautiful black girl who loved to wear her hair in Afro puffs, like she was a black Minnie Mouse. She had incredible skin. She was sixteen in a month and possessed almond shaped hazel eyes, full lips, and an athletic build. She liked to dress like a girl, most of the time, but Bird was a basketball and track star 100% of the time.

Bird chased me around the front of our apartment, and I ducked and dodged her for as long as I could. She caught me and instead of beating the snot out of me, she put me in a headlock.

"Take it back," Bird said.

I didn't know what to take back so remained silent.

"You are just so frustrating," Bird said. "You know." She said, releasing me.

I smiled and studied Bird on the sidewalk.

Mom pulled the Toyota around with a U-Haul attached and Bird's scooter poking out of the boxes, I couldn't help but think how Mister Gilbert losing his business set off a host of events for our family. One thing led to another. Bankruptcy led to my mom losing her savings and our apartment. The loss of Mom's savings had led to us to heading to Effingham, for the summer.

I tried to think when the last time I had been in Effingham, Illinois. In my head, all I could remember, or recall was that there were lots and lots of cornfields. There was just so much corn. Acres and acres of corn for as far as the eye could see. There was a lot of corn in Effingham.

Okay, beyond the corn there was Grandpa Clark in Effingham. My memories of Effingham were dominated by the big bear of a man. When Bird and I stayed in Effingham, grandpa would wake me up early in the morning and he and I would drive out to his special fishing hole. That fishing hole was somewhere on the edge of a dam or irrigation system. We fished from the banks and spent hours there.

I hoped that grandpa didn't mind us staying with him for the summer. He lived in a big house by himself. I couldn't imagine how our showing up would go over. Mom said that Grandpa Clark was looking forward to seeing us.

Grandpa was going to have a lot to deal with, I thought. He was, based on my calculations, in his sixties, and a bit of an eccentric. Grandpa Clark was a loner and a veteran. He had been in one of the wars. He had a tattoo of a lightning bolt on his shoulder from his travels overseas.

He liked talking about traveling, but not about what he did while he was there. All I knew about what grandpa did was when I was there one summer we went to the Veteran's center, and I listened to the men he talked to there. He was always telling stories to his friends. I liked going to the Veteran's center because there was always food to eat or TV to watch.

"You looking forward to seeing grandpa?" Mom asked as she drove.

"Yeah," Bird said, petting the ever-curious Bo.

I looked through the back window of the Toyota and into the back of the U-Haul and scratched my head at the sight of Bird's scooter. She had an old non-working scooter she got from Uncle Benny. She decided to bring the scooter to Effingham.

"Think you'll get it working while we're here?" I questioned.

"Hope so," Bird said.

As we drove away from Chicago and toward the cornfields that made up much of the Midwest, I wasn't angry. I wasn't mad. I was just trying to understand my mother's plan.

"The way I see it, guys," Mom said as she drove down the interstate, the music low and barely audible. "We have the summer to figure things out. We get three months for me to figure things out. We all get three months to figure it out. Worse come to worse and you spend a year in Effingham. The schools down here are strong. They have an excellent sports program. Their academics are good, too."

Bird rolled her eyes.

"Look at it this way," Mom said. "We're on an adventure this summer."

"It's a change," I announced aloud.

Bird looked at me like she wanted to kill me when I spoke. I grinned in the face of imminent death.

"I hate this," Bird complained from the passenger seat.

Bird didn't like change. Me, I didn't mind too much. I mean, I was twelve years old, and every day was thrown into a world that continually demanded me to change or die. One of my teachers had suggested that our ability to change was the reason we were alive today.

I looked at Bird and then mom at the wheel of the Toyota. She was dressed in a wide brimmed hat, sunglasses, a blue button front blouse and tweed blazer.

We were just a few miles from Champaign, Illinois when Bird offered another thought.

"Mom, I have to say it," Bird said. "I know that Zee is thinking it. We are worried about you."

"Don't worry about me," our mother said. "I just need a little time to figure things out. I promise you before the end of the summer I will have this all figured out."

Bird moved her head side to side.

"Mom, you know what people are saying?"

"Bird, people always are saying something," Mom said.

"Yeah, but Missus Kay and Miss Mary were saying that you were having a break down," Bird said.

"That's not true, firstly," Mom said.

Bird looked up from her cell phone as she sat in the front of the Toyota.

I looked up seeing Bird looking away from her phone. The disturbance got the attention of Bo, our black tongued Chow, who laid on my lap. Bo was seventy pounds of muscle and furry protection that thought he was a lap dog.

"Mom, are you having a break down?" Bird asked.

"Bird, I am not having a break down, no matter what those crows say," Mom said. "I just need to regroup." She looked at me and the road ahead and smiled mirthlessly. "I lost my job. It was unexpected. I made some mistakes. I just need a little time to figure things out."

"Mom, this summer doesn't feel like a regroup or figure things out kind of summer. It feels like we're running away and that we're the victims of your bad decisions."

The flatlands of Illinois were peppered with small towns. None of the towns notable or memorable compared to the one-time second largest city in the nation. The only notable city south of the Chicago was the home of the University of Illinois and the Fighting Illini in Champaign, Illinois. When we reached Champaign, we were less than thirty minutes from Grandpa Clark. The entire drive to Effingham took just three hours from Chicago.

Mom exited the interstate and made her way to the city limits of Effingham.

"We're here," Mom said as she turned onto South Banker Street of Effingham.

"We are definitely here," Bird said, looking out the window as mom turned off National Street and onto the four lanes that made up South Banker Street. We drove down the street and on one side of the street there was two restaurants, a pharmacy, a grocery store, a clothing store, and a bank. On the opposite side of the street there was an office building, a diner, another clothing store, and a Dairy Queen. Eight buildings made up the head of South Banker Street, I saw as mom steered the Toyota left and drove toward the western side of Effingham.

As we stopped at a light on the street, I noticed that there were the blank faces of people staring at me taped on street poles. The strange thing was that they all looked to be all white men in their early thirties or late forties.

"Weird," I declared aloud to Bird, pointing to the missing persons on the street poles.

Bird moved her head side to side.

"Small town drama," Bird said with a shrug of her shoulders.

I didn't think any more of it.

"How many people live here?" I questioned. Bird moved her head side to side. Mom did not answer. Not having that answer irked me. It was something that I needed to know.

At East Eiche Avenue mom turned left and drove down the tree-lined street. The drive was short and after two stop signs mom slowed the Toyota.

"Look who's waiting for us," Mom said as she pulled into the driveway.

On the porch stood our bigger than life grandpa. He was dressed in a dark blue collared shirt and overalls. On his head was a Chicago Cubs baseball cap.

Mom parked the Toyota behind grandpa's Jeep.

By the time mom turned off the car's engine Grandpa Clark was standing by the U-Haul.

Mom and Bird ran to Grandpa Clark and were embraced by the giant. I climbed out of the car with Bo. Bo seeing the yard made a beeline to relieve himself. I chuckled. I stepped into the yard and watched as Bo found a place to pee and poop. I watched as Bo sniffed the trees and the bushes that marked the end of the property. Between grandpa's yard and the neighbor's yard was an eight-foot-high hedge that ran from the edge to the street.

Releasing his daughter and granddaughter Grandpa Clark stepped to my side. He didn't hug me like he had Mom and Bird. Instead, grandpa placed a heavy hand on my shoulder. Bo watched grandpa silently. I smiled. Bo seeing me smile sniffed at grandpa's leg.

"Put your dog in the backyard," Grandpa said, his voice deep and bassy and sounding like the rumble of thunder. "He'll need to get used to the area before we let him off leash."

I looked at Gramps and agreed. I found Bo's leash and put him on it. Bo looked at me with his big eyes studying me.

"It's not for long," I declared aloud.

"Come inside," Grandpa said to us all. "We'll unpack after you take a moment to tell me about your trip down from Chicago."

"Grandpa, can I bring Bo inside?"

"Is he housebroken?" Grandpa asked.

"Yes," I declared aloud with a smile.

He gave a slight nod.

I walked Bo up the back stairs on leash.

"Okay, be good," I said. Bo nearly bowled me over when I opened the back door. Bo ran through the entire length of the house sniffing and checking out every room on the first floor. Finding Bird in the small living room he jumped onto her lap.

"Bo," Bird said with a feigned protest. "You know you are too big to be jumping into my lap?"

Bo cuddled with Bird.

"Okay, there are four bedrooms upstairs," Grandpa said. "I have a bedroom upstairs, but usually, I end up sleeping in the living room with the TV watching me."

"So, we have the choice of rooms?" Bird asked.

"I suppose you do," Grandpa said.

"Bo, come on," I said. Bo hearing my voice jumped off Bird's lap and followed me upstairs.

Running upstairs, I turned left at the top of the stairs and ran to the end of the hall with Bo on my heels.

Chapter 3.

My new bedroom was a big box. There was a small desk with a rolling chair near the bedroom door. A dresser sat against the wall. Beside the dresser was a door that opened into a small closet. A bed sat in the middle of the room beside the window that looked out toward the backyard. The room that was twice the size of what I was used to and had a pair of windows. One window looked out and toward Eiche Street. The window opened and offered the chance to sit on the roof of the overhang in the front of the house. The second window opened out and onto the backyard. There was a small balcony to sit on over the porch below.

"Hope you're okay with the room," Grandpa Clark smiled broadly from the doorway. I agreed. I saw mom's eyes and smile in grandpa's face. "I'll be back to check on you."

"Yeah, thank you, grandpa," I smiled easily and laughed. Grandpa left without a word.

I agreed and checked out my new summer bedroom. I had to admit I was impressed with the sheer size of the room. Bo walked around the space sniffing at everything. He sat down in front of a door at the far end of the room.

As I was taking in the room, I heard Bo grumble. I looked. Bo was looking at the door he was lying in front of annoyed. The door I had not opened moved only to give a little as Bo lifted his head and pushed against the door but did not move.

"Move Bo," I said.

I watched as the Chow we raised from a puppy climbed to his feet and padded toward me. Bo was a lovable fluffy bear with a black tongue. He was friendly and loyal. Bo was like his breed, protective and fearless. Standing nearly three feet high he was a truck of a dog. I watched Bo brush up against me. I grinned broadly. Bo looked up at me and turned to watch the space he vacated.

The door opened and Bird stood in the doorway with Bo studying her. I held Bo by his collar.

"How's your new room?" Bird asked.

"Love it," I declared aloud, with a determined grin. I released Bo and looked behind Bird and into the darkened bathroom that we now shared. I smiled at my sister as she stepped into my new bedroom. I was sitting in the rolling chair with Bo now by my side.

"It's definitely bigger than Chicago," Bird said.

Grandpa Clark appeared again at the bedroom door with a grin on his chestnut brown face.

"Well, we need to move in the boxes," he said to me and Bird.

Bo looked up and at me and laid his head back on the floor.

"Okay," I responded aloud. I knew that the moving of boxes was not going to take too long for me. Mom, in her organized and overly orderly fashion, had labeled all the boxes. Now that our rooms were sorted out, all we had to do was move boxes to each assigned room.

"So, we move in the boxes first," Grandpa said. "Think you have to take in the boxes with your names on it. I'll help." There were kitchen boxes, bathroom boxes, Mom, Bird, and my boxes. I liked that Bo even had a box.

"Mom has this on lock," Bird said, adjusting her box in her arms. I agreed. Mom and Bird had the most boxes. Bo had just a box. Me, I had less than a dozen boxes. For the next few hours Bird and I moved our boxes to our rooms.

When I finished unloading my boxes I kept unloading and putting the labeled boxes in the appropriate rooms. Grandpa Clark moved boxes as well. Mom helped too.

After me, Bird was the first to finish putting all her boxes into her room. She was unpacking one of her boxes as I finished bringing up mom's last box of things from Chicago. Mom was in her summer bedroom adjusting boxes and trying to figure out which box to open first. Bo was nipping at my heels as I dropped off the last box at my mom's door.

Bird took her boxes to her room. I took my boxes to my newly claimed room. It took most of the day to move all the boxes into our rooms. By seven o'clock all the boxes were unloaded from the U-Haul. The last thing on the U-Haul was the scooter.

"Let's put the scooter in the garage," Grandpa Clark said with an uneven grin. The three of us pushed and pulled the scooter past grandpa's Jeep and into the two-car garage.

Inside the garage sat Grandpa Clark's 1965 Porsche Speedster. He had bought it a long time ago from someone in Champaign and towed it back here and been tinkering on it ever since. In the three years I had been to Effingham the Speedster had sat, in that exact spot.

"Grandpa, I thought you were done trying to restore that car?" Bird asked pushing the scooter in front of a storage bin.

"I think that when that bug bites you it's not that easy to shake," Grandpa said, with a grin.

I studied all the mechanical parts and tools in the garage. His garage looked like a miniature auto garage. The only thing missing were the car lifts and oil pits. It looked like grandpa could rebuild an engine with all the equipment he had.

The scooter sat on the far side of the garage, where a car would sit if grandpa ever used the space for the Jeep.

"Hey, grandpa, you think we can get this working?" Bird asked.

"Maybe," Grandpa said with a crooked smile. He stopped and looked at Bird. "If you unpack and get rid of all the boxes so that my place doesn't look like the inside of a packing and shipping company," Grandpa said. He waited and looked at us both. "I'll give the scooter a thorough once over and if there's nothing too serious, I should have it up and running by the end of the week, if not the following week."

"Deal," Bird said.

The scooter had not started since Bird had it. She had gotten it from Uncle Benny, and he had it for years and never ridden it. I shook my head at the idea of getting the non-working machine running.

"Think it needs some new wheels and maybe a tune-up," Grandpa Clark said. "It doesn't look too bad."

Grandpa Clark ushered Bird and me out of the garage. Bird and Grandpa Clark headed toward the rear of gramps house. Bird sat on the couch in the living room, and I sat near her. Bo, seeing us lounging jumped on the couch and stretched out with his head on my lap and his feet on Bird.

"You know Bo is too big to be doing this?" Bird asked with a shake of her head.

Mom appeared and seemed pleased with herself. She smiled and gave me a pat on the shoulder. She patted Bird on the back.

Grandpa Clark had begun cooking dinner.

"Finish up," Mom said as she carried a small box to her new bedroom. "We're going to eat in an hour."

Bird was the first to climb to her feet and head upstairs. Bo watched Bird but didn't move.

"Come on," I declared aloud.

I climbed to my feet and Bo and I walked upstairs to my now crowded room that had nearly a dozen storage boxes with all the items of my life.

I rested in my room surrounded by boxes. I knew that inside of the boxes were my jackets, coats, and sweaters. In another box was my winter clothing, which I wasn't going to bother with that summer. In a box were my trousers, jeans, and shorts.

Looking at the boxes and knew I had to find my shoes, jeans, and T-shirts. I also wanted to find the box where I kept my comics, music and chess set.

As I climbed to my feet, I studied the pyramid of stacked boxes. I tried to remember which box of the boxes held my T-shirts, jeans, and shoes. I touched the boxes. I didn't open any. Instead, I tried to decide which boxes to open.

"Zee," Mom said from downstairs. "Come down to dinner. Wash your hands before you come down."

By dinner I was tired. It sort of hit me that I had been on the go, moving boxes and going up and down the stairs for four hours. The U-Haul was empty and as I sat at the dining table, I felt physically exhausted.

We ate, our first night in Effingham, pan-fried chicken, black-eyed peas, greens, mashed potatoes, cornbread, and sweet tea. For dessert we had peach cobbler.

After dinner I headed back to my room and unpacked two boxes, I decided were the boxes that needed to be opened before going to bed. The first box I opened contained my ten T-shirts, four pair of jeans, four basketball shorts and two pair of basketball sneakers, a pair of boots, a pair of dress shoes and a Chicago Bears hoody. Also in the box were my pajamas and underwear.

The last box I opened that night had my comic book collection. I removed the sixty books and placed them gingerly on the desk in the room. There was a sweatsuit mom bought me for my birthday the year before in the same box. I removed the CD player and like the comics sat it on the desk. The last thing I pulled out of the box was my chess set. I sat the chess set along with the thirty-six chess pieces on that suddenly cluttered desk before going to bed dressed in a Dead Pool pajama set.

*　　*　　*　　*　　*

The next few days I woke up and methodically unboxed and put away clothes and personal items in my closet and set of dresser drawers. It didn't take long, but the process was mentally challenging. I had to find a particular place for everything in my new bedroom for the summer.

Mom would call me down to breakfast and I would head downstairs with Bo. I would feed Bo and let him outside in the backyard while we ate breakfast.

Grandpa cooked for us every morning. He was an incredible cook. He loved making filling meals.

At the table, he would sit and read the newspaper and drink a coffee while Mom, Bird and I ate. Grandpa Clark subscribed to the Daily Effingham Record. It was a local newspaper that was located downtown.

After breakfast, Bird and I were tasked with the responsibility of cleaning the kitchen. I cleared the table. I wiped down the stove, counters, and refrigerator. Bird washed the dishes and the pots. I helped sweep the kitchen. I also had to take Bo for a walk after cleaning the kitchen. That was my morning responsibilities in Effingham.

The remainder of the day, those first few days, were spent straightening my room and unboxing clothes. The sun and heat were unbearable from noon to three o'clock every day. So, Bird and I stayed indoors during those hours or went to the garage to check on the progress of grandpa's tinkering with the scooter. We usually did not set foot outside the house until after four most days that first week in Effingham.

27

At night we might sit on the front porch and watch the sun set or listen to the katydids screaming in the night. Sometimes we might eat ice cream outside, but that first week in Effingham we, Bird and I, concentrated on unpacking and organizing our rooms, breaking down the boxes, and storing them in the garage so grandpa's house didn't look like a storage space.

My first Friday since leaving Chicago I woke in Effingham, Illinois. Effingham was known as the Crossroads of Opportunity. It got its name for the number of roads that ran through Effingham. The I-57 ran from Chicago to Missouri. I-70 cut through Effingham and if you picked it up you could go west to Utah or east to Maryland. US Route 45 went from Michigan to Mobile, Alabama. US Route 40 was known as the National Road from Atlantic City, New Jersey all the way to Silver Summit, Utah. In Effingham there was also Illinois routes 32 and 33. There was a railroad junction in Effingham as well. There was the Pennsylvania Railroad that ran from Indianapolis to St. Louis.

The town was also the home of a 198-foot cross. They called the cross the Cross of the Crossroads. That was the highpoint. It was in South-Central Illinois and an hour away from Springfield, the state capitol. It was also an hour away from St. Louis.

Effingham sat in a flat ten square mile bit of land. There was Salt Creek and several lakes in the area. The population of Effingham was 12,310.

I learned all that from reading the daily paper grandpa received.

In just three days I was unpacked, and my newly crowned summer bedroom was neat and tidy. I walked past Bird's still cluttered room and checked on her progress. She had made a significant dent in putting clothes away that first week in South-Central Illinois. I figured she would be finished by the end of the week, if not by Saturday.

"Are you finished?" Bird asked.

I looked at my sister and grinned. I didn't have as many boxes to unpack as her.

"Well, I'm not," Bird said. She had half a dozen boxes that she needed to unpack. "Go and... do something while I finish."

I returned to my bedroom. On my desk was my chess board and small comic book collection. Sitting on top of my valuable comics was my iPod and earphones. In a corner was deconstructed box I needed to take to the garage.

I walked downstairs with Bo by my side. There was no one in the living room. There was no one in the kitchen. I stopped and looked around the heart of the Clark house. It was kind of odd to not find grandpa at the stove or sitting at the kitchen table.

On the kitchen table sat the daily news, the Effingham Daily Record. On the front page was a square faced man with the word: Missing under his picture.

I didn't stay in the kitchen exceptionally long. Bo stood at the door waiting for me. I made my last trip to the garage and before I reached it found gramps sitting in the shade of the garage overhang in a folding chair in front of an old folding table.

"Grandpa," I announced aloud. He looked up as I walked into the garage. After depositing the flattened box in the garage, I walked to see what my gramps was doing.

He was arranging his fishing hooks and fishing equipment.

Bo sniffed around the garage and sat then laid down between me and grandpa.

"How'd you end up here?" I inquired leaning on the side of the garage.

He was dressed in khaki trousers and a Chicago Cubs baseball jersey. He had repaired Bird's scooter and was onto his next project. Gramps loved to fish. That day, he was preparing his fishing tacklebox for an early morning fishing adventure.

Grandpa Clark stopped arranging his hooks and weights and looked at me. He looked back at his fishing equipment on the folding table. Grandpa wearing his Cubs baseball cap looked at me and smiled.

"Why?" He asked.

"I was wondering," I uttered aloud. "I wouldn't have picked this place first."

"Well, Zion, when I got out the Army I came back to Chicago," Grandpa said. "I was in Chicago, and it seemed too loud and too big. I had a friend, David Walker, who was living in Champaign. He invited me to come down and visit. I went down there and liked the slower pace. I guess I didn't want to live in Chicago anymore. Too much noise. Too much... everything. I liked being away from Chicago, but Champaign was a college town," Grandpa said.

Bird appeared. She was dressed in basketball shorts, a cartoon T-shirt and basketball sneakers. She was carrying her basketball.

The sun was giving way to the night. Lightning bugs were just appearing in the shadows near the hedges.

"Where you going?" Grandpa Clark asked Bird.

"Nowhere," Bird said. "I was just going to dribble the ball on the driveway."

Grandpa Clark gave a slight nod.

"What were you talking about?" Bird asked dribbling the basketball and getting the attention of Bo.

"Grandpa was talking about not wanting to live in Chicago," I declared aloud. I watched as Bo climbed to his feet and padded to Bird and the basketball. Bird seeing Bo held the basketball in her arms.

"Yeah. I couldn't live in Chicago, and I liked and hated Champaign. There was the college town feeling there. I guess I wanted an even slower pace than Champaign. Walker told me about Effingham it was just a few minutes away from Champaign. He told me it was the Crossroads. I liked the idea. I visited and fell in love with the place," Grandpa said with a slight smile. He checked his watch and looked at the sky. He gave a faint nod. "That's how I ended up here."

I grinned, satisfied.

"Do you ever go to Springfield or St. Louis?" Bird asked, tossing the ball from one hand to the other.

Grandpa Clark chuckled.

"Too much noise," I reported aloud. Bird looked at me sideways. I grinned knowingly.

"How often you go to Champaign?" Bird asked, hoping for a different answer.

"Almost never," Grandpa said with a grin.

"I have everything I want here," Grandpa said, contentedly.

"Well, that's good and great for you," Bird said, impatiently. "But I'm sixteen. What about me?"

"What about you?" Grandpa Clark asked.

"What is there to do here?" Bird asked, pointedly.

"Well, there's all sorts of activities here," Grandpa said with an irregular smile. "June there's the Moccasin Creek Festival. July there's the Fourth of July celebration sponsored by the VFW and then there's the Artisan Craft Fair and EffingHAM-JAM. August there's the biggest event of the year, the Harvest Moon Festival."

Bird moved her head side to side, unimpressed.

A week later, on Wednesday, after Bird and I came back from the park with Bo and found Grandpa Clark sitting on his porch swing sipping lemonade. Seeing him there, I detoured to the porch and sat on the swing with my giant grandpa. Bird climbed onto the porch and sat on the brick wall in the shade of the overhang.

"How was the park?"

"Good," Bird lied. There was no one there except for Bird and me. Bird shot a few baskets until it got too hot, and we sat under a tree, in the shade and just relaxed. While we relaxed Bo laid in the strip of shade and watched us. We were at the park for maybe two hours.

"You know one of the biggest events of the year is this weekend?" Grandpa asked with a wry grin.

"What's that? They got a cow tipping tournament next weekend?" Bird asked sarcastically.

"The Moccasin Creek Festival," Grandpa said. "I've never gone, but I hear it's one of Effingham's biggest events."

"We should go," I declared aloud. We had been in Effingham a week and after arriving and setting up our rooms and disposing of the boxes in Grandpa Clark's garage we had only been downtown and to the park, which was only a few blocks from Grandpa's house.

It was the summer and in my mind the summer was made for adventures. So, having wasted a week putting our rooms in order and grandpa fixing Bird's scooter, as promised, I wanted to do something exciting.

"It's not too far," Grandpa said.

Chapter 4.

Bird and my first adventure involved going to Lake Sara in Summit Township. It was only five miles from Effingham. The lake, like most in South-Central, was created by man and not natural. Lake Sara was created in the 1950's from five creeks that ran through the basin.

When we arrived, I knew there might be an issue. There were a bunch of RVs and trucks parked on the bank of the lake and very few faces that looked like Bird or me.

"Stay close," Bird said.

I agreed. I did not hold Bird's hand, but I thought about it as the people at the Moccasin Creek Festival seemed to be surprised by our appearance.

The outdoor event was fenced in to provide control of entry and exit. There was a main entrance and exit. There were several other side exits as well. Bird decided to go in the main entrance.

As we walked toward the entrance, I again noticed that there were the blank faces of people staring at me taped on the light poles around the gated entrance to the festival. The same men or women that were taped up in Effingham were on display here at the Moccasin Creek Festival.

I wanted to stop and study the faces, but Bird did not slow down. She plowed ahead and after a brief wait, we were inside. It was an odd feeling to be the one black pearl in the sea of white faces with blue, brown, and green eyes. The blonde, red and auburn hair that was straight, slightly curly, and long and short was jarring.

I reached out to Bird.

"Don't worry," Bird said. "We'll stay for a few minutes, if we don't like it, we'll leave," she said.

I didn't like it already. I didn't say anything. I couldn't say anything. My sister had told me repeatedly that if she wasn't worried then I should not be worried. Between the two of us Bird was the fighter. She was never one to back down from a fight. So, with all that floating around in my head I didn't say anything. I just stayed close to Bird.

"Check this out," a straight blonde, pie-faced girl dressed in short shorts, cowboy boots and plaid collared shirt tied just below her ample chest said. She was looking at Bird like she was dessert.

Behind the pie-faced farm girl were two Barbies, one brunette, the other a curly haired blonde.

"What brings you here?" The straight-haired blonde Barbie asked.

Bird grabbed my arm and continued to walk.

The lead Barbie stepped in front of Bird with a toothy smile.

Bird stopped short. She released my arm and flexed her fingers in preparation for a fight.

"Hey, I was trying to be friendly," the straight, shoulder length blonde girl said. She raised her hands, showing she meant nothing malicious by her earlier question.

"I don't know you and you're in my way," Bird said, looking left and right at the other Barbies who were smiling, amused by the conversation.

"What? People aren't friendly where you come from?" The nameless Barbie asked.

Bird was watching everything. She was like a cat with its hair standing on end. She just needed a reason to launch her attack.

"*Where I come from?* What you trying to say?" Bird asked narrowing her eyes and watching the girl in front of her and the two others.

"Easy," the pie-faced girl said, her hands still open and palms facing Bird.

I reached out and placed my hand on Bird's hip.

"We should leave," I said under my breath.

"Bump that," Bird said. "They ain't going to run us off. I bought a ticket and we're going to listen to some music and enjoy ourselves despite them."

"Okay, maybe we got off on the wrong foot," the pie-faced Barbie said with a wicked grin, lowering her hands. She placed an index finger on her chest and tilted her head to the right. "My name is Amber. Amber James. I'm the daughter of the mayor."

"And," Bird said, unimpressed.

"And this is where you calm down and realize that I am not trying to do anything but be nice," Amber said. "And tell me your name."

"Okay, Amber," Bird said. "Get out of my way so that me and my brother can sit down and enjoy the music."

"That's your brother? He's cute," one of the Barbies said behind Amber.

Bird narrowed her eyes at Amber. She was once again on guard. She checked her surroundings and grabbed me by the shoulder and pulled me past Amber and the Barbies and into the crowd of adults and children milling about the food stands and T-shirt and hat vendors.

Standing in the crowd was a tall white man wearing a light blue police uniform with his thumbs hitched in his gun belt, his pistol against his hip.

Instantly, seeing the deputy, I took a breath and then before that breath was completely out of my lungs, I tensed. I looked at the man there smirking at us as we approached him. He looked like he either was going to laugh or spit.

"Hey," the deputy said with a thin smile. "What brings you here tonight?"

"Does everyone ask that question?" Bird asked. She moved her head side to side and pouted. "Do you ask that question to everyone?" She studied the deputy.

I studied the tall and slender man in front of us as well.

"What brings you here?" Bird asked the deputy, annoyed.

The deputy frowned at Bird's words. He looked over Bird's head at the three girls behind.

"Is there any trouble?" The deputy asked. "Saw you talking to the mayor's daughter."

"No trouble," Bird said. "Just going to sit down and listen to some music. Is that a problem?"

"Don't think so," the deputy said.

"Okay," Bird said and began to push past the deputy.

The deputy extended his hand to stop Bird and me.

Bird stopped short. I stopped and looked around us. Being close enough to the deputy I could read his nameplate. It read: Kenner.

"Be careful, little one," the deputy said. "Strangers aren't always welcomed. Especially down here in the farmlands."

The Moccasin Creek Festival was so strange in that there were only pale faces with thin eyebrows, thin noses and pointy chins milling around us but no one that resembled Bird or me. I scanned the crowd looking for anyone who might come to our rescue.

Bird did not respond. Instead, she just pushed past the deputy to the stage area and found a piece of grass to sit down. I sat beside Bird concerned.

We watched three women come on stage and sing and play their own instruments. I tried to enjoy the three women's songs, but it was hard with all the eyes on Bird and me. I felt uncomfortable from the moment we sat down. It seemed like everyone was more interested in us than the people on stage.

"Can we leave?" I questioned.

"Not yet," Bird said. "We'll leave after they end their show," Bird said. She was trying to prove a point. I understood. I didn't necessarily agree with her thinking but since she was my ride home, I sat there and tried not to squirm.

The three women did three songs. At the end of the third song by the women Bird climbed to her feet and looked at me. She didn't have to say a word. I was on my feet and walking with her toward the exit.

We made our way to the exit and saw the tall thin deputy again. He smiled emotionlessly and grinned at us as we left. Bird did not acknowledge the deputy or anyone else as we made our way back to her scooter. I looked back as we reached the exit and found Kenner watching us.

Bird marched out of the Moccasin Festival and thankfully, when we reached the scooter, the engine started. We left the festival unmolested.

We drove back to Effingham silently. The scooter had a headlight that brought us back safely to Eiche Street. Bird parked the scooter, and I was never happier to be standing in grandpa's driveway than I was that evening.

"How was the Moccasin Creek Festival?" Mom asked when we returned to Grandpa Clark's house.

I didn't say a word.

Bird did not say anything, and mom knew something was up as a result.

"What happened?" Mom asked, concerned.

"Nothing," Bird said. "We met some interesting people. It was a short ride out to the lake and back." Bird stopped, thinking. "Definitely realized that we aren't in Chicago."

I agreed.

"Well, Effingham definitely is not Chicago," Grandpa said. "This weekend I'll be barbequing. Hope you're hungry. I have two days of sampling and perfecting to do."

"What are you perfecting?" Asked Bird.

"My sauce," Grandpa Clark said with a wry smile.

Bird gave a weak nod. Mom leaned in and put an arm around her father's bullish neck.

"This guy is an Effingham legend on the grill," Mom said.

I smiled broadly at the idea of eating grandpa's barbeque.

Bird pouted. She didn't say anything immediately.

"This weekend is Juneteenth," Bird said. "Are there any events or celebrations for that here?"

"I don't think so," Grandpa Clark said, uncertain. He looked at Mom and Bird confused. "What's Juneteenth?"

"Juneteenth," Bird said. "Our freedom celebration in this country," Bird continued. "It is celebrated by most of the black nation during the second week of June. It commemorates when the Union Army finally arrived in Texas and emancipated the last slaves under the slave laws in this country."

"I don't know anything about that," Grandpa Clark said.

"How is that possible?" Bird said looking from grandpa to Mom.

Grandpa Clark shrugged his shoulders.

Bird looked at grandpa unbelieving.

After dinner, mom pulled Bird to the side. I listened.

"Baby, need you to tread lightly while we're here," Mom said.

"What do you mean?" Bird asked.

"We are in my dad's house. We're guests here. If he doesn't know about Juneteenth then let it go," Mom said.

"Mom," Bird said.

"Bird, your grandfather is sixty-four years old," Mom said. "He's a different kind of man."

"What? Are you saying that grandpa can't learn?" Bird asked.

"No, I'm not saying that," Mom said. "I'm just saying that you should tread lightly with someone who watched you grow up."

Bird tilted her head at mom's words.

"What do you mean? You think that older people know everything?" Bird deliberated. "You know that's not true. We all are supposed to be open to learning. If we stop learning, then we might as well be dead."

"Bernadette," Mom said, unsettled.

"I know that grandpa opened his house to us. I know that he's my grandfather. He's my elder. But I also know that as much as I learn from you or him, you and he can learn things from me," Bird said.

"Yeah," I declared aloud.

Mom hearing me talk looked and smiled awkwardly. She looked back at Bird. "Just tread lightly."

Chapter 5.

Bird had a look in her eyes. She was determined. She was angry. When she stormed off from mom and headed to her bedroom, I knew Bird's argument wasn't over by a longshot.

I mounted the stairs and Bo and I tried to just walk past Bird's room unnoticed.

"Zee? You understand?" Bird asked.

I paused and Bird was sitting on her bedroom floor with her head against the closet door. I looked in, curious.

"So, what do you think?" Bird asked, wiping at her eyes.

"About what?" I asked.

"About being here?" Bird asked.

"It's fine," I said.

"*It's fine*? We came down here and it was supposed to be better. It's the same. Or worse," Bird said.

I did not comment.

"Mom is telling us to tread lightly," Bird said, angry.

I listened. I did not feel it was necessary to point out that mom was talking directly to Bird.

"No one should be afraid to hear the truth," Bird said.

I could not disagree. So, I nodded.

"How can grandpa not know about Juneteenth?"

I pinched my lips.

"How can anyone black not know about Juneteenth?"

I looked at my older sister, uncertain what to say.

"We have to go to the library," Bird said.

A couple of days later Bird and I went to the Effingham library. Bird loved riding on her now working scooter. I didn't mind. I just wished that it was a car. In a car I felt safer.

The Effingham Public Library was not on the Southside of Effingham. It was on the Northside of the town. Fayette Street divided Effingham in half. On Bird's scooter the trip one way was as long as going to the Moccasin Creek Festival.

The two-story dark building looked more like a factory than a library as Bird parked her scooter and locked it up at the bike stand.

"This is pretty small," I reported aloud, thinking of the libraries I had been used to in Chicago.

As I walked toward the entrance, I again noticed that there were the blank faces of people staring at me taped on one of the light poles near the entrance to the library.

"Look," I announced aloud pointing to the pictures.

Bird laughed. She shrugged her shoulders and entered the small public library. Bird walked to the reference desk and the librarian sitting behind the desk looking at the monitor. I looked around the reference desk and grabbed a few pamphlets. I stuffed them in my back pocket mindlessly. One of the pamphlets was the Effingham Events Calendar.

The woman, dressed in a pink print dress with ruffles looked at Bird from behind her glasses and smiled affectionately. The woman had arched eyebrows, almond shaped brown eyes, and wide mouth. Instantly, she reminded me of one of my teachers at Faraday, back in Chicago.

"Hi, I'm looking for books on Juneteenth," Bird said.

The bibliognost frowned at the request.

"I'm not sure if we have any books on that subject," the woman said. "If we do, I think it would be in African American History. You can find that in the History section of the library." She directed us to the area of the library and wished us luck in our search.

"Doesn't she look like Missus McGrady?" I posed the question to Bird, after the curator left.

Bird looked back at the retreating librarian and moved her head side to side.

"Okay, Zee, you know what I'm looking for," Bird said. "You look from everything this level and lower." She pointed to the stack of books in front of us. The books stretched six feet in either direction. I took a deep breath. I liked a mission. I was looking for a book on Juneteenth. All I had to do was find a book with June in the title and hope that it was about Juneteenth.

I scanned the hundreds of books in the History section of the library and found nothing that dealt with Juneteenth. I was surprised. After Bird's clear explanation I thought there would be at least one or two books about the subject.

"Nothing," I reported.

"Did you find anything?" The reference librarian asked.

Bird and I both shook our heads.

The archivist lifted up a plain cover that said: Juneteenth on the cover.

"This is by Ralph Ellison," the librarian said. "It's not history. It's fiction, but I recalled it was in the library. I don't know too much about it other than that he wrote Invisible Man."

Bird extended her hand, and the library-keeper handed the novel to her. I looked at the book and then found myself looking at the attractive older woman for recognition.

"Thank you," Bird said, looking at the book. She turned and saw me looking at the woman oddly.

"Can I ask you a silly question?"

"Sure," the curator said with a gentle smile.

"Do you know a teacher in Chicago named Missus McGrady? She teaches at Faraday," Bird asked. "My brother thinks you look like her," she added.

Instantly, I wanted to run. I looked at my shoe tops and those of Bird and waited for an answer.

"No, I don't know anyone in Chicago," the round cheeked woman said. "Is that where you are from?"

"Yep," Bird said. "We're here for the summer. We're staying with our grandfather."

Bird fished out her library card and handed it to the woman curator. The bibliosoph looked at Bird, weirdly.

"Who is your grandfather?" The archivist asked.

"Thomas Clark," Bird said. I looked up at the mention of Grandpa Clark.

The wide mouthed woman smiled broadly.

"Tell Mister Clark that Stephanie Graham said, 'Hey,'" the woman dressed in a pink print dress with ruffles chirped.

Bird smiled and gave a thumbs up. "Will do," Bird said.

The wide mouthed woman smiled and handed Bird the novel. Bird slipped the novel in her backpack.

When we returned to grandpa's house Bo acted like we had been gone forever. Bird gave grandpa the Juneteenth book and told him about the librarian.

Grandpa Clark grinned.

"She's your cousin," Grandpa Clark said.

Mom appeared in the living room. Bird grinned broadly at mom dressed in periwinkle blouse, oversized belt buckle, and a dark blue skirt that showed off her legs.

"Who are you talking about now?" Mom asked.

"They went to the library today," Grandpa said, lifting the Ralph Ellison novel.

Mom looked at the book.

"They ran into Stephanie while they were there," Grandpa said.

"Stephanie Graham?" Mom asked.

Grandpa Clark agreed.

"Do she and Darryl ever come over?"

"Sometimes," Grandpa said.

"Maybe I'll invite them over for dinner next week," Grandpa Clark said.

Bored with the conversation, I took Bo for a walk. Bo loved running around without fences. I had to put him on a leash. Bo was well-trained, but when he saw open ground, he was going to run as far and as fast as he could. I loved that about Bo.

When we lived in Chicago, he was limited to the dog park. His dog run was just a block in length. So, being in Effingham was heaven for Bo.

That Thursday, after dressing in a T-shirt and basketball shorts, the first thing I did was take Bo for a walk. Off leash, Bo went running across the field that separated Eiche from Blohm. The distance had to be a thousand yards of open space. I walked, following the bouncing ball of fur as it bounced over the grassy field.

Bo stopped and was sniffing the ground when I showed up.

There was a mound of freshly dug up ground. I studied the topsoil and Bo digging at the ground.

"Come on Bo," I said, looking back toward Grandpa Clark's house and attached the leash and began to head back to the house.

Before dinner, I asked Bird a question in the bathroom we shared.

"How is the librarian related to us?"

"Who knows," Bird said. "You know how it is with us. When we become friendly, we become family," Bird explained.

       "So, you think they are really related to us?" I wondered aloud.
       "Who cares?"
       I agreed.

Chapter 6.

The end of June Grandpa Clark saw me sitting on the back porch with Bo. Bird and mom had gone shopping and I didn't want to tag along.

"Hey, Zee, you want to go with me to the VFW?"

Of course, Grandpa Clark didn't have to ask twice. I agreed and climbed into grandpa's Jeep. He drove us to the corner of his block and turned left onto Fourth Street. We drove past the Hendelmeyer Park where Bird schooled me every time we went to play basketball. The Jeep slid down South Fourth Street and behind the Village Mall. The VFW was on the corner of Blohm and Veterans Street.

Although I loved driving in the Jeep, I always had a secret desire to have grandpa drive across the field that separated Eiche from Blohm but in all the time I climbed into the Jeep with grandpa he never drove over the curb or into the field.

The VFW as a low-slung brown roofed building that had a parking lot and sat on the edge of a field. The closest building was Southside Baptist Church, where my Gramps went every Sunday.

We entered the front door and were greeted by various memorabilia of wars. There were several display cases. In one was a mannequin dressed in an old-fashioned soldier uniform with a helmet.

Grandpa saluted the mannequin and entered the second door that opened into the main area of the hall. Along the left wall were the offices of the VFW. Sitting in the main hall were two dozen men sitting at tables and talking. Most were wearing baseball caps with the war they fought in.

Grandpa walked and waved to some of the men as he made his way to a table near the west side of the building.

"Clark, good to see you," said a dark man with a big toothy grin dressed all in black. On his jacket was an Iraqi lapel pin. He was seated with three other men. One of the men was the color of chestnuts and bearded. The man next to the toothy grin was sandy hued with curly salt and pepper haired and had a speckled broom brush mustache. The third man was wearing rectangular glasses on his rectangular face. He was clean shaven and tone but not extremely muscular. On his head was a baseball cap with Desert Storm embroidered on the front.

"We got our assignments for the Fourth," chestnut beard said, handing Grandpa Clark an index card. Grandpa Clark squinted and looked at the card.

"I got Kreke Avenue. I hope there's a restaurant nearby, so I can go to the bathroom when I want," the salt and pepper curly-haired man said.

"I'm sure you can talk your way into one of the houses on that block to let you piss if you need," Iraqi lapel pin said.

"Me, I found out last week," Desert Storm said. "I'm posted at Enterprise Rent-A-Car." He smiled smugly. "Easy job."

That was Gramps's posse. They had been friends forever. The only one I sort of recalled was the one wearing the Desert Storm baseball cap. We had gone fishing together once when I was here for the summer. I thought his name was Morris.

"Zee, go get you something to eat or watch TV," Grandpa Clark said, looking at me standing there not knowing what to do. "I'll come get you when I'm ready to go."

I gave a thumbs up. I scanned the room and found the buffet. There was always food at the VFW. That day I loaded up on two hotdogs, a bag of Ruffle potato chips and grape soda.

Not wanting to be a bother I sat in the shaded back area of the VFW and watched three veterans talking over the TV.

The three veterans sat at one table. They were small men. One wore a Korea/WWII baseball cap. The dark-haired veteran of the three wore an Iraqi baseball cap. The third veteran had a Persian Gulf baseball cap on his head.

The TV was mounted on one of those swing arms that was positioned so everyone could see it in the corner of the back area of the VFW.

I sat down at a table and began eating. As I ate, I watched the veterans talking amongst themselves.

"You know when I came here the crossroads was busy," old vet wearing a Korea/WWII baseball cap said. "Now, it is borderline dangerous. It's like we're living in Chicago or..."

"Don't try and claim that Effingham is as crowded as Chicago," the Iraqi Veteran baseball cap wearer said.

"There are just so many people down here now," said the vet wearing a Korea/WWII baseball cap.

"What are you talking about? Effingham is a small town and will always be a small town," Persian Gulf vet said. He was an average sized man with blue eyes and a straight nose and thin lips. He was dressed in a dark blue Navy collared shirt with a white T-shirt beneath, matching trousers and black polished dress shoes. On his head was well-worn Persian Gulf embroidered baseball cap.

"There's a lot more crime here nowadays," the Korea/WWII baseball cap wearer said. "Lot more than I remember."

"There's always crime. People are always looking for opportunity," the big eared Iraqi Veteran baseball cap wearer said.

"Yeah, you are right about that," the Navy Persian Gulf vet said. "I saw someone drop a dollar and a kid picked it up and didn't even think twice about returning it to the man. The kid just pocketed that money."

"What are they teaching them in school?" big ears said.

"What are they teaching them at home is more important," Korea/WWII vet with a diagonal scar through his lips said.

"They being taught to care only about money and what it can buy," the blue-eyed Persian Gulf vet said.

"There used to be a time when if someone dropped a dollar a kid would have picked it up and given it back," Korea/WWII said.

"You talking about Honest Abe?" big eared vet asked with a smile. "That was a helluva a long time ago."

"No, I am talking about how things are changing in front of our eyes," the Korea/WWII baseball cap said.

"Things ain't changing. Things have always been this way. You just got old. Now, you can sit back and see what you didn't want to or didn't think was going on," the blue-eyed vet wearing the well-worn Persian Gulf baseball cap said.

"I maybe the oldest at the table, but that don't mean that what I am seeing isn't happening," Silas said.

"No one said that you were wrong, Silas," the Persian Gulf vet said. "It's just that your perspective might be a little off."

"Off? How?" Silas asked.

"This place is a small town," the vet wearing a Persian Gulf baseball cap said. "People come through our little town on the way to other places. Simple as that. We have crime. Everyone has crime. This ain't nirvana. So, we're going to have problems."

"But you know that the little problems in Effingham are nothing compared to Chicago or St. Louis," the vet wearing the Iraqi baseball cap said.

There was a lull. I looked up from my hotdog and watched the table. Two veterans sat at the table. Silas sipped on a beer. The Iraq veteran was sitting and drinking from a glass.

The Persian Gulf veteran had climbed to his feet. He was standing near the rear of the back area. He looked around and fished out his cell phone and talked quietly. After a few minutes he slipped his phone back in his pocket and returned to the table.

"Thought you were the cock of the block?" Silas asked.

"I am," the Persian Gulf veteran said with a smile. "I just need to make sure my house is standing when I return."

"It's just you and Vera now?" Silas asked.

"Yeah, but she seems to need something every time I'm out," the Persian Gulf vet said.

"That's how it is," the Iraqi vet said with a laugh.

"You signed up for this," Silas laughed.

"We all did," the Persian Gulf vet said with a knowing nod.

The three married vets laughed.

"You know there was a disappearance last month?" Silas asked.

"Oh, hell, Silas," the Iraqi veteran said with a shake of his head. "I didn't come here to hear you telling us all your fears from living in Effingham."

"It's not like that," Silas said, defensively.

"It is," the Persian Gulf vet said. "Every time we are together you always focus on the negatives."

Silas sulked. There was an extended tense moment at the table.

"You want to go to St. Louis and catch a baseball game?" The Iraqi vet asked, changing the topic.

"Who're they playing?" Silas asked.

"Does it matter?" The Persian Gulf vet asked.

"No, not really," Silas said with a smile.

"Yeah, we go there and just enjoy the trip," Iraqi vet said.

"Who's going to drive?" Silas asked.

"Vera's nephew is in town," the Persian Gulf vet said. "He is always looking for an excuse to drive somewhere."

"So, last month I read there was a tow truck driver that didn't come back to his tow truck," the hook-nosed Silas said. He was wearing creased khakis and a matching short-sleeved shirt. He looked to be much older than Grandpa Clark, I thought.

"What happened?" The dyed black-haired vet with big ears said, wearing an Iraq Veteran baseball cap.

"Like I said, I was reading about this tow truck driver, and he just parked his truck and never came back to it. The police searched the truck. They searched around the area. No sign of him." Silas paused. "Ain't that a little odd?"

"Yeah, it's odd, but people get fed up with their jobs every day and quit," big ears said.

"Just leave his truck in the middle of the shift?"

"Yeah, that's odd," the Persian Gulf baseball cap wearer said. "But people do odd things."

"So, why you bringing this up?" The vet with big ears asked.

"It's just odd," Silas said. "I mean, It's another... disappearance."

"That really a disappearance?" The Persian Gulf baseball cap asked.

"He disappeared," Silas said, smugly.

Persian Gulf baseball cap smiled and bobbed his head.

"How many is that now?" The vet with the big ears asked.

"Hell, Tobias, who knows the exact number of how many are missing? All that matters is that they're more than two," Silas said.

"I just think that something has to happen," Tobias, the vet with the big ears, said looking at the hook-nosed vet. "It's a shame."

"What are the police doing?" The Persian Gulf baseball cap wearer asked.

The two vets shrugged their shoulders.

"Come on, Zee, we're heading home," Grandpa Clark said as I sipped on my grape soda and tried to watch TV while listening to the old veterans.

We left the VFW and just as fast as we got there, we were gone.

"Did you get enough to eat?"

I chuckled in response. It was one of the benefits of knowing Gramps. Wherever he went there was always food or the hint of food to eat.

Just a week after going to the VFW I looked up and watched the beginning of a new month. July in Effingham was the month that Grandpa Clark perfected his barbeque sauce. It was the same month that every dinner was barbeque something or other. I loved it. Bird enjoyed it despite her attempt to be a vegetarian. No one could be a vegetarian at Grandpa Clark's house in July.

July was also the month that Effingham celebrated the Fourth. It was a big production. The town had a pancake breakfast, a parade, and a fireworks display.

Grandpa and most of his VFW friends were street marshals. They were given the responsibility of making sure that people didn't cross South Banker Street during the parade.

"I'll be gone most of the day for the parade," Grandpa Clark announced. "I am a street marshal."

"We know," Bird said.

Grandpa smiled, a little annoyed at Bird's response.

"Where are you going to be camped out?"

"I'm on West Douglas Avenue, next to Fox Holler Coffee," Grandpa Clark said.

Mom appeared dressed in a blue and white striped top and jeans.

"Are you coming to the parade?" Grandpa Clark asked us.

"We don't celebrate the Fourth of July," Bird said.

"What?" Grandpa Clark said, looking at Bird questioningly. "Who is *we*?"

Bird, dressed in green T-shirt, shorts and basketball sneakers smirked and pointed to me and then her.

"Why?" Grandpa asked.

"Yeah, it isn't a celebration for us," Bird said to Grandpa Clark.

"What? Why not?" Grandpa asked, puzzled.

"Well, it's a lie," Bird said.

Grandpa Clark frowned.

"The worse part of the Fourth of July is that this nation pretends that in 1776 on July Fourth everyone in this country was liberated and freed from tyranny," Bird said. "That isn't true. It's a lie."

"But I have always celebrated the Fourth. I mean, I make barbeque. I shoot fireworks. I drink a few beverages. Enjoy the day," Grandpa said, baffled.

"You can do all that, I guess," Bird said. "But don't pretend that the Fourth of July means that this nation believed or believes in freedom and liberty for all."

"It does," Grandpa Clark said.

"It doesn't Grandpa," Bird said. "Every day we see the two nations and two different treatments in this country."

"I don't believe that," Gramps said.

"It's true," Bird said.

Grandpa frowned again at Bird.

"I think you can enjoy the celebration and not believe in the beliefs that they're celebrating," Bird said. "But most who are celebrating today are celebrating the lie of freedom and justice and liberty for all."

"I don't believe that," Grandpa Clark said.

"Well, then we're fine," Bird said, grinning broadly.

"No. I don't believe that the Fourth of July is not about freedom for everyone in this nation," Grandpa Clark said.

"History says different. History says that in the thirteen colonies when the country was celebrating freedom there was nearly three million slaves in the colonies." Bird looked at Grandpa. "I won't celebrate America's freedom when they were and unapologetically enslaved our ancestors."

"I don't know if you're right," Grandpa said.

"You don't have to believe me. Look it up," Bird said.

Grandpa looked at mom and shook his head. He went to his bedroom and dressed in a white collared shirt, khaki trousers, and comfortable shoes. On his head was his Desert Storm baseball cap.

Grandpa before he left invited us to the VFW parade and fireworks show.

Mom, Bird and I did not go. Instead, we hung out with Bo and tried to keep him calm while the fireworks popped outside. Bo did not like the firecrackers too much, but he was not jittery or completely freaked out from the firecrackers and fireworks like he was in Chicago.

For the Fourth Mom made us dinner. We ate Spinach and ricotta lasagna for dinner. For dessert we had mini raspberry custard muffins in the backyard. That day, when Gramps returned from being a street marshal we sat in the backyard and watched fireworks and fireflies.

A week after meeting Stephanie Graham in the Effingham Public Library, while Bird and I were walking around the Artisan Craft Festival in the Effingham County Courthouse Museum Stephanie Graham showed up. I waved at the Effingham librarian.

"Who is that Zee?"

"The librarian that knows grandpa," I reported.

Mom went to meet the Effingham librarian.

"Hope you come by the house soon, my dad would love to have you over," Mom said.

My mom had made the dinner a reality. The Grahams were coming for dinner on a Thursday night.

Chapter 7.

Stephanie Graham, that night, didn't look like a librarian. She was still the same person with arched eyebrows, almond shaped brown eyes, and wide mouth, but she seemed different. She was dressed in a wine-colored dress that showed off her tone arms. On her wrists were silver bracelets. In her hands, a small bouquet of pink and yellow flowers.

Her husband, Daryl Graham, was dressed in a dark blue suit with light blue collared shirt. He had a peanut shaped head with dark eyes and round nose above his bearded face. Darryl Graham seemed incredibly smart.

According to Grandpa and Mom he worked and owned five of the million gas stations in Effingham. He was a round cheeked bearded man with a noticeable pot belly. Darryl Graham had been a high school athlete and fallen in love with Stephanie Green while in high school.

When Stephanie went to the University of Illinois and got her degree in Library Studies Daryl Graham went to Eastern Illinois University and decided to study business and then dropped out and began working at a gas station. By the time Stephanie graduated Darryl Graham owned three gas stations.

The bibliothecary offered Mom the small bouquet of flowers. Darryl Graham had brought a bottle of wine. He handed it to our mother. Mom and the Grahams smiled. Mom handed Bird the wine. She handed me the flowers.

"Take the wine to the kitchen and find a vase and put the flowers in them," Mom said to Bird who was pulling me with her toward the kitchen.

Grandpa Clark was puttering around the kitchen when Bird and I entered.

"Grandpa," Bird began, handing him the bottle of wine. "This is from the Grahams." Before I could speak Bird continued. "We need a vase for the flowers."

I lifted the bouquet of flowers wrapped in cellophane.

Grandpa gave a crooked grin, taking the wine bottle.

"Think there might be a vase in the lower cabinet near the refrigerator," Grandpa said.

I looked around the kitchen, found the refrigerator, and made a beeline to the cabinet. Opening the cabinet, I found a small clean glass vase about two feet tall.

"Be careful," Bird said, watching me retrieve the vase.

I stood up and brought the vase to Bird and Grandpa. Grandpa took the vase and studied it.

"Okay, go back and entertain our guests," Grandpa Clark said. "I'll be there in a minute."

Bird and I returned to the living room where Mom was sitting and talking with the Grahams. Bird stood at the end of the couch and smiled at the Grahams. I did the same. I marveled at the light sound of music coming from somewhere in the living room. In the handful of days in grandpa's house I had not even heard the television let alone music playing.

"Music," I announced to Bird. She chuckled and moved her head side to side.

The front two main rooms of grandpa's house looked inviting. Bird and I had spent all day making both rooms presentable.

Grandpa Clark appeared. Darryl seeing grandpa climbed to his feet and formally greeted grandpa. The two shook hands and the handshake turned into a bear hug from grandpa.

"Good to see you, Mister Clark," Darryl managed to say, as grandpa released him.

"Likewise," Grandpa said, turning and walking to the Effingham librarian.

Stephanie attempted to extricate herself from the couch's overstuffed cushions, but grandpa was quicker. He extended his hand and Stephanie took it. He lifted her effortlessly from the clutches of the couch.

"Mister Clark, it has been a while since we have had some of the best cooking in Effingham," Stephanie said.

Grandpa Clark stood looking at Stephanie with a small, crooked smile on his face.

"You trying to butter me up?" Grandpa Clark asked, seriously. "Because it's working."

Everyone laughed.

"You and Darryl are always welcome here," Grandpa said. "And speaking of food, let's move this dinner to the dining room and feed some folks."

We moved to the dining room. The dining room table could seat ten comfortably. That night it sat six. Grandpa Clark sat at the head of the table. On either side of him was Mom and Bird. Next to Mom sat Darryl Graham. Across from him was Bird. Next to Darryl was his wife. Next to Bird was me.

"This is kind of cool," I stated aloud as we sat in the dining room and listened to the adults talk.

Grandpa Clark was in charge of the food. As soon as he sat everyone was able to eat.

That night Grandpa Clark did not disappoint. At dinner, we ate Southern green fried tomatoes, classic Southern fried chicken, red beans and rice, sweet tea, and real banana pudding.

"You know that when I first moved here it was your family that welcomed me?" Grandpa Clark asked Darryl.

"My mom was always going around the neighborhood and welcoming in the new residents," Darryl Graham said with a chuckle. "She felt that everyone deserved a good welcome. It was like a warm hug or pat on the back for the people moving in."

"She was definitely unique in a town like Effingham," Grandpa Clark said.

"I miss her every day," Darryl said.

After dinner, Grandpa Clark ushered everyone outside and into the backyard. In a corner of the backyard there was a small firepit and chairs to sit around. He did not light the firepit. Instead, we sat around the firepit and studied the stars and talked.

It was one of those crystal-clear nights in Effingham, I recalled. There was not a cloud in the sky. In the sky there was a bright, fingernail thin sliver of moon overhead.

"There's nearly no moon," Daryl Graham said, seeing me looking up at the sky.

I agreed.

"You know what they say about sides of the moon," Daryl Graham said with a slanted grin. Before I could answer he spoke. "Everyone is a moon and has two sides. There's the light side, the side that people want everyone to see. Then there is the dark side that they do not show to anybody or want people to see," the man dressed in a dark blue suit with light blue collared shirt said.

"How is your summer going?" Stephanie asked mom.

"Well, Effingham is some place to get used to," Mom said with a smile. "It is a truly unique place," Mom added.

"It is definitely a bit of culture shock coming from Chicago. It has to be a trip to be here this summer," Stephanie said with a smile to our mom.

"It's definitely different," Mom said.

There was a pause.

"It's got its good points and bad. Just like everywhere. They want this small town to be some place to stop and visit on the way to St. Louis or Indiana," Stephanie said.

"How is that going?" Mom asked.

Stephanie shrugged her shoulders in answer.

"How is the business, Darryl?" Grandpa Clark asked.

"It's good, but you have to always be vigilant," Darryl said. "They are always trying to sabotage you when you aren't looking."

"That's why you have to hire people you can trust," Grandpa Clark said.

"Right," Darryl Graham said. "Of course, they try to get you and try and say I'm reverse discriminating against them."

"You can't trust everyone," Grandpa Clark said.

"Agreed," Darryl Graham said.

"Enough business talk," Mom said to the relief of Stephanie.

"Are you and Stephanie thinking about the future?" Grandpa Clark asked. We were in the backyard, under the stars.

"We're always thinking about the future," Darryl said.

Grandpa Clark smiled.

"You know since I been here this place is a good crossroads place," Grandpa Clark said.

"But there are some places where it seems like we are back in the 1940's. So, be careful where you go at night," Darryl Graham admitted.

"Daddy, I thought this place was better than the last time I came down here?" Mom asked.

"It is but there are still problems. Problems don't just go away because you go away. You have to fix problems. It takes time,"

Grandpa Clark said. "That's why I am always happy to have Darryl and Stephanie come by. They know the problems aren't over just because they own a few gas pumps."

Everyone agreed.

"So, Clark, you entering the HAM-JAM this year?" Asked Darryl Graham.

Grandpa Clark shrugged his shoulders.

"What is the HAM-JAM?" Bird asked.

"It's just something that we do to celebrate the best cooks in Effingham," Stephanie said.

"Darryl, are you going to compete?" Mom asked.

"I'm not on that level," Daryl Graham said.

"The EffingHAM-JAM is a big deal around here," Stephanie said.

"Bragging rights," Darryl said. "I'm surprised they haven't convinced you to open a restaurant or sell your barbecue sauce to someone Clark."

"I'm not interested," Grandpa Clark said. "I'm still just an amateur. I'm doing it for fun."

"And bragging rights," Darryl said with a laugh.

Grandpa Clark smiled.

"There's the KCBS Championship, which is a really big deal," Stephanie Graham said, looking at Grandpa.

"That's for the pros," Darryl said.

"The Hometown Throwdown though is where the locals get to compete for bragging rights for the year," Stephanie said. "Your grandfather has won a bunch of times."

"Really?" Bird asked.

"Yeah," Daryl Graham said.

"How many times have you competed?" Stephanie asked.

"Ten times," Grandpa Clark said.

"How many times have you won?" Mom asked.

"Nine," Grandpa said.

Chapter 8.

The Thursday, the day before the HAM-JAM, I woke up to the sound of a door opening and closing downstairs. I climbed out of bed and was surprised to find that Bo was not by my bed. I stretched and scratched and headed for the stairs. When I came downstairs the kitchen lights were on. I walked into the kitchen, and it seemed that grandpa had been up for hours. He was wearing his Cubs baseball cap, a T-shirt, and khaki pants. Gramps was seated near the backdoor and removing his wet boots. Bo was sitting next to grandpa. Grandpa looked up and grinned and rubbed Bo's head. Bo padded to my side. I watched as grandpa placed his wet boots near the door. He slipped on his house slippers and moved to the stove.

Grandpa began to make breakfast. I watched as he washed his hands and started cooking breakfast for us. I just sat and watched. I loved watching the big man moving in the kitchen, mixing things, checking the heat, playing with dough in front of the kitchen window with the sun starting to shoot strands of light into the kitchen.

By seven, breakfast was made. Grandpa Clark made sweet potato dumplings, cheesy grits, and southwest hash with eggs for breakfast. Grandpa always had milk, apple, and orange juice available for the morning.

Mom appeared with the Effingham newspaper in hand and dressed in a light blue dress with an embroidered monogram over her heart. Her hair was brushed back to show off her round forehead, big brown eyes, and full lips. Hanging from her earlobes were hoop earrings.

"I'm going to Eastern this morning," Mom said, looking at me and Bird.

"Can I go?" Bird asked. She looked at me after asking.

I shook my head at the idea of leaving Effingham.

"Sure, be ready to go by nine," Mom said.

"What are you going to do today, Zee?" Bird asked.

I shrugged my shoulders as I ate.

"Don't you want to go to the college with me and Bird?" Mom asked sitting at the kitchen table and placing the newspaper on the table. She smiled as she ate one of the Sweet Potato Dumplings.

"Leave the boy alone," Grandpa said. "He'll be fine here. I can always use a little help around here." He sat down at the kitchen table with a cup of coffee. "We might go to Salt Creek after I finish packing the wagon." Gramps looked at me over his coffee cup. "Sound good, Zee?"

I twisted my lips into a smile and gave my grandpa a thumbs up.

Mom and Bird talked about Eastern Illinois and having lunch before returning to Effingham. After breakfast Bird and I washed the dishes and cleaned up the kitchen while Gramps and Mom talked.

"What you doing at the university, Jess?" Grandpa Clark asked leafing through the newspaper.

"Just checking on some things," Mom said.

"You thinking about going back to school?" Grandpa Clark asked.

"It's an idea," Mom said to grandpa.

Grandpa Clark didn't press. He just looked at my mom and his daughter, knowingly.

"Bird, go and change if you going with me," Mom said, and Bird threw the rag she had been using to wipe down the kitchen table at me as she ran to the stairs to change.

A few minutes later Bird came downstairs dressed in a floral button front blouse and jeans. On her feet were basketball shoes.

Mom smiled at the subtle transformation.

"You sure you don't want to come to Eastern?" Bird asked.

I smirked. The idea of being with my mom and sister was not an option usually. I was always with them whenever they decided to go somewhere. I liked the idea of not being forced to shadow the two. It was just a different experience. In my head, it was not an insult, it was more a need for space.

"Suit yourself," Bird said, heading to the back door for her day trip to Charleston, Illinois.

"Zee don't get in daddy's way," Mom said. "He has a lot to do to prepare for tomorrow."

I smiled at my mom's advice. I agreed.

By a quarter to nine Bird and Mom were on their way to Charleston and Eastern Illinois University.

I waved goodbye from the front porch. As the Rav4 drove down the street Grandpa Clark patted me on head and spun on his heels and headed through the house toward the kitchen. I followed. In the kitchen Gramps turned and found me just a few feet behind him. He grinned.

"You get dressed. I'll be in the back packing the wagon. You can help. Maybe a little after lunch we can go to the creek?"

I gave a quick nod. Gramps nodded too. He walked out the backdoor. I walked up the stairs to my bedroom with Bo following. Dressed in T-shirt, basketball shorts and sneakers I made my way back downstairs.

Grandpa Clark was organizing his equipment. I walked out of the backyard and Bo slipped out with me. I stopped and looked at Bo seriously.

"Okay, Bo, you stay here if you get into trouble," I stated. "No running around or you have to stay in the backyard."

Bo listened and I looked at him for some understanding. He leaned against me and pushed me a little to the side. I gave Bo a beat to understand and then headed to the garage and grandpa. Bo followed silently.

On one side of the garage wall were all of grandpa's barbeque equipment and tools. He had two suitcases that hung on the wall, identical in shape and size. Also, on the wall hung a dozen grill thermometers. There were also several wire mesh baskets on the wall. Against the wall was grandpa's black portable grill. It was on wheels and had locking brakes. Next to the grill were four bags of charcoal and two cords of chopped wood. Sitting on top of the wood pile were bags with spices. Gramps had a mini fridge in the garage as well. Next to the mini fridge was Bird's scooter.

On the other side of the garage sat the Porsche Speedster convertible without a passenger door or an engine hood. The Speedster was silver with a black and red leather interior. It looked like a rocket with wheels.

"You need any help?" I said aloud, looking at my grandfather.

Grandpa Clark was at a cabinet against the wall. He turned and looked at me with a big smile.

"Sure, sure," he said. "What do you feel like doing?"

"Anything," I stated.

"Okay, can you get the lights for the Jeep and set them behind the rear wheels?" He asked, pointing to two portable lights that sat on a shelf near the front of the garage. "Then, you can help me pack the wagon."

I grabbed the heavy lights and took them to the Jeep. Bo followed interested. We carefully walked the lights to the rear of the Jeep and placed them gingerly on the driveway behind the rear wheels.

When I returned from the Jeep Grandpa Clark and I walked to the side of the garage and got to work uncovering the wagon he used for carrying his equipment to the barbeque contest. Gramps was methodical. He sent me to get a broom to sweep out the dried mud and dust that had settled in the wagon before we attached it to the rear of the Jeep. After attaching the wagon, I got to learn how to attach the lights I had brought out to the Jeep.

"You see, these lights signal anyone behind us of what we're doing. I have lights on the wagon, but I have always believed it was better to be safe than sorry," Grandpa Clark said.

Bo whined and I looked at the big baby. He had been incredibly good the whole time we were out helping grandpa.

"Grandpa, I have to feed Bo," I announced, with a shrug of my shoulders. Bo hearing his name climbed to his feet. "I'll be back after he's fed."

"Okay, feed him and come back," Grandpa Clark said with an easy smile, looking at Bo and then me.

"Come on Bo," I declared. Bo instantly was by my side. He brushed up against me like he was a cat and not seventy pounds of muscle. He nearly bowled me over.

We, Bo, and I, went into the back of the house. I got Bo some food and refilled his water bowl. He drank thirstily from the bowl like he had been in the desert for years. I sat at the kitchen table in the quiet house and watched Bo lapping up his water and then eating his food. While Bo ate, I decided to explore the house, just a little, while I waited for Bo to finish eating.

I walked to grandpa's den. The den was just on the other side of the kitchen and had a window that looked out to the side yard. In the center of the room was a wooden desk and behind it two bookcases with books. A bookcase sat on either side of the desk. There were a set of shelves that connected the bookcases. On the three shelves were ten ribbons, grill sets, and aprons. Also, on top of the shelves were seven silver hog replicas. The hogs were 12-inches tall and just as long. On each hog's side was etched the words: Top Hog followed by the four Arabic numbers of the year.

I wondered where the other three silver hogs were? I scanned the small room and did not find the missing hogs. I looked on the bookshelf and saw one of the missing silver hogs being used as a bookend. I grinned finding the eighth silver hog.

I looked up and down the books and found that many of the books in Grandpa's library were cookbooks. The ninth silver hog sat on the third shelf of the bookcase between two cookbooks.

I stood in the den, where Grandpa Clark would sit and read the newspaper, or the book Bird brought him and wondered if the tenth silver hog was hidden on the bookshelves somewhere. I scanned the bookcase and decided that the tenth silver hog was not in grandpa's den.

Bo showed up while I was looking for the last missing silver hog. He shouldered me as was his way of getting my attention. I gave him a rub on the head and pushed the beast out of grandpa's den. I headed to the backyard with Bo in tow.

While we worked grandpa and I talked. I didn't talk too much with many people but being around my gramps was different. I felt comfortable and I found myself asking things aloud that I usually only thought in my head.

"Grandpa? How long you had that car?" I asked, tossing my head back to the garage.

Grandpa Clark shook his head. He scratched at his jaw thinking. He shrugged his thick shoulders.

"I don't know," he said finally. "Maybe ten or twelve years."

"Have you ever driven it?" I asked.

"Not yet," he said.

"You think it'll be drivable soon?" I asked.

Grandpa Clark grinned reluctantly at the question. He looked at me with those big brown eyes and did not answer immediately.

"Why you asking all these questions about something I'm tinkering on?" The giant of a man asked.

I shrugged my shoulders, uncertain how to answer. Grandpa Clark stared at me seriously like he was trying to decide something. He smiled and after securing something in the wagon looked at me with a different expression.

"Well, I have a laundry list of things to get to make my Sweet Chica ready," Grandpa Clark said.

Chica? Gramps named his car? I smiled at the idea of Gramps naming his car.

"What? You think that's funny?" He smiled and paused. "Anything of value has a name," Grandpa Clark said. He grinned and returned to cataloging his grilling equipment and preparing them for the HAM-JAM.

I thought about what Gramps said. Anything of value has a name. I have a name. I am valuable. Bird has a name. She is valuable. Bo has a name. What Gramps said made sense. I searched in my head for the most valuable things I owned, and they too had names.

My comics, the most important ones, were named for the action in them and not the character on the cover. I let all that sink in as I shuttled back and forth from the garage to the wagon and back helping my grandpa.

Walking outside and into the heat of the day I looked left and right, and a question came to mind. I placed the chopped wood where my Gramps instructed me and returned to the shade and coolness of the garage.

"Grandpa? You ever want to live anywhere else?" I asked.

Grandpa Clark was a straightforward kind of man. He either answered or didn't. If he didn't want to answer, he didn't. There were no ifs, ands, or buts with him.

"You know before you or Bird were born, I considered moving," he said, opening the cabinet only to close it without taking anything out. He turned and looked at me. "I thought about it long and hard, but things didn't work out. So, I stayed here."

"Where did you want to live?" I asked holding a grill brush.

"For the longest time I thought about living in Las Vegas," Grandpa Clark said, leaning against a beam holding up the garage. "I'm not a gambler or anything but I like all the entertainment there."

I understood. I looked at Gramps. He was nearly two times my height and had to weigh one hundred pounds more than me, if not more. Grandpa Clark looked like a man that could have been a football player, a boxer, or a firefighter long ago. His hands were three times my hand size. He was the biggest man I had ever seen up close. Now, I knew there were bigger people, but I only knew my Gramps.

"Grandpa," I pronounced, frowning for a moment, to the gigantic man with biceps as thick as my thighs. "You ever play any sports or... go to see the Cubs play?"

Grandpa Clark smiled broadly. He looked like a big kid suddenly. I grinned seeing him smile so easily. We had boxed the spices and placed them in the corner of the wagon. It, the wagon, was not more than six feet long and four feet wide. The wagon had a three-foot-high railing around it. The rear had a gate and a short ramp.

"When I grew up there were all these great baseball players; Hank Aaron, Ernie Banks, Lou Brock, Bob Gibson, and Fergie Jenkins. Then things changed. Basketball took over. It is easier to play by yourself or with one other person. You don't need to get two teams together. I get that, but something got lost. Me." Grandpa Clark paused, grabbing a bag of sugar. "I've always liked baseball. I like the team idea of the game." He hesitated, thinking. "Team sports passed me by and then I went to the Army," Grandpa Clark said. He halted. "I like the Cubs. I grew up watching them. So, I go and see them play now and then," Grandpa Clark said. He looked amused and looked toward the front of the house.

"You like watching them play?"

"I go to the Cardinals games when they play the Cubs, since it isn't too far from here." He stopped and gave a crooked smile. "It's nice to just sit and enjoy the day away from things," Gramps said.

We packed the wagon in layers. On the outside were the charcoal and wood. The spices and the two grill sets, not in the cases, sat in the corner of the wagon. There were five folded chairs that lined the side of the wagon as well. There were four sandbags to hold down the pop-up tent.

"Zee, can you go in the garage and get the tarp? It's bright blue and folded up near the cabinet you saw me at earlier," Grandpa said.

I remembered and went into the garage to find the tarp. I located the blue folded material and was surprised that it was heavier than I imagined and incredibly bulky. I tried to bring it to Gramps folded but by the time I had returned to him the tarp was partially unfolded.

"How come you don't use the one we took off earlier?"

"This one has my name on it," Grandpa Clark said proudly. He took the tarp and placed it neatly on top of the charcoal and chopped wood. I looked at the tarp and noticed that there were ten-inch decals with Chef Thomas Clark on them.

Around three o'clock Mom returned from Eastern Illinois with Bird. For the next hour Bird and mom told us about their day trip. Mom had spent most of her time at the Eastern Illinois University library doing research and then going to the university occupational center.

"You should have come with us," Bird said. "We walked on campus and looked at all these buildings. Mom went to the library and there were all these books inside."

I smiled.

"We had lunch at the faculty lounge," Bird said. "It was nice."

Mom laughed as grandpa straightened up the garage.

"We went to the Liberal Arts building," Bird said to me as if I would care.

"Yeah, Sharon took us to lunch. After lunch we walked around the campus and went to a few buildings. The last hour we went and found Sharon and told her to come by, but she said she was going to California for a month," Mom said to grandpa.

Grandpa pouted.

"She ever come by?"

"No," Grandpa Clark said. "You know that she's your friend? Right?"

"I know. I just," Mom began only to stop herself. Mom changed topics. "She always tells me to come by if I ever get down here. So, we went and found her. She told me to tell you: Hey." Mom smiled. "It was nice to see her."

"Who's Sharon?" I asked.

"A friend of mom's, I guess," Bird said. "She worked in the Economics department."

I listened and tried to care. Grandpa came in and went to wash up. When he returned from the bathroom, he began to prepare dinner for us. Mom tried to make dinner, but grandpa would not hear of it.

"I need to keep my skills up for tomorrow," he said as he whipped up another great dinner.

"Go and wash up for dinner," Mom said to me and Bird.

Bird and I headed upstairs, and Bo followed us. He was a constant shadow for me. I liked that about him, even though Bird thought that Bo loved her more.

"I found a bunch of books on Juneteenth. I asked the librarian if I could copy the names and authors down for Gramps. She said yes," Bird said smugly.

"You going to give the list to grandpa?" I asked.

"Yep," Bird said. She smiled like she was trying out for a toothpaste commercial. "I also copied something from an encyclopedia that told a little bit about Juneteenth." She took a breath. "I'm giving him that too."

I washed my hands and face and shrugged at Bird's library research.

That night we ate honey BBQ chicken skewers, peach BBQ baked beans, fried pickles, creamed corn, and honey cornbread muffins. Grandpa was testing his various barbecue sauces, trying to decide which to use at the HAM-JAM.

After dinner Bird and I cleaned up the kitchen. While we were finishing the dishes and sweeping the kitchen grandpa headed back outside to the small wagon that was covered and tied down attached to the Jeep.

"Mom," Bird said, from the kitchen. "We're done. Is it all right if we go out and help grandpa?"

"Don't get in his way if you go out there. He has work to do to finish before tomorrow," Mom said from the living room.

Bird gestured and we went out the back door. Bo followed.

Grandpa was checking his equipment. Bird leaned on grandpa's Jeep.

"I'm going to take Bo for a walk," I pronounced. Grandpa Clark was focused on his wagon. Bird looked at me and Bo and then returned to watching grandpa.

I took Bo for a walk. When I returned to the backyard, I let Bo climb into the back of the Jeep. He immediately laid down on the backseat and napped.

Bird sat on the fender of the Jeep, and I climbed in the Jeep and onto the hood next to my sister. We watched as grandpa finished packing the wagon for Friday morning.

"Grandpa? When does the cooking start?"

Grandpa Clark was placing his pop-up tent in the wagon when Bird asked her question. I slid off the hood and helped grandpa. So, I was pulling the pop-up tent into the wagon against the folding chairs. There was a designed space left open for the portable grill grandpa was going to put in the wagon last before he left for the HAM-JAM in the morning.

"Thanks Zee," Grandpa said and looked to Bird. "Well, they say that you can set-up at eight and start cooking after," Grandpa Clark said. "So, my plan is to be ready to set-up when I get there. I won't have too much to set-up."

"When do they pick who wins?" Bird asked.

"They judge at five and then there's a public food tasting," Grandpa Clark said as a matter of fact.

While Grandpa Clark was locking down all the things he was going to take to the HAM-JAM we watched. I was trying not to get in the way but help wherever and whenever I could.

I got tired and Bo and I left grandpa and Bird in the dark. Once inside, Bo and I headed upstairs. I found my pajamas. Bo climbed onto the bed.

"Get down," I declared, climbing into bed. I turned off the lights and fell asleep a few minutes later.

The next morning Bo was sleeping at the foot of my bed as usual. I climbed out of bed and as soon as my foot hit the ground Bo was up. He climbed to his feet and followed me out of the bedroom and down the stairs to the darkened kitchen.

I looked around and found the stove warm, but not hot. I walked to the back door and opened it to the cool of the South-Central Illinois morning. Mom's Toyota was parked in the driveway, but Grandpa Clark and the Jeep and wagon were gone.

I panicked for a moment and then remembered that EffingHAM-JAM was that morning.

I let Bo out and went to the guest bathroom. By the time I was done so was Bo. I let him back in the house and we headed back upstairs. I thought about watching TV but after getting upstairs decided against going back downstairs to watch the only TV in the house.

Mom woke up a little after seven and by eight we were eating breakfast.

"Has grandpa checked in?" Bird asked, sitting at the kitchen table. On the table was the latest Effingham newspaper.

"Yes," Mom said. She smiled from the stove. "He has his spot and his pop-up tent up. He said that he should be up and running in an hour."

Mom made praline-pecan French toast with strawberries and blueberries and scrambled eggs. We poured milk, orange, and apple juice for breakfast. Mom put down four wedges of praline-pecan French toast in front of Bird and me. She sat a bowl of scrambled eggs on the table. In front of Bird was a glass of apple juice. I had a glass of milk.

"Do you think that grandpa is going to win?" I asked.

Mom sat down and ate a wedge of Praline-Pecan French Toast. She scooped a spoonful of Scrambled Eggs onto her plate. She did not answer.

"Grandpa has won ten times," I voiced.

"Yeah, that's true," Mom said.

"He has a target on his back now," Bird said. "Everyone wants to knock the king off their throne."

"That ain't nice," I mentioned to Bird.

"I don't know about that," Bird said. "It's just the way people think."

"Finish eating and clean up the kitchen and we'll head down to the HAM-JAM after lunch," Mom said. She waited. "Maybe, if you do a good job on the kitchen, we can go down a little early and have lunch there. Of course, once we get there we're going to stay until the winner's announced."

Bird ate and I tried to keep up. It was our unspoken daily eating contest. Bird was the undefeated eating contest winner. There were no real rules. I did not think that Bird recognized the eating contest. Perhaps, the contest, like many things that were unsaid were actually just my perspective and my contest in the end.

Mom climbed to her feet, rinsed her plate, and put it in the sink along with her now empty cup that had been filled with coffee.

"Okay, clean up the kitchen, Zee, take Bo on a walk and get dressed," Mom said as she left the kitchen.

"Should I take Bo for a walk first?" I asked Bird climbing to my feet.

"We have to clean up the kitchen first," Bird said with a snort.

I sat back down and finished eating my French toast and scrambled eggs.

Bird finished her juice and climbed up from the table. She rinsed her plate and placed it in the sink. She quickly removed the pots and pans left on the stove and kitchen counter and placed them in the sink. Bird washed the dishes first and then the glasses. The flatware was the second to last thing washed and cleaned.

By the time I was finished eating Bird was starting on the pots and pans that needed to be cleaned. I dried the plates and glasses and put them away. We worked as a team.

"Sweep the floor," Bird said, looking in the direction of the broom closet. I gave a small nod. I peeled off and found the broom and dustpan.

"When you're done, wipe down the refrigerator and the stove front," Bird said, while I was sweeping and picking up the trash.

I helped Bird clean up the kitchen and then took Bo out for a walk. The sun was out, and it was warm but not incredibly hot. Bo walked alongside me and sniffed and looked for places to tinkle or poop. I walked him on a leash when we walked down Eiche Street.

People saw me and Bo and thought he was dangerous. So, to avoid the stares and the people crossing the street, more than usual, it was just easier to walk Bo on leash. I preferred walking Bo than having him poop in the backyard. When he pooped in the backyard, I had to clean it up. On the street Bo did his business and the city of Effingham cleaned it up.

We walked to South Banker Street before turning around and heading back to the house. It was a Friday, and most people were off to work or indoors as we returned to grandpa's house. There were a few people climbing in or out of their cars as I walked Bo back to Grandpa Clark's house, but no one said anything to me either way.

Back at grandpa's house I entered through the backdoor of the house with Bo. Bo headed to his dog bowl and lapped up his water like he had been in the desert.

"You thirsty boy?" I asked Bo.

Bo did not look up. He just lapped up his water.

I sat at the kitchen table and studied Bird and Mom. Bird now was dressed in a blue cartoon T-shirt, shorts, and comfortable basketball sneakers. Mom was wearing a floral summer dress and comfortable flats.

"When are we going?" I asked.

"Well, I figure that the best time to get down there is just a little before lunch," Mom said. "By then dad will have had time to set up everything he needs, and he will have texted me his list of items he might have forgotten."

Bird and I chuckled at the idea of Grandpa Clark forgetting something.

"Well, we will need to bring a case of water, just in case," Mom said. "And we're going to get two bags of ice on the way." Mom paused. "He asked to bring the bag of wood chips he left in the garage. He said Zee would know where they were."

I gave a knowing nod. I climbed to my feet.

"Get the chips, Zee, and then go change into a clean T-shirt," Mom said routinely.

I went to the garage and retrieved the bag of wood chips and placed them in the rear of the Toyota. I headed inside the house and to the second floor, thinking what T-shirt I could wear. I didn't have too many choices. So, I picked a shirt I had not worn since we had been in Effingham.

I helped Bird carry the case of water to the Rav4. When Mom unlocked the car, I grabbed the bag of wood chips and placed them inside the Toyota on top of the case of water.

"We're getting two bags of ice," Mom said once we were headed to South Banker Street.

We stopped at a gas station owned by Darryl Graham and bought two bags of ice. I grabbed one bag and Bird grabbed the other and we placed them in the rear of the Rav4 on top of the case of water after I moved the wood chips.

"How you know this is Darryl's gas station?" I asked.

"It's got a sign that says: Graham Gas right over there," Bird said, pointing to the lawn sign sticking out of the small patch of grass.

By the time we arrived at the HAM-JAM there were knots of people moving back and forth on the street in pairs and groups of four. There was a DJ playing music when we parked. I noticed we were across the street from a bank. When we climbed out of the Toyota the heat washed over us. It was oppressively hot, and the sun was still climbing into the sky. By two, according to Bird, the sun would begin to descend and by seven it would be down, and the day would cool off a bit.

The DJ was playing some instrumental music which added to the surreal feeling of all the people walking around the cook off. It was busy and hot when we arrived. The walk to grandpa's pop-up tent was not too far. We walked past the local cooks all wanting to win the Top Hog championship on the Effingham Veterans Memorial Park.

There were five rows of contestants, five deep. Each contestant had a table with their name and number taped to the front. Most contestants had pop-up tents. I walked around and unlike the Moccasin Creek Festival the HAM-JAM had a sprinkling of black and brown faces.

Grandpa Clark sat on the third row and the second contestant under his bright blue pop-up tent. When I saw grandpa, he was dressed in an all-white chef outfit with one of those white stovepipe hats and a white apron. He was all smiles.

Mom carried the wood chips, Bird and I managed to carry the case of water between us with the two ice bags on top. We had to be a sight.

Daryl Graham, who was sitting behind the table, seeing us jumped to his feet and ran to our assistance. He took the case of water from us effortlessly, leaving Bird and I holding the ice bags.

"Thanks for all this," Grandpa Clark said. He hugged Mom. He looked to Bird and me and pointed to the cooler beside the table. "Sit those there."

Darryl Graham placed the case of water beside the table.

"Dee, open that case and line the cooler with those waters, then pour in some ice," Grandpa said.

"Sit down," Grandpa said, dressed all in white. He gestured to the five chairs in a semicircular under the shaded protection of the pop-up.

I looked around and in one corner of the pop-up sat the portable grill closed and smoking. All his supplies were in easy reach. Grandpa had a prep table on the other side of the grill. There was a propane tank attached to the grill. It all looked very professional.

Mom sat down. Daryl Graham sat down after putting in the water and the ice. Bird sat down after looking around the pop-up tent. I was the last to sit. Before I sat, I found the missing tenth silver metal hog sitting in a glass case on the table.

"This your last trophy?" I asked.

Grandpa Clark gave a crooked grin. He smiled.

"Have to show them what they messing with," Grandpa Clark said with a confidence that surprised me.

He seemed to be in his element. Grandpa Clark was glad handing all those that came to the pop-up tent. He offered them barbeque chicken, sausage, and ribs. Each contestant was supposed to offer chicken, shish kabobs, sausage, and ribs.

Grandpa Clark smiled from ear-to-ear. He looked so happy. That day, while I was there, he never sat down.

"So, dad, this looks amazing," Mom said with a smile that seemed to stretch from ear-to-ear.

"Yeah, Grandpa," Bird said, beaming. "Very pro."

"There's all these eyes on me," Grandpa Clark said with a chuckle, gesturing to the other cooks. "When I got here there were all these Looky Lous trying to see what I had. They wanted to know what I was going to be cooking with today."

"Wild," Daryl Graham said with a shake of his peanut head.

"Excuse me," Grandpa Clark said, seeing some people wanting to have a taste of his barbeque. Grandpa had samples ready for a few dollars. While we sat there was steady stream of people paying for the samples.

"Dee, is Stephanie here?" Mom asked.

"Naw," Daryl Graham said. "She'll be here when it cools off a little."

"Can we go and check things out?" Bird asked.

"Sure," Mom said. "Hopefully, dad has something for us for lunch?"

"Yeah, of course," Grandpa Clark said with a giggle.

"So, be back in an hour," Mom said. "Because I'm starving."

We laughed and walked down the aisle toward the far end of the Hometown Throwdown. On either side of the wide aisle cooks were cooking.

There was barbeque smoke everywhere. Luckily, the wind was blowing westward and toward St. Louis. The smoke billowed out and over our heads and not into our eyes.

The cook off was more diverse than the Moccasin Creek Festival, I thought but didn't say.

"I'm glad we came to this," Bird said.

"Yeah, me too," I stated as we reached the bottom of the aisle and turned left to head back up the next aisle.

I stopped. I immediately reached out to get Bird's attention.

Standing at the entrance to the next aisle was Amber James and the three Barbies from the Moccasin Creek Festival.

Amber James was dressed in red designer T-shirt, blue distressed jeans, and red sneakers. The Barbies were dressed in designer T-shirts, shorts, and tennis shoes. Behind the Barbies appeared three pale faced boys dressed in T-shirts, baseball jerseys and a polo shirt.

"Well, ain't this cute?" Amber James asked with a painted-on smile. She looked left and right to the Barbies and grinned a toothy grin.

Bird seeing Amber stopped short. Instantly, Bird balled her hands into fists ready for battle. She frowned seeing the daughter of the mayor of Effingham and her friends.

"You going to be all 'tude? Here too?" Amber James asked, with a feigned hurt.

"You going to be all bitch? Here too?" Bird asked.

I shook my head at the cattiness of the two girls. The Barbies oohed at Amber's question and oohed again at Bird's cap. The three boys hearing Bird's words looked at each other.

One of the boys, the one wearing a high school baseball jersey, stepped around Amber, and pushed her behind him.

"What did you just call my girl?" The boy asked in a growl. He was a big-eyed boy with thick eyebrows and pencil-thin nose above his thin-lipped mouth. His brown hair was combed back and away from his flat face.

"I said--," Bird began only to be interrupted by the appearance of a black girl the color of coffee with her hair braided and piled on top of her head wearing a black spaghetti string top, cut off shorts and high-top sneakers. Beside her appeared two boys, one wearing a Chicago Bears T-shirt and jeans and the other wearing a Chicago Bulls T-shirt and matching basketball cap. The boy wearing the Bears T-shirt was average sized with a tight fade and big ears. The boy in the Chicago Bulls T-shirt was a peanut-colored brute of a boy, six foot tall and weighing easily two hundred pounds. He had a Chicago Bulls baseball cap flipped backwards on his neatly trimmed black head.

"Amber James, what you doing? Is your daddy coming? There some photo shoot I don't know about?" The nameless girl asked, placing a hand on her hip.

Bird did not back down but the three stepped forward.

"Where's what we call the paparazzi?" The boy in jeans asked.

I watched the giant, and the two others, stop the boy who was taking up for the mayor's daughter. Amber's nameless boyfriend stopped in his tracks and stood looking daggers into the face of the three new arrivals.

"Paris, this ain't got nothing to do with you," Amber said to the spaghetti topped girl.

"Naw, snowflake, that's where you're wrong. You can't try and punk my fam and think I'm going to let that ride," Paris said.

"Fam? You related to her?" Amber asked.

"Yeah," Paris said with a wicked smile.

"Besides, we don't care if you're the mayor's daughter," the smaller boy wearing the Chicago Bears T-shirt and jeans next to Paris said.

Amber moved her head side to side. She looked at Bird menacingly.

"Just know that I ain't going to be happy if my cousins tell me that you're messing with them," Paris said.

"It ain't got to be like that," Amber said. "I tried to be all friendly with your cousin and all I got was attitude. Now, that ain't right," Amber said, looking at the Paris and the giant.

"Well, I don't know shit. I don't care who did what. All that matters is you trying to punk my cousin. I ain't going to let that ride," Paris said. "For now, you don't say: Boo to my fam. I will talk with my girl and see what is what."

"You know me Paris," Amber said. Amber moved her head side to side and turned on her heels and into the Barbies. "Come on," Amber said. "Let's go the other way." She pushed through the girls and boys, and they made their way away from the trio and toward the other side of the HAM-JAM.

Paris and the two boys watched as Amber and her group walked away from them.

The black girl with her hair braided and piled on top of her head turned and looked at Bird and me. She grinned and adjusted her spaghetti string top on her shoulder.

"I'm Paris," the black girl wearing high top sneakers and cut off shorts said.

"I'm Bird," my sister said.

"Hi," I stated aloud.

"This is Zee," Bird said.

"I'm Trey" said the boy in jeans wearing the Chicago Bears T-shirt.

"This is Donny," Paris said pointing to the big boy with the Chicago Bulls basketball cap. The big boy looked at Bird and I through his dark eyes.

"Are you really our family?" I asked.

"Yeah, little one," Paris said with a laugh. "I was just at Grandpa Clark's tent, and they told us you had just left," Paris said, watching the people walk past them. "Where were you going?"

Chapter 9.

I walked along with the group and tried to gauge everyone. Paris was easy. She was the bad girl. From the looks of her she was the fighter. She didn't look like someone who would back down from a fight. Then there was Trey. He was the negotiator. He looked like he wasn't afraid to fight but preferred to talk his way out of anything physical. The giant, Donny was the cartoon tough guy. I was sort of surprised that he didn't have a T-shirt on that read: Goon. He was the hammer that solved all problems with his fists. So, I didn't expect him to talk too much.

"So, what is the deal with that snowflake?" Bird asked.

"She's a rich girl in a small town and doesn't know what to do about it," Paris said.

"Think she wants to be an influencer," Trey said with a shrug of his shoulders. "Here in Effingham. What can she influence? Boredom?" He shook his head.

Paris chuckled at the idea.

"She wants to get out of here and go to anywhere but here," Trey said with a chuckle. "The problem is that she has two more years before she can."

"Why do you care? You're only here for the summer," Paris said to Bird.

"Yeah, I shouldn't care but I ain't going to let some chicken head, mayor's daughter or not, punk me," Bird said.

I smiled at Bird's toughness. Paris was tough too. If Paris and Bird got together it would only mean trouble was soon to follow.

"You live by my grandpa's?" I asked.

"Sort of," Paris said. "We live on Park."

"They related to you?" I asked, pointing to Trey and Donny.

"No," Paris grinned. "Trey and Donny are my crew. We look out for each other."

"We live over by East Kreke," Trey said, tossing a thumb over his shoulder toward Donny. I grinned and agreed, acting like I knew where East Kreke was in Effingham.

We walked up the rows of cooks and checked out Grandpa Clark's competition. As we walked Bird told Paris about going to Moccasin Creek Festival and meeting Amber and the Barbies.

"Don't nobody I know go to that lame festival," Paris said. "We go to the HAM-JAM, the Pumpkin Hunt, the VW Car show, and the Harvest Moon Festival. But not much else."

Paris and Trey pointed out the three biggest competitors at this year's HAM-JAM.

There was Travis Stillman who had come in second last year at the HAM-JAM. Stillman was a triangular faced man with salt and pepper hair and ears that seemed to want to run away from his head. Unlike Grandpa Clark, Stillman was a small shouldered, average sized man who looked like a schoolteacher more than a barbeque cook.

There was Missus Katie Barber who was a local favorite and first-time contestant. Missus Barber owned a restaurant in Effingham. She looked like someone's fat auntie. She had a round stomach, big hips, big chest, and fat arms that made her look like she could have been a professional arm wrestler. When we walked by her table there was a line to get to eat her barbeque.

The third competitor was Mister Casey Arnold. He had been an on again and off again contestant for the past five years. He liked his food a little spicy and most locals found his barbeque sauce highly seasoned. There were half a dozen people eating Mister Arnold's spicy barbeque.

Chapter 10.

When we returned to Grandpa Clark's tent there was a serious looking young man with the shadow of a mustache behind the table. He had a tight fade with a thin lightning part cut into the right side of his head. In his ear was a Cubic Zirconia diamond stud earring. Around his neck was a thick gold chain. On his wrist was a gold bracelet.

"Where did you go?" The young man asked as Paris and the others walked past the front table.

"Had to find my new family," Paris said.

The young man smiled.

"This is my brother, Frankie," Paris said.

Unlike Paris, Frankie seemed to be a combination of rapper and thinker. Brash and reflective. Dressed in a collared dark blue short-sleeved shirt, designer jeans and nice basketball sneakers Frankie smiled and greeted Mom and Bird and me. He seemed friendly but simultaneously a little closed off.

"So, do you think that the competition is more fierce than last year?" I asked.

"Grandpa Clark knows that they are always gunning for him," Frankie said. "The best thing about a real fighter is that they don't run from a challenge."

Grandpa Clark grinned at Frankie. "No one can stay on the top forever," Grandpa Clark said.

"When the king loses his crown, the choice is always difficult," Frankie said. "Keep fighting to regain the crown or to slink away." Frankie looked at Grandpa Clark. "I don't think you're the kind of person to slink away."

Grandpa Clark grinned.

Frankie was two months from eighteen. He was tall and possessed with a confidence that suggested that he would succeed at whatever he put his mind to achieve. Meeting him and listening to him talk I wanted to hang out with Frankie.

As the sun began to set and the heat broke, just a little, Stephanie showed up to the delight of Mom. The two became fast friends. Well, they had been friends already and they resurrected their friendship.

"I think I'm going to take a walk," Frankie said from his seat. He looked at everyone but did not move. "I know I just want to be back for the judging."

Everyone agreed with Frankie and decided to stretch their legs.

Frankie climbed to his feet. So, did I. Frankie noticed me by him.

"Can I go with you?" I asked.

Frankie shrugged his shoulders as an answer.

Paris, Trey, Donny, and Bird walked in another direction. I walked with Frankie.

Frankie walked to the head of the HAM-JAM and paused looking across the street and toward the Effingham Police Department. I stood by Frankie and looked across the street and at the sun descending from the sky.

Again, I noticed the blank faces of the people staring at me on the light pole on the sidewalk.

"Hey," I stated aloud, reaching out to touch Frankie's forearm. "What's up with them?"

"What?" Frankie said, looking down and finding my hand on his arm. He smiled and looked at the light pole I was looking at. Frankie smiled at the question. He shoved his hands in his pockets.

He looked at the people walking past before saying anything.

"You heard of Tommy Crawford?"

I shook my head.

"What about the South-Central Werewolf?" Frankie asked.

I laughed.

"I'm serious," Frankie said.

He was kidding. Right? I shook my head. My cousin was pulling my leg. Right? He had to be kidding. I liked a good joke as much as anyone but there were a dozen people missing. That wasn't a joke. I mean, I was twelve. I knew that there were no such things as werewolves, vampires, or mummies. I started to smile only to find Frankie looking at me seriously.

"Those people are a bunch of people that Effingham cares about," Frankie said. "They all disappeared during the full moon," Frankie said seriously.

"What? Seriously?" I asked.

"Seriously," Frankie said. "Look it up." Frankie looked around, suspiciously. "There are rumors about the disappearances, but I think that someone knows what's going on."

I was having second thoughts about wanting to walk with Frankie. I shook my head.

"In Effingham and South-Central Illinois there is a story about a werewolf stalking the cornfields," Frankie said as we walked past the DJ booth and a woman dressed in a leather jacket and a purple high collared zip front shirt with a yellow and white design on the front. She had a pair of earphones pressed to one of her ears as she bobbed to the music she was playing. While I was looking at the DJ Frankie kept talking.

"So, there's a werewolf?" I began cautiously. "In the cornfields," I repeated. This had to be a joke. Frankie was trying to see how far he could go before I called him on his fairytale.

"No. Seriously," Frankie said. "The disappearances happen usually during the full moon," Frankie said.

"When is the next full moon?" I asked., curious

"Tonight," Frankie said.

"You know I just met you and all and it would be bad to say something stupid, but no one believes in werewolves," I stated.

"Suit yourself," Frankie said. "Just be inside tonight."

I shook my head. I looked up and around us. We were outside.

Frankie smiled.

I walked with my new cousin who believed in werewolves and wondered if Paris or Donny believed in fairies or aliens or Big Foot.

To bring my new cousin back off the ledge I asked:

"Who is Tommy Crawford?" I asked, confused.

"Right," Frankie said, looking at me concerned. "If you ask anyone," Frankie said, looking around. "They should be looking for him, but they can't be bothered."

I was suddenly confused.

"Tommy Crawford played football and baseball at our high school," Frankie said. "He was a blue-chip athlete and came up missing. No one blinked an eye. No one investigated. Nothing."

"What?" I asked, suddenly confused. I had asked about the four pictures of the men on the light pole. How we got to Tommy Crawford confused me.

Chapter 11.

The stage for the live music was on the side of the Effingham Veterans Memorial building. The local bands began performing at half past five. The judging ended and the announcement was planned to happen on stage at the HAM-JAM stage.

The three-girl band that Bird and I had seen at Moccasin Creek Festival performed.

At the conclusion of their performance the HAM-JAM Hometown Throwdown champion was announced.

The announcement was delivered by Alice Poland a member of the City Council. Poland was an entertainer. She appeared on stage dressed in a blazer, an I Effing Heart HAM- JAM T-shirt, jeans, and comfortable boots. Poland was a dark-haired woman with thick eyebrows, small eyes, broad nose, and thin lips. The council member grabbed the microphone and smiled at the gathered audience before speaking.

"I want to thank all the contestants that participated this year. It was a great turnout. We have twenty-five of the best local cooks around," Poland said. "Don't forget to come by tomorrow to check out the KCBS Grill Off. If you enjoyed today, tomorrow will knock your socks off."

Poland moved her head side to side and fished out the index card she had been given to read.

"Without further ado. The third-place winner for HAM-JAM this year is Casey Arnold. Congratulations on this distinct honor. You receive along with a third-place trophy and a ribbon, a hundred-dollar Amazon gift card and a hundred-dollar gift card to our sponsor BBQ Guys."

Casey Arnold climbed on stage and accepted his ribbon, gift card and cup trophy.

"Second place this year goes to newcomer and chef extreme Katie Barber who impressed everyone this HAM-JAM. She might be the next champion in the making.

"As the second-place winner for HAM-JAM Katie receives a two-hundred-dollar gift card to one of our sponsors at this year's event, Walmart. Katie also receives a ribbon and a plaque for her efforts and this grill set from our sponsor, BBQ Guys." Katie Barber climbed on stage and received her ribbon, plaque, gift cards and grill set.

"The final and champion of this year's HAM-JAM is the seemingly unbeatable Thomas Clark. Thomas Clark everyone. He has won the HAM-JAM for the unprecedented eleventh time in a row. Thomas receives the coveted Top Hog metal trophy, five hundred dollars in prize money, a five-hundred-dollar Amazon gift card and a two hundred- and fifty-dollar gift card to Walmart and a two-hundred-dollar gift card from our sponsor BBQ Guys.

Grandpa Clark climbed on stage, and everyone clapped and cheered. Grandpa Clark received his trophy, prize money, and gift cards.

"Let's give everyone a hand who participated in this year's HAM-JAM."

Everyone remained on stage to be photographed. After the photos were taken the chefs were ushered off stage and the musicians climbed on stage.

The next performance was by another local band who thought they were an eighties group. They were dressed like the big hair bands of the eighties in makeup and elastic tights. It was a spectacle. They were the definition of a one-hit wonder.

The four-member band with the name of Poison Snake had a hit on the radio. I didn't like the guitar heavy music, but they were fun to watch trying to entertain the crowd.

The live show ended at ten o'clock with the most successful local band, Moonwalk, that had a radio hit, "Breakfast Club," and opened for The Broken Pumpkins a moderately famous Chicago group for one summer.

After Grandpa Clark received his awards all the family helped breakdown the pop-up tent and extinguished the grill. All the customers crowded the pop-up tent and seemed to hunger for the championship bits of Grandpa Clark's food. Grandpa made another six hundred dollars before beginning to pack up.

The Grahams were the first to leave after helping Grandpa Clark put the portable grill on the wagon. Stephanie and Mom made a lunch date for the next week.

Paris, Trey, and Donny helped breakdown all the big things and the pop-up tent while the music played.

Bird and Mom took off a little before Frankie.

Frankie packed the mini fridge and propane tank on the wagon before saying his goodbyes.

Grandpa Clark stopped his last bits of packing to give Frankie a hug.

I watched the two hug and smiled at their affection. Grandpa Clark was a hard man, and he did not hug everyone. He liked Frankie. That said a lot about my newly minted cousin.

After Frankie left it was just me and gramps.

"Check to make sure I didn't leave anything important," Grandpa Clark said.

I walked around the area where Grandpa Clark's stall had stood. Now, there was nothing there but an empty space. I looked around the space and returned to my grandfather.

"Grandpa," I announced. "What do you think about Frankie?"

"He's okay," Grandpa Clark said. "He's a little intense at times. It's growing pains."

"What's that mean?" I asked.

"You know," Grandpa Clark said. "The whole youth is wasted on the young thing."

I listened not knowing exactly what grandpa was talking about.

"He wants to do something important. He's just busting at the seams to figure out what that is. Growing pains," Grandpa Clark said.

I smiled and understood.

Grandpa and I finally packed up and were finally ready to leave.

"Frankie told me this crazy story," I announced to grandpa.

Grandpa Clark checked around his spot where his pop-up tent stood one last time before climbing into his Jeep.

"What did he tell you?" Grandpa Clark asked.

"He told me that there's something called a South-Central Werewolf," I muttered skeptically as we drove away from the Veteran Memorial building and onto the darkened streets.

Grandpa Clark chuckled and pointed up and into the night sky. There in the partly cloudy sky hung the full moon.

"Yeah, I know," I remarked smiling. "You think he was just kidding?"

"Don't know," Grandpa Clark said. He drove down Jefferson Avenue to South Banker Street and turned left toward home. "You know this is a small town. Small town people fill their days and nights with foolishness. So, maybe they make things up to stay entertained." He paused. "That make sense?"

I understood.

"Some people believe things no one else believes to make them feel important," grandpa paused and looked at the road ahead. "Zee, you know what a martyr is?"

I shook my head.

"Well, there are some people that are being prosecuted for telling the truth. You know about Martin Luther King and Malcolm X?" He paused.

I raised and lowered my chin.

"There are good people that die telling the truth. Then there are others that believe they are telling the truth, but it's a load of crap," Grandpa Clark said as he drove. "So, like everything there are two sides to this martyr thing."

I listened. I didn't say anything. Was Frankie trying to be a martyr? Did he believe he was telling the truth? Or was grandpa saying that Frankie was telling me a load of crap?

"What you think?" Grandpa Clark asked.

"You mean about werewolves?"

"Yeah," Grandpa Clark said.

I didn't believe Frankie, at first. But I didn't know. I shrugged my shoulders.

"Well, I don't believe in werewolves or vampires or things like that. I ain't got time for that kind of nonsense," Grandpa said. "There are too many things in the real world to worry about, than a bunch of made-up fake stuff," Grandpa Clark said.

I agreed. As we drove down South Banker Street, I looked around the streets a little tired after being in the sun and then packing the wagon. I leaned back and let grandpa drive. As we approached a light, I was surprised to see Frankie crossing East Wabash Avenue against the light heading away from Southside. Now, I wasn't one hundred percent that the person I saw was Frankie, but it looked a little like him. I looked back as we drove, but the dark figure disappeared as quickly as he appeared.

The next morning when I woke up Bo was missing. I walked downstairs to find grandpa in the kitchen making breakfast. He was at the stove making grits and bacon. Bo was laying by the kitchen door. When Bo saw me, he climbed to his feet and padded across the kitchen to me. I gave Bo a pat on the side as I sat down. Bo stood wagging his tail.

"Morning grandpa," I said.

Grandpa smiled and bobbed his head in reply.

I sat at the kitchen table and found The Effingham Daily Record on the kitchen table.

I looked at the newspaper and saw that Grandpa Clark was on the front page of the Effingham Daily Record. The five-column front page had a picture of Grandpa Clark smiling on the right side of the bigger story that read: Two Vanish During Full Moon.

I didn't read the missing persons article thoroughly. Instead, I just scanned it for keywords.

Grandpa turned from the stove.

"Go wake up your sister and wash up and then come down for breakfast," grandpa said. "By then everything will be ready."

I climbed to my feet and headed upstairs. Bo followed.

I tapped on Bird's door as I walked past her bedroom. I grabbed some shorts and a T-shirt and went to the bathroom to wash up. I brushed my teeth and cleaned up and stepped out of the bathroom as Bird stepped into the bathroom dressed in a pink and blue pajama set.

"Grandpa is making pancakes and scrambled eggs," I said.

"I'll be down in a minute," Bird said closing the bathroom door for privacy.

Bo and I returned to the kitchen, and I filled Bo's dog bowl.

Sitting at the kitchen table I looked at the newspaper.

"When did you talk to the news?" I asked.

"I can't remember," Grandpa Clark said. "I didn't read it all the way through. I just thought it was nice to have as a memory of the win."

I looked down at the paper. I skimmed the HAM-JAM article. The article was only about three paragraphs long on the front page and continued on page 9 of the Local News.

Thomas Clark makes it ten in a row, the front-page article began. *The perennial winner of the Effingham HAM-JAM has once again won the coveted amateur cook off with his one-of-a-kind barbecue sauce. Clark's competition included: Casey Arnold and Katie Palmer. Katie Palmer was a HAM-JAM newcomer and chef extreme. Barber impressed everyone this HAM-JAM. She might be the next champion in the making.*

On the front page as big as life was a pair of pictures of two men, with their names beneath their pictures. I read the article and found that the details were startling. These two men had been at a local bar during the HAM-JAM. The first man, John Hartman, worked at Subway as a manager and his disappearance was reported when he did not report for work last night. His phone was found near a dumpster behind Comfort Suites. The other man, William O'Neil, was a tow truck driver. O'Neil simply disappeared and his tow truck was found in the parking lot on West Fayette Avenue. His wallet minus money was found near his tow truck but nothing else was found. Neither man had been found. The reporter mentioned the full moon and there was a question about the South-Central Werewolf. I couldn't believe it.

Bird arrived and sat at the kitchen table and grandpa made me put the paper away for breakfast. As was the custom, Grandpa made a sensational breakfast. It was a breakfast of Easy Cheesy Loaded Grits, Brown Sugar Oatmeal Pancakes, chopped up pears, Fluffy Scrambled Eggs, Bacon and apple and orange juice.

"Congrats, grandpa," Bird said sitting down at the table.

Mom came downstairs and joined us at the table. Seeing the newspaper, she scanned the front page and smiled.

"Congratulations pop. You're a big deal down here," Mom said with a big smile. "You think you can keep repeating?"

Grandpa Clark did not respond.

"Grandpa is the undisputed champion of the HAM-JAM," Bird said.

"You know no one can stay undefeated unless they quit," Grandpa Clark said looking at Mom.

"Yeah," Mom said.

Grandpa Clark shook his head, sitting down and eating a pancake and a couple of forks full of scrambled eggs.

"I think you can keep winning," Bird said to grandpa.

Grandpa smiled at Bird. Grandpa climbed to his feet and poured himself a cup of coffee. With his cup of coffee Grandpa Clark returned to the kitchen table. He sipped at his cup and smiled.

"What do you want to do today?" Grandpa asked me.

I looked at everyone at the table and shrugged my shoulders.

"I think I'm going to go to the lake and get away," Grandpa Clark said. He looked at me out of the corner of his eye. "You want to come?"

"Wait," Mom said. "Aren't you going to the KCBS cook off?"

"I probably will, eventually," Grandpa said, scooping a bit of egg into his mouth.

I looked at Bird and Mom. Bird frowned, thinking.

"Grandpa, you don't want to go to the professional event?" Bird asked. She turned and looked at Mom. "Do you think Paris is going?"

"I'm not sure. Give her a call and see what she's doing," Mom said.

Bird fished out her cell phone and called Paris. The two talked for a few minutes. Bird rung off the phone and talked to Mom. As Bird and Mom talked, I half-listened to them talking about the KCBS cook off.

"They said that they are going to be at the cook off. They invited us to meet them," Bird said.

Instantly, I thought of Paris, Trey, and the non-talking Donny. I smiled thinking of wacky Frankie and his belief in werewolves. I wanted to see my cousin's and the others, just because.

I looked to grandpa and tried to think of a way to back out of going to the lake with him. I suddenly wanted to listen to and ask Paris a million questions and especially pick Paris's brain about her brother and werewolves.

"Okay, Zee, after you and Bird clean up the kitchen, get dressed and we'll head to the lake for a couple of hours. Then maybe we'll get lunch and head to the HAM-JAM before heading home and maybe stopping at Dairy Queen for a Blizzard," Grandpa Clark said with a grin.

Bird and I cleaned the kitchen. I cleaned up and dressed in my summer wear. For the whole summer I had not worn jeans or pants. I wore T-shirts and gym short or cut off shorts and gym shoes every day. Occasionally I wore basketball shorts.

So, dressed in a Chicago Bears T-shirt and basketball shorts I took Bo for a walk. Bo loved to run in the field, and I didn't mind walking and sometimes chasing him through the uncut grass field that sat on the other side of Eiche Avenue and stretched all the way to Blohm Street.

That morning Bo found a rusted bicycle frame. I was a little surprised by the find, but it seemed like people used the empty lot for trash and rubbish disposal. I kicked the bike frame that was just the diamond frame all beaten up and with flecks of green paint near where the front fork would have gone. I studied the frame and noticed that there were no round spots on the frame. It looked like someone had methodically stomped the bike frame flat for some reason. It looked like someone had been incredibly angry at the bike and beat it up with no mercy.

Bo did his business and we walked back to grandpa's house. I looked back at the field and where the bike lay. I figured that if I walked the whole field, I would find all sorts of odd things. At the edge of the field, I stopped and tried to think what else might be hidden in the field.

I crossed the street and walked to the rear of grandpa's house. Bo walked alongside me. He paused and waited for me to open the back gate before bounding into the backyard and up the stairs to the back door of the house. I opened the door and Bo scrambled inside.

After walking Bo, Mom and Bird were preparing to go and have lunch with Paris and her family.

"We're going to meet them at the HAM-JAM," Bird said.

"We're making a day of it," Mom said beaming, dressed in a light blueprint dress that showed off her arms and legs. "Stephanie and Darryl are going to show up and we're going to sit out and listen to some music."

"Sounds fun," Grandpa Clark said, with a grin.

"Grandpa are there any cooks that you recommend?" Bird asked.

"No, not really," Grandpa Clark said, dressed in a polo shirt, khaki trousers, and comfortable shoes. He was wearing a pair of Ray Ban sunglasses and his well-worn Chicago Cubs baseball cap. "Today is for the professionals who get paid to cook. So, it should all be good."

Chapter 12.

The route to the lake was unfamiliar to me as Grandpa Clark drove toward the west and Bo sat in the back looking at everyone and everything. We made our way to the edge of Effingham. Grandpa Clark was in no hurry. We drove up North Keller Avenue and out past the Flying J and TA Travel Center to Lake Pauline.

Lake Pauline was only three miles outside of Effingham. We parked on the side of the road under a handful of trees that gave off shade and walked to the edge of the lake. From the bank of the lake, I could see a bunch of RVs, a store, and some people walking around the edge of the silvery water. There was also a small sturdy pier that jutted out and into the water.

Grandpa Clark had a cooler and two folding chairs. He marched by me as I looked at the four boats on the lake. Bo, on leash, stood by my side.

"Are we fishing?" I asked, trying to keep up with grandpa as he walked along the bank.

"It's too late in the day to fish now," Grandpa Clark said, never looking back. "The best time to fish is early, in the cool of the morning, when the fish are hungry."

I listened, agreed, and looked at the lake on my side with Bo brushing against my leg. Bo was a curious dog. He liked the water. So, taking him to the lake meant that he would eventually end up in the water. The question was when not if he would end up in the water.

I felt a tug on the leash and found Bo standing chest deep in the lake's water. He was looking out at the wide-open water, longingly.

"Grandpa," I said, seeing Bo in the lake. "Bo is in the lake."

Grandpa turned with those words. He didn't seem angry or upset but amused. His lips curled into a soft grin as he stood looking at me holding the leash and Bo standing in the lake.

Grandpa Clark snorted and bobbed his head at the sight of Bo standing in the water. He adjusted the folding chairs and cooler in his hands and turned on his heels.

"We don't have too much further to go," grandpa said, continuing his march along the bank.

"Come on, Bo," I said, giving the leash a tug and getting Bo's attention. Bo splashed his way out of the lake and onto the bank. Once out of the water Bo proceeded to shake himself dry and douse me.

True to his words, Grandpa Clark stopped underneath the shade of two trees that seemed to be leaning on each other. He put the cooler on the ground and unfolded the chairs to sit on. To the left of us, maybe one hundred feet away were a group of anglers with their reels and rods and lines cast into the lake hoping for a bite. I scanned the lake's surface for where the anglers were fishing, looking for the telltale signs of bobbers and stoppers floating on the silvery surface. Maybe three hundred feet from the bank were a handful of fishing floaters. Just beyond the furthest were two other bobbers.

"You think I can let Bo off leash?"

"I don't see why not," grandpa said, sitting and enjoying the lake and the slight breeze that moved the grass blades at our feet.

I let Bo off leash and immediately Bo walked to the edge of the lake and ran headlong into the water. I watched nervously as Bo nearly disappeared in the lake only to reappear as the water settled. He was not completely soaked. Somehow, Bo had managed to keep one ear dry.

"Sit down," Grandpa Clark said, gesturing to the chair.

I sat.

"You need to relax," grandpa said behind his Ray Ban glasses.

I sat and took a deep breath. I exhaled looking at the stillness of the lake. Bo, in dark water up to his chin, was looking at me and grandpa. I looked to the left and my grandpa, who seemed to not have a care in the world. I listened to the indistinct sound of the voices one hundred feet to our left. The sun was up and though it was warm and leaning toward becoming hot, there, on the bank of Lake Pauline, everything, that moment, was pleasant.

"You know the difference between intelligence and genius?" Grandpa Clark asked.

I shook my head.

"Quiet," Grandpa said.

I frowned, not understanding the answer.

Grandpa didn't speak for a moment.

"There's too much noise and distractions around people nowadays," Grandpa Clark said. "The people, the children, that might be able to solve all the problems we face are too distracted by the latest and greatest thing. They don't get time to just be quiet." Grandpa paused. "The greatest inventions and discoveries didn't happen at a concert or on a dancefloor. They happened in the quiet of a lab or a library or place like this."

I agreed, understanding what he was trying to say.

"How often do you just stop and get quiet and think?" Grandpa under his Chicago Cubs baseball cap breathed. He seemed in no hurry. "You want to solve real problems? Get quiet."

I sat and listened to the quiet all around me. Bo, having cooled off in the water was lying by my side, resting.

Grandpa had packed us a lunch. He had packed cornbread, baked beans, and Sweet Tea Fried Chicken. For drinks he had brought two Arizona Peace Teas. I fed Bo cornbread.

We sat on the bank of the Lake Pauline for a couple of hours before grandpa stirred. Bo periodically returned to the lake and nosed around the edge. He pawed at the shore and for no apparent reason jumped seeing something in the water.

We ate lunch and after Bo sprinkled us with the lake for the fourth time we headed back to Effingham.

"Grandpa, Bo is still wet," I said as we walked back to the Jeep.

"It won't be the first time that the Jeep has had a wet passenger," Grandpa Clark said.

Bo jumped into the back of the Jeep. I could not help but smile as our seventy-pound overgrown puppy laid down on the backseat of the Jeep until the engine started. Even though the ride from Lake Pauline wasn't very far from Effingham Bo was nearly dry when we parked at the pro cook off.

When grandpa parked the Jeep on the other side of the bank it seemed the Hometown Throwdown was little league compared to the turnout for the KCBS EffingHAM-JAM. The crowd was in the hundreds the day before. The crowd now was in the thousands.

Like the day before there was a DJ playing music when we parked. The sun was already starting to descend when we crossed to the Veterans Memorial building. It was still hot, but not scaldingly hot and according to Bird, the sun would set by seven and the day would cool off a bit.

The DJ was playing some house music that reminded me of Chicago for some reason. The music was funky but fun which made returning to the HAM-JAM feel more like a club.

The pro HAM-JAM was definitely busy when we arrived. The walk to the tents where contestants cooked and fed people was wall-to-wall people.

"Now, you see why I didn't want to come?" Grandpa asked me.

I gave a nod. Bo looked at everyone and everything. He stayed by my side on leash.

We walked past the black and brown and various shades of colors of faces. There were all sorts of people at the professional cook off that afternoon. I couldn't help but smile at the range of ages of people gathered for the food and the contest.

"They said they were going to be listening to music," I said to grandpa about Mom and Bird.

Grandpa Clark gave a thumbs up. He took the lead. He pushed through the crowd and the people parted seeing the giant of a man wearing a Chicago Cubs baseball cap and Ray Bans walking toward them.

We, Grandpa Clark, Bo, and I, crossed the crowd thick area where the food was being served to the music stage, which was now in the front of the Veterans Memorial building. Jefferson Street was blocked off from South Third Street to South Second Street so people could walk on the streets.

In the front of the Veterans Memorial building Grandpa found Bird and Mom with the Grahams and a beady eyed woman the color of a chocolate milkshake with braided pig tails that fell to her round small shoulders. She had sharp features and was dressed in orange leggings, knee-high boots, and a blue and brown high necked sleeveless blouse.

Seeing Grandpa Clark, she ran up to him like she had not seen him in years and gave him a long hug. Grandpa Clark hugged LaShay Brooks back. The two separated and smiled at each other.

"Hey Clark," the woman said with a smile.

"Hey LaShay," Grandpa Clark said.

When LaShay and Grandpa stopped their hug, Mom introduced me to Miss Brooks. Miss Brooks smiled one of those catbird smiles that felt like she knew everything about me before I said: Boo.

"Is this Zee?" Before I could respond she bent down and patted Bo on his head. Bo, who usually, didn't like to be patted by anyone he didn't know, didn't growl, bark or flinch.

"I've heard a lot about the quiet boy from Chicago," LaShay Brooks said with a toothy grin.

I looked at my mom.

"Not everyone is all loosey goosey when it comes to people," LaShay Brooks said. "For some it takes time and patience." She paused. "It seems like Effingham has been good for you."

I didn't respond.

"You talking now that you are here? Right?"

I raised and lowered my chin.

"Use your words," LaShay Brooks said.

"I am," I said, feeling all eyes on me suddenly.

"It just takes time and patience," she repeated.

"Well, nice to meet you, Zee," LaShay Brooks said.

"Nice to meet you too," I said.

I looked to my grandpa. He gestured to the street. On the other side of the street stood Bird and Paris with Trey and Donny. I looked back to Mom and grandpa.

"Go ahead," Grandpa said. "I'll be here for another hour then I'm heading back to the house." He paused, looking at his daughter. "If you ain't here when I leave, your mom can take you home."

"I ain't going to leave my baby," Mom said as I turned and walked across the street with Bo toward Bird and the others.

As I crossed the street I could see that Paris, Trey and surprisingly, the giant Donny, were a little uncomfortable seeing Bo with me.

Bird bent down and hugged Bo as we arrived on the other side of the street.

"What's up Bo? Did you have a good day?" Bird asked.

I rolled my eyes. I watched Paris and the boys tense up seeing Bird playing with Bo.

"It's okay. He's friendly. He ain't going to bite unless you try and hurt me or Zee," Bird said.

I stood there with Bo by my side and waited for everyone to exhale and relax around my dog. Bo was not intimidating, but if you tried to hurt me or Bird, he simply became protective. A protective Bo was a dangerous and scary thing.

Paris climbed to her blue Converse covered feet and looked around. Trey stood up as well. He was wearing a windbreaker that night. Paris, Trey, and Donny started to walk down the sidewalk in front of the Effingham Police Department. They crossed the street and sat on the bench on the sidewalk. Bird sat next to Paris. I stood and then knelt next to Bo.

"You hear about the missing people?" I asked pointing to the light pole.

The four older kids looked at me skeptically. Paris moved her head side to side. Trey smirked. Bird looked like she wanted to laugh. Donny just studied me with his dark eyes.

"What?" I asked.

"No one worrying about those men," Trey said.

"Why?" I asked. "I mean, they are people... with families."

"They're people," Paris said, with a thin smile. "But they ain't all good the way I hear it."

I opened my mouth to respond but stopped.

"Well, what about the full moon?" I asked.

"What about it?" Trey asked, looking at me sideways.

"Frankie told me that people think there's a South-Central Werewolf," I said.

Trey and Donny laughed. Donny, sitting near Paris, leaned on the smaller girl. Paris looked annoyed as Donny leaned his bulk on her shoulder. Paris tried to push Donny off. Trey shook his head. Even Bird giggled.

Paris freed herself from Donny's bulk and again climbed off the bench and to her feet. She looked scornfully at Donny.

"You have to stop listening to dumb stuff my brother says," Paris said.

"Yeah, none of that nonsense is real," Trey said.

"Even I know there's no such thing as werewolves," Donny said, his voice deep and bassy.

"They make up stuff all the time down here to make people stop by and buy stuff on the way to St. Louis," Trey said.

"Yeah, the whole creature feature thing sounds like a way to get tourists to stop and spend money," Paris said.

I looked at Paris and studied her for a moment. She seemed so confident. Yet, as she spoke there was something there beyond her attitude, hoop earrings, and ponytail made of a bunch of braids.

Just then a white man with a square chin dressed in a blue suit and tie appeared surrounded by four other men dressed in suit jackets and sunglasses. They moved methodically down the street, the square chinned man shaking hands and taking pictures with people.

"Who's that?" Bird asked.

"That's the mayor," Trey said.

"That's Barbie's father?" Bird asked.

"You mean, Amber?" Paris asked.

"Yeah," Bird said.

"Yeah," Paris said.

"Why he got so many people around him?" Bird asked.

"They act like he god down here. They love him," Trey said.

"He used to be some Chicago investor and then got caught up in something," Paris said. "So, he moved his show south."

I looked as the mayor shook hands with people who were trying to shake his hand or take a picture. His security was very alert. There were three men dressed in suit jackets shadowing the mayor.

"He got enemies down here," Paris said. She leaned toward Bird. "They said he made some shady deals before becoming mayor, the way I hear it."

"But no one runs against him," Trey said.

"Yeah, he's all about using the police down here to threaten people," Trey said.

"I'm surprised the chief of police ain't out here taking pictures with him," Paris said.

"You know that the newspaper is going to have something about him in the paper. He uses the paper for his own re-election campaign," Trey said.

The mayor and his entourage passed and turned into the festival. A few minutes later, on the speakers the DJ announced the arrival of the mayor.

"How's it work down here?" Bird asked.

"What you mean?" Paris asked.

"I mean, in Chicago, we know there are certain things that we can't change and places not to go," Bird said. "We don't trust everyone. You know?" Shrugging her shoulders.

"I know," Paris said. "Down here, the mayor is the law. He has the police in his pocket. They do what he tells them."

"What about the newspaper? Or the TV station?" Bird asked.

"There's only two newspapers," Trey said. "One is run by some old white family. The other is run by a black family. You can guess which is the most popular."

"How'd it get like this?" Bird asked.

"Like what?" Trey asked, confused.

"You know," Bird said, waving her hand in the general direction of the street.

"It's always been like this," Trey said. "Since I been breathing."

"That's why anyone that is old enough gets out of this place," Paris said.

"As soon as I graduate, I'm going to New York or Chicago," Trey said.

"Quick. Fast. In a hurry," Paris said with a smile.

Paris and Trey laughed.

"Well, before you leave," I began. "What do you know about Tommy Crawford?" I asked.

"What?" Paris asked, curious.

"Frankie told me about him," I said.

"His uncle came down from Chicago," Trey said. "He got a news team to follow him to the ranch where Tommy was last seen."

"Yeah. I heard about that," Donny said.

"He said that he was going to find his nephew and that he was going to make sure that people knew what was going on down here," Trey said.

"What happened?"

"The police threatened to arrest him," Trey said. "They tried to say he was interfering with an ongoing investigation."

"That's bull," Donny said.

"The weird thing is his uncle said that no one is looking for Tommy. Tommy just disappeared and that's it," Trey said, looking at me.

"They don't care about our missing," Paris said, a little choked up. Paris turned away.

"What happened?" Bird asked.

"Well, according to his sister, he went to a party at a farm," Trey said. "He was the only black shell on a white beach. You know?"

"Damn," Bird said. "That's a recipe for trouble."

Everyone shook their heads.

"Is his uncle still around?" I asked.

"Yeah, I think so," Trey said.

"What happened to him? Didn't anyone say?" Bird asked.

"Yeah, Tommy was at this party because he was this big deal athlete, and everyone liked him," Trey said. He looked at Paris and frowned. "Something happened."

"Something happened," Donny said.

"Yeah, he came up missing," Trey said.

"What do they think happened?" Bird asked.

"No one knows," Trey said. "I think that of us all, Paris liked him and knew him a little bit better than any of us."

Paris looked at Trey with red rimmed eyes menacingly.

"So, he rode out to the farm with a bunch of people he knew, but never came home?" Bird asked.

"Yep," Trey said.

"Is he dead?" I asked.

"Nobody knows," Trey said.

"When was this?" I asked.

"End of last year," Trey said.

"And no signs or newspapers, ever?" Bird asked.

"Nope," Trey said.

Grandpa appeared on the far side of the street. He paused, caught eyesight with me and gestured toward the Jeep. I climbed to my feet. Bo climbed to his feet as well.

"Got to go," I said, and walked away from Bird and the others.

"Watch out for werewolves," Trey said with a chortle. Donny growled and laughed. I smirked.

Grandpa Clark and I drove home with Bo in the back of the Jeep. He parked the Jeep and placed the cooler and chairs in the garage.

"Grandpa? You know Tommy Crawford?" I asked.

He shook his head as an answer.

"He disappeared last year," I said, hoping he might know him.

"No," he said.

"Last year. He went to a party at a ranch and disappeared," I said. "A black kid."

Grandpa Clark scrunched his face like he was smelling something distasteful. He looked at me and Bo curiously.

"A black kid," grandpa said. "Yeah, I think I remember something about some kid disappearing, but it was long time ago."

Chapter 13.

When I woke it was Sunday and that meant we went to church with grandpa. On Sunday grandpa made us a light breakfast. We had bacon, eggs, and toast before church.

Grandpa was a faithful member of the New Beginnings Church on South Willow Street. So, while we were staying with grandpa, we were faithful members of the New Beginnings Church on South Willow Street too.

I liked going to church on Sundays. I liked dressing up. I got to wear my collared shirt and jeans. The people were friendly. They all had smiles on their faces when we showed up. Everyone seemed nice. The music was lively. The band of four men with beards, tattoos, and earrings were good. The singers, usually one or two of the women, were good too. There was a bunch of clapping, singing, and dancing. The service was run by a short, broad nosed preacher with short dark hair and a booming voice.

The church service was long. I sat with Bird and the rest of the family. The preaching was long and about heaven and hell. When the preacher ended his message there was a short song and the service ended.

After church service we climbed in grandpa's Jeep and usually went to brunch at a local restaurant, owned by one of his war buddies. After brunch, we headed back to Eiche and grandpa's house. By the late afternoon we returned home, and I changed out of our Sunday clothes. Mom and Bird sat around and chatted with grandpa.

Bo, having been left alone for most of the day acted like he hadn't seen us for years. He nosed everyone. He placed his head on everyone's lap until he was patted and recognized.

I would take Bo for a walk when we returned home. Bo, having not seen us for half of the day, was crazy affectionate. He had abandonment issues, Bird said. I didn't agree. I just thought he hated when he didn't know where we were. So, after church when we stopped at the field, Bo didn't just run off. He stood by my side and seemed reluctant to leave.

"Go on," I said to Bo every Sunday, but every Sunday he seemed to forget that we went to church in Effingham. He looked up at me with his big black eyes and hesitated. I stepped into the field and walked Bo a few steps across the field.

"You know I'm not going to leave you, silly," I smiled at my overly needy dog. Bo stayed near my side. He trotted along and the more we walked the more my Black Tongued Chow relaxed. Before we reached a dozen steps Bo was running like he usually did in the overgrown field. In the field one Sunday, during the walk with Bo, I found a broken green pebbled material sofa sitting on its side. Again, while Bo did his business, I looked across the field and wondered how many things were just out of sight under the two-foot-high grass cover.

Bo and I had never walked to the far end of the field, I thought.

"Bo? You want to walk to the other end of the field?"

Bo looked at me, curiously.

"Okay, it's not that far," I said, looking at the span of green that stretched from Eiche all the way to Blohm. Standing just a hundred feet from Eiche the distance to Blohm seemed at least ten or a hundred times as far. It wasn't as if the distance was pancake flat. The field was lumpy, at least close to Eiche.

Bo and I had gone ten percent across the field before turning around and returning to Eiche and grandpa's home. I looked at Bo again. Bo stood by my side.

"Okay, let's go," I said. Bo looked from me to the field and back to me.

I stepped forward and Bo walked ahead. We skirted the broken sofa. I took in the six-foot length of fabric and springs and the still attached green pebbled arm of the one-time sofa. A dozen springs poked through the fabric where the cushions should have been. The sofa nearly matched the two-foot-high grass.

I led Bo slowly toward the far end of the field. I pushed away from the sofa and into the unknown of the undiscovered or explored part of the grass field. The grass was at my hips as I walked. Bo, usually curious, walked behind me, allowing me to cut a path through the grass. Just twenty feet from the sofa I found a broken yellow and green piece of pottery that had been a lamp at one time. I looked at the broken parts and saw the metal cup where the light bulb would have rested.

Bo sniffed at the broken parts. I looked back and smiled at my dog investigating the pieces.

"Come on, Bo," I said.

We were just one hundred feet from the sofa when I heard something move ahead of me to the left. The sound was not me stepping on plastic. It was something that wasn't me or Bo. I stopped. Bo stopped.

I tried to imagine what was hiding in the tall grass.

I looked left and then right and then left again. I tried to look through the thigh high grass in the direction of the noise. I didn't know what I was looking for, but I thought that seeing what made the noise would calm my suddenly jittery nerves.

In the grass I heard scurrying. Well, I thought that I heard scurrying. Bo pressed against my leg.

"Easy, boy," I said to Bo. Bo pressed forward and growled.

I backed up.

"Bo, come," I said.

I continued backing up, keeping my eye on Bo and the grass. I paused at the broken lamp.

"Bo, come," I repeated.

Bo turned and seeing me farther away from him circled the area growling. He spun around again before heading back toward me and the sofa.

Standing at the green remains of the sofa I watched Bo approach. Seeing my dog coming to me made me feel better suddenly. I felt a nameless dread standing in the field for some reason. As Bo approached, I realized that the field that seemed so innocent and harmless only moments before had transformed into a scary place.

It was, in my mind, like the beach that I had visited in Chicago. The sand, where everyone sat and talked was safe, generally. Yet, there were the seeming brave who splashed in the water. Those people were braver than the people on the shore. They played in the water's shore. Yet, again, the real dangers lay farther out, in the deeper and darker waters. Fewer people were there.

The grass field, in my head, was like that beach. I thought all this before turning around and fast walking from the field with Bo by my side.

"Maybe tomorrow," I said, unsure.

Once on Eiche I turned around and looked at the dark field.

"Gramps, who owns that field over there," I asked, pointing to the vacant field.

"I don't know," Grandpa Clark said.

"Why?" Mom asked.

"I nearly tripped over a sofa out there," I said.

"Be careful, Zee," Mom said. "I don't want you playing in that field."

"I'm not playing in the field, mom," I said.

"You know what I mean," Mom said.

Later that Sunday, after dinner, I thought to ask a question thinking I knew the answer to despite never asking it. Bird and I had cleaned up the kitchen and we were out in the backyard sitting around the firepit, just enjoying the night.

The dinner was sensational.

Mom was mentally planning out her week. Bird was sitting in her seat holding onto her basketball. The basketball had become a part of Bird since HAM-JAM. Every day Bird went to the park to work on her skills.

Grandpa Clark was sitting in his Adirondack chair and just smiling.

"Grandpa, do you have a computer?" I asked when Bird climbed to her feet and went to the bathroom.

"Yeah, sure," Grandpa Clark said. "I think it's in one of the rooms upstairs."

I bolted upstairs with Bo in hot pursuit and searched each room for the computer. I knew that there was no computer in my summer bedroom. I had checked every nook and cranny while unpacking my clothes. So, there were two choices; Mom's room or Bird's.

I headed to Bird's room and immediately found that grandpa's computer could have been in the cluttered bedroom under a pile of clothes. I methodically searched her room concentrating on the desks and closet. Bo nosed around the room and found a part of Bird's bedroom to lie down and watch me.

I looked under the bed and there, found the box for a MacBook laptop. I dragged the box out and lo and behold it was empty. Bo seeing me pull something from under the bed climbed to his feet to investigate.

"This could be it," I said to Bo. Bo watched as I opened the box.

Of course, it was empty. Grandpa Clark had a MacBook laptop in his house, and he probably didn't even use it. Immediately, I wondered why he bought it. It seemed as if Grandpa Clark did well without technology. He had cable and in the whole time, two weeks, we had been in Effingham I had seen him turn the TV on only once.

Bo sat down beside me and the empty MacBook box. I scanned Bird's room for the laptop. Knowing Bird, if she had found the laptop, she would be using it. I climbed to my feet. Bo, curious followed me.

I searched the most obvious places and then the most absurd places. I checked the closet again. I looked in the bathroom. I returned to the bedroom and searched behind the door.

Hanging behind Bird's bedroom door was what looked like a filing system. I counted four distinct storage holders. Each looked sturdy enough to hold a laptop. Each had a snap front lid atop of it. I opened the bottom compartment first. There, to my surprise, was the MacBook. Next to it was the power cable.

I giggled aloud. Bo, by my side, watched silently.

I took the laptop and the box that it came in, with Bo by my side, to my room and sat on my bed and plugged in the computer.

"This could take a while," I said to Bo. I looked at the black screen and looked at Bo. Bo placed his lion-like head on my leg.

I opened the MacBook box and looked for any literature on the twenty-year-old computer that grandpa would have kept. On a yellow piece of paper were the username and password for the MacBook Air. On the paper was also the Wi-Fi password. I wrote the Wi-Fi password on a separate piece of paper and headed downstairs.

Chapter 14.

The following day, Monday, I woke and tried to start up the MacBook I tapped the space bar and the black screen blinked on. The screen was no longer black. Instead, it was the picture of rocks and a cliff.

I typed in the username and password on the start page. I hit the return button.

The screen blinked and a progress bar appeared. I watched as the bar pushed from left to right quickly. Instantly the picture of rocks and a cliff changed. Suddenly, I was looking at a blurry picture of four men dressed in Army uniforms in the desert. At the bottom of the screen appeared twenty icons. I scanned them and tapped the Internet browser.

The screen opened and suddenly the computer screen read: You are not connected to the Internet.

I checked the screen and noticed that the computer was charging, but there was no Wi-Fi connection. I referred to the yellow paper and clicked on the Wi-Fi connection icon. There was a drop-down window that had more than a dozen choices.

Finding Grandpa Clark's Wi-Fi connection, I tapped on it and entered the password.

Instantly the computer, router, and password connected, and the MacBook suddenly was connected to the Internet.

We had breakfast.

Mom said she was heading to Champaign.

"Anyone want to go?" Mom asked.

Bird did not seem interested. I had other plans, waiting to see what I could do with a fully charged and Internet ready MacBook.

"We're going to the library this morning," Bird said. When my sister said those words, I instantly recalled that I had asked her to take me to the library before learning that Grandpa Clark had a computer in the house. Instead of canceling our library trip I gave a thumbs up. I was going to wait until I found out if the computer worked. If it didn't work, I could get the information I needed from the library. If it did work, I could get even more information after a visit to the library.

Bird rode me to the Effingham Public Library. The two-story dark building looked more like a factory than a library. Bird parked her scooter and locked it to the bike stand.

"We're here for two hours at most," Bird said. "I am supposed to meet Paris at the mall today."

"That's fine," I said, thinking of the information I needed to look up at the library.

As I walked toward the entrance, I again pointed to the faces of people taped on one of the light poles near the entrance to the library.

"Look," I said pointing to the pictures again.

Bird moved her head side to side.

"Paris told you not to worry about them," Bird said with a scowl.

I agreed. I recalled what Paris and Trey had said, but I still thought that it was interesting to have so many people missing in Effingham.

Bird walked into the library, and I followed. She waved to the librarian who was seated at the reference desk. Miss Graham, dressed in a striped blouse smiled affectionately and waved at Bird.

"Hi, Miss Graham, I'm looking for newspapers," I said timidly.

The librarian smiled at the request.

"Well, Zee, we have a few newspapers we get every day," the woman said. "Do you have a particular newspaper you want to read?"

"I want to read the last month of the Effingham Daily Record," I said. "Well, we have the last week of most of the newspapers on display. If you need a specific date, tell me. But before you ask for the whole month, check out the papers on display."

I agreed.

She directed me to the area of the library and wished me luck in my search.

"You good?"

I agreed.

"I'm going to sit down over there in the magazine area. When you are ready to leave," Bird said, heading to the small area that had a few round tables and chairs. "Just come get me."

105

I headed to the newspaper area. In the newspaper area of the Effingham Public Library there were four long tables were half a dozen men and two women were reading newspapers and magazines. I scanned the area and found the newspaper stand. The newspapers were on newspaper holders. The stand held a week's number of newspapers.

I grabbed the Effingham Daily Record and scanned it from the front page to the last looking for keywords. I found an article that mentioned the two missing people I had read about at grandpa's kitchen table. That was last Friday night. I checked the weather and found that night there was a full moon.

I walked back to the librarian and asked when were the last three full moons?

Miss Graham typed in the question and instead of answering said two words: Farmer's Almanac. She looked back behind her and pulled down a thick tome.

"Do you have a library card?"

"Yes," I said, then I frowned. "I left it at grandpa's house."

"Okay, I'm not supposed to do this but I'm going to loan this to you. Do not leave the library with this. When you are done bring it back to me."

"Okay," I said with a smile.

I took the Farmer's Almanac and headed back to the newspaper area of the library. I opened the Farmer's Almanac, read the introduction, and learned too much about the book I had in front of me. I went to the rear of the book and looked for the glossary. In the glossary I found moon phases by month and year. I looked at the cover and realized that this was just for this year.

There were full moons every month, usually in the last week of the month the Farmer's Almanac suggested. I wrote down the days from the end of the last year until August when the full moon appeared. I returned to the reference desk with the tome.

"Can I see the newspapers for these days?"

I handed my list to the librarian. She looked over the list. She smiled and took a deep breath.

"It'll take me a few minutes to find these," she said.

I went to one of the library computers and tried to search for information on Tommy Crawford.

Two entries appeared.

I tapped the article about Tommy Crawford and found that the article was brief. In the Effingham Daily Record newspaper and the article was located on page 9 in the Local News section.

Junior at EHS Thomas Crawford has been reported missing. A few days before the New Year, he was reported missing by his family. He was last seen at a high school party with friends at a house in Green Creek on a Friday. Friends, all minors, were not available for interview.

I read the article again, thinking that I missed something.

I frowned. The article was written by Ben Sherman.

The second article was found in the South Central Defender.

The disappearance of Thomas Crawford, a junior at EHS, remains unsolved. Days before New Year Crawford and some friends went to a high school party at a house in Douglas Country in rural Green Creek and did not return home. The high school party reportedly included drinking and possible illegal activities. Friends of Crawford, all minors, suggested that Crawford left the party and caught a ride with other friends' home, and they did not suspect foul play. When Crawford did not return home the next day, his parents contacted EPD and filed a missing person report. As of the writing of this article no information has been attained from the authorities.

I noted the reporter was Zada Gallamore.

A few weeks ago, there was another article written by the same reporter about Joshua Pernell, the uncle of Thomas Crawford.

Joshua Pernell, the uncle of Thomas Crawford, came to Effingham armed with a camera crew and questions about his nephew's disappearance. His nephew has been missing since December 30 of last year. Pernell and his camera crew went to the house in Green Creek just off County Road 1525 East and was denied entry into the property. His sister, Georgina Gibson, Thomas Crawford's mother, was there as well but gave no comments. Pernell told this reporter "The owner of the house did not live there," Pernell said. "The owner of this place lives in Chicago. It's some weird Airbnb that had only been rented a handful of times." Suspicious? Douglass County Sheriff deputy Louis McCauley barred Pernell's attempts to enter the property. Not being able to investigate the property and under threat of arrest by the Douglas County Sheriff, Pernell left the last known location of his nephew unsatisfied. Pernell has vowed to return and uncover the cause of his nephew's disappearance. "I just want to know what happened to Tommy. I think that something is going on down here and someone has to get to the bottom of it," Pernell

While I waited for the librarian, I opened another window and typed in South-Central Werewolf.

Almost instantly, there were ninety-nine plus entries available on that subject.

I looked at the earliest date and was shocked to find that the subject had been going on since the 1900's. I looked at the most recent and noted that there were six articles in the last month on the South-Central Werewolf.

I opened another window and typed in Green Creek. Green Creek was in Douglas County. It was an out of the way place. The main road was County Road 1525 East. I did a satellite search of the main road and found a farm with a half dozen buildings. It was too big. I then moved a little father from those buildings and found a big building and paused. There at the bend of the road, hidden behind a grove of trees was a pond. I zoomed in on the pond and paused.

Miss Graham appeared and handed me the six newspapers I had requested.

"Thank you," I said to Miss Graham.

"Sure, if you need anything else just ask," the woman smiled.

I read the six newspapers and all the werewolf stories were found either on the front page or page two of the newspapers. There was incredible detail. The reporters, John Bell, Henry Riley, and William Scoggins interviewed no less than three people per article.

The difference was stark. There were hundreds of articles about nothing or what Paris and the others suggested was a long game for a tourist attraction. In stark comparison to the long game there was the most rudimentary, perfunctory, and reluctant of reports on the welfare of a missing teenager.

I wrote down the names of the six missing persons and the dates of their disappearances along with Tommy Crawford's information on a scrap of paper. I slipped the information in my shorts and tried to think if I had missed anything.

I looked up at the clock, gathered the newspapers, and walked back to the reference desk.

"Thank you for your help," I said to Miss Graham.

"You could have left them on the table," Miss Graham, the librarian, said. "That's my job."

I smiled awkwardly.

"Can I ask you what you know about Zada Gallamore?"

Miss Graham looked at me oddly. "You mean the reporter for the South Central Defender?"

I smiled stiffly.

"I wondered if you knew how to contact her? I wanted to get some information on Thomas Crawford?" I asked.

Miss Graham looked at me confused. "You mean Tommy Crawford?" Miss Graham tilted her head at me. "I don't know too much. Just that he went to a party with some friends and never came home after a party in Green Creek."

I listened and looked at her steadily.

"What happened to him?"

"I don't know. It happened a while ago," the librarian said seriously. "Everyone has an opinion about things, even if they don't know exactly all the details. But I don't think I have anything to add to the question you are asking. I simply don't know." She paused. "As for Zada, she works at the Village Mall. Her family has a clothing store there. You can find her there most days. Just look for the Gallamore shop."

I smiled uneasily. Bird walked up to the reference desk. She smiled at me.

"We're leaving," Bird said. "Good to see you again," she said, looking at the librarian.

"Good to see you too," Miss Graham said as Bird and I left the library.

Bird raced us back to grandpa's house like she was being chased. I held on like the scooter was life.

"Slow down," I screamed as Bird tore down South Fourth Street. Thankfully, she had to slow down as we stopped to cross Wabash Avenue.

"Bird, I don't want to die on the back of this scooter," I screamed as she took off across the street and made her way to grandpa's house.

When I got off Bird's scooter, she laughed like she was crazy.

"That was crazy," I said.

"Later," Bird said. I shook my head. Bird drove away and back down the street and toward the mall.

I stood in the driveway and thought about what I was going to do while Bird was away and with Paris. I looked to the grass field and saw a boy standing there, about halfway in the middle of the field. I looked back to grandpa's house and then back to the field.

I shrugged my shoulders and crossed the street to the field. I walked into the two-foot-high grass and made my way toward the boy in the field. He was closer to the street and halfway between Eiche and Blohm. As I got closer the boy turned and I was surprised to find Frankie standing in the field about one hundred feet from the street.

"Hey," Frankie said.

"Hey," I said. I looked at the loose dirt mound he was standing in front of. "What you doing?"

Frankie shrugged his shoulders.

I looked down at the mound and kicked at the soil, bored.

"Hey, don't do that," Frankie said, suddenly protective of the mound.

"Why?"

"Just because," Frankie said. "That dirt ain't done nothing to you. It was just sitting there being dirt. It don't deserve you trying to disturb it."

I smirked at Frankie's words. It seemed as if Frankie had a bunch of words for a pile of dirt. I shrugged my shoulders.

"What you doing out here?" I asked.

Frankie did not answer. Instead, he just looked at the dirt mound.

"Where you been? I haven't seen you since the HAM-JAM," I said.

"I been busy," Frankie said.

"Busy?" I asked, looking at Frankie dressed in a cartoon T-shirt, jeans, and basketball sneakers. He was not as big as grandpa but maybe just as big as Donny but at seventeen he was still not overly muscular. In his short-sleeved T-shirt he had visible muscles where his biceps rested but not overly muscular arms.

"Yeah, this summer I have a part-time job," Frankie said. "Not too many people know about it."

"That where you were going when we saw you that night?" I asked.

"You saw me?" Frank said, curious.

"Yeah, grandpa and I were heading home from the HAM-JAM, and I saw you walking across Banker," I said, hoping I named the right street.

Frankie frowned and shrugged his shoulders.

"What you doing for a part-time job?" I asked.

"It's a secret," Frankie said.

I didn't push.

Frankie looked up from the mound of dirt.

"I was heading to the mall," Frankie said. "You want to go?"

I twisted my lips and looked back at grandpa's house.

"What you worried about? Grandpa Clark? He won't mind," Frankie said.

I smiled uncomfortably.

Frankie and I went to the mall. We went to the food court. Frankie sat down at a table near the Hot Dog on a Stick.

"Frankie, I got a question," I said, sitting at the round table with the high schooler.

"Shoot," Frankie said.

"Why did you tell me about werewolves?"

"I think that you should know," Frankie said with a wry smile. He was looking around the mall for something. I looked around because Frankie was looking around.

"Why?" I asked.

"I think that people cannot hide who they are, even when they're werewolves," Frankie said. "I have noticed that sometimes you can catch a glimpse of people with red eyes." He paused and looked across the table at me. "You know what I'm talking about?"

I didn't. I was confused.

"There are killers walking around us all the time. We just don't notice. Or, we just don't want to notice," Frankie said.

I nodded. I sort of understood what Frankie was saying.

"Well, I was trying to work out who these red eyed individuals are in the daylight," Frankie said.

"Frankie? I got a real question for you?"

"Sure," he said.

"You know where the Gallamore shop is in this mall?"

"Sure," Frankie said with a smile. "What you religious?"

I shook Frankie's question from my head.

"Can you take me to it or point it out?"

Frankie pointed across the food court to a small mall shop with a red arrow pointing to the entrance.

"That's it," Frankie said.

"Okay, thanks," I said and climbed to my feet.

I walked across the food court to the small shop with the red arrow over the door. In the window were three mannequins dressed in religious sweats that read: Chosen. On the mannequins' heads were baseball caps with the same branding.

The small store that had a main aisle that led to the rear of the store where an older woman wearing cat eyeglasses was sitting behind a sewing machine. On either side of the main aisle were rounders with T-shirts and sweatsuits on them. It looked like on the left side were the men's clothing and on the right the women.

As I entered an audible bell rang from inside the store. I looked down and noticed the sensor and laser light that announced my arrival in Gallamore Fashions.

"How can I help you?" Asked a woman a little younger than my mother. She was the color of beechwood. She had big brown eyes and slightly upturned nose above her full lips. The woman was wearing a Chosen sweatshirt and blue jeans.

"Hi," I said. "I'm looking for Zada Gallamore."

"I'm Zada. How can I help you?"

I told Zada I was curious about the disappearance of Tommy Crawford. I told her I had gone to the library and the visit had only made me more curious. Zada told the woman behind the sewing machine that she was going to take a break.

Zada walked me out of the store, and she pointed to a bench just outside her family's fashion store.

She and I talked. Well, she talked more than me.

"You know he's been missing now for nearly seven months," Zada Gallamore began.

I gave a small nod.

"Why you want to know about this?" Zada asked.

"I think that a new set of eyes on an old problem can help," I said.

Zada Gallamore studied me slowly.

"This ain't some game," Zada said. "Tommy Crawford is someone's son. I think that me telling you anything or saying more than you already know might be bad."

"I plan on talking to his family," I said.

The South Central Defender reporter remained quiet.

"You know that no one has found him yet," I said, with a shrug of my shoulders. "What is the worst that can happen? I find him? I figure out something someone overlooked?"

"What makes you think you can find Tommy Crawford when no one else has been able to?"

"Well," I began, thinking. "I'm a kid. Most people ignore kids. They let slip things that they would never let slip if they were around other adults. They don't take me seriously." I paused. "That's my advantage."

Zada Gallamore smiled at my explanation.

"Let me think about it," the reporter said. "Come back here in a couple of days and by then I will make a decision if I'll help or not."

I shrugged my shoulders. I looked at the reporter. "By that time," I said. "I should have talked to Tommy's family, and they will be one hundred percent behind me trying to help find and bring Tommy home."

I climbed to my feet and walked away from Zada Gallamore and the Gallamore Fashion store.

I sat with Frankie in the food court for a while and after he offered his insights on red-eyed possible doppelgangers or aliens or whatever he thought the people were, Bird and Paris showed up and saved me from Frankie's ranting. I pointed to my sister and climbed to my feet to leave Frankie once again.

"Suppose you're heading home?" Frankie asked.

I gave a tiny smile. I left Frankie at the table. Frankie did not seem too bent out of shape at my leaving. Paris gave a thin smile to her brother.

"What's up Frankie?"

"What's up sis," Frankie said, sitting at the food court table.

"Zee?" Bird said, looking at me and not too happy to see me. "What are you doing here? Does Mom know you're here?"

I did not answer.

"You need to go home," Bird said.

I smiled. I walked with Bird and Paris through the mall. Paris seemed amused. Trey and Donny were at the ice cream store in the mall waiting.

"You need to go home," Bird repeated. "You know Mom and grandpa are going to be worried."

I tried to ignore Bird.

Trey seeing Bird upset stepped in.

"You upsetting your sister," Trey attempted. He was suddenly protecting Bird. I wanted to laugh. I didn't know if Bird had a type, but it felt that she was more into thugs and bad boys than anyone else.

I took in Trey for a long moment. Trey was dressed in Chicago Bulls T-shirt and jeans. He didn't give off the bad boy vibe to me.

So, I shrugged my shoulders at Trey and said: "So?"

"I like this version of Zee," Paris said with a giggle. "He's a little spicy." Paris reached out and patted me on the back. "You rubbing off on him, Bird."

Bird moved her head side to side. Donny smiled. Trey stared at me unsmiling. I wanted to laugh at Trey but hid my smile and swallowed the laugh that bubbled up inside me.

"My question is: How did you end up with my brother?" Paris asked.

I explained.

"Be careful, Frankie is a little high strung," Paris said. "He can be a bit much but generally; he isn't anyone to worry about."

"He is cool and all, but thinks he knows everything," Trey said.

Donny bobbed his head.

We continued walking through the Village Mall. I knew that this was the best time to ask a tough question. So, I did.

"Paris? You know Tommy Crawford's family? Right?" I asked.

"Yeah. Why?" Paris asked.

"I want to talk to his mom or uncle if she's willing or he's still here," I said.

Paris looked at me for a beat before speaking.

"Why?"

"I think I know something, but I need to be sure," I said.

The teenager looked at me doubtfully.

"When was the last time you talked to Tommy?"

Paris knitted her eyebrows.

"Right before he disappeared," Paris said, reluctantly.

I nodded my head.

"You got a lot of questions," Paris said.

"Yeah, but the real questions are for Tommy's family," I said.

"Well, I'm not sure if she would be up to it or if he's still here," Paris said. "Let me check. I'll tell Bird a little later."

"Thanks," I said.

Bird looked at me like her friends in Chicago did when I appeared unexpectedly. Trey looked like he was trying to think of a way to strangle me. Donny, being Donny, did not say anything. I could only smile.

Chapter 15.

I left the mall after Paris told me and Bird that Grandpa Clark sort of adopted her mom when she was struggling. So, according to Paris, when Paris' mom was pregnant with Frankie and barely making it Grandpa Clark reached out to help. He's been in their lives ever since.

"He's unofficially, officially, our grandpa." Paris looked at me with those big brown eyes of hers and held my attention. "That make sense?"

"I suppose," I said.

When I finally climbed onto the front porch and opened the front door Bo practically bowled me over. Bo was so excited to see me. He was a fur covered seventy-pound ball of muscle. When he got a full head of steam it was like trying to stop a locomotive.

Grandpa Clark stood in the front room and watched amused at Bo's antics. I fell on my butt and nearly tumbled back onto the front porch as I tried to fend of the affectionate attack by my faithful dog with abandonment issues.

"He's been waiting for you," Grandpa Clark said with a big smile on his face.

"Yeah, I can tell," I said, pushing Bo away and climbing to my feet. Bo pawed me and tried to nuzzle. I hugged the big dog that thought he was still a puppy.

"Did you take him for a walk?"

"No," Grandpa said.

I smiled weakly and walked through the house with Bo by my side. I grabbed his leash and walked out the back door of grandpa's house and toward the field. I stopped on the edge of the field, just on the opposite side of the street.

I stopped and studied the big plot of land. I walked Bo, purposefully onto the field. I revisited the place where I first saw Frankie.

The plot of land was as it had been earlier. I stopped where Frankie was when I saw him. There on the ground, I could see maybe seven feet of loose rectangular earth. Bo sniffed around the soil. He walked around the pile of dirt curious.

I kicked at the soil and let Bo off leash. Instantly, Bo ran away from the street and deeper into the field only to stop twenty yards away and turn and look at me.

"Go on," I said, with a shake of my head. "I ain't going to leave you."

While Bo sniffed around the field and did his business, I revisited the loose earth at my feet. I kicked at the dirt and paused seeing something in the dirt. I bent down and was alarmed to find the broken case of a watch just hidden beneath the dirt where Frankie had stood. I hesitated to pick up the watch case. Instead, I walked around the disturbed land and looked slowly to see if there was anything else there but there wasn't.

Before Bo returned, I picked up the broken watch and slipped it into the napkin I had from my ice cream earlier. Instead of slipping the watch case into my pocket I examined the bit of glass and metal. With a cursory glance I knew it was expensive. Even covered in dirt there was a glimmer and weight to it. The watch was not made of plastic or cheap parts.

Bo returned and we walked back to grandpa's house with the watch in my shorts. As always, as we reached Eiche I looked back and wondered what was hidden beneath that two-foot-high sea of grass.

I took the watch to my room and examined it. I cleaned it up as best I could without damaging it. I needed to examine it more closely. Bo, sat by my side and then realizing I was going to be sitting at my desk for some time, laid down and rested.

The old-fashioned watch had a shattered cushion shaped broken face covering, and if I was not mistaken, a golden case and matching little gold knob on the side of the watch to manually wind the mechanism. The dirt and mud were caked and on the front of the watch dial, but it looked as if the time was sometime after one o'clock. I didn't want to destroy the watch, so I left it in its muddied condition.

Flipping the watch over I could make out some writing. I held it to the light and saw that the scratches were uniform. It was an engraving that read: To David, From Your Biggest Fan, Reita.

David? David York? The name sounded familiar.

I scanned my room for all the notes I had taken when Bird took me to the library. I knew I had notes somewhere. I had written down the names and dates of the missing. I climbed out of my chair and Bo climbed to his feet thinking we were leaving.

"Relax, Bo," I said to my dog. "I'm looking for something."

I remembered that I had left my backpack when I went outside. I was wearing this outfit. Was my information in my shorts?

I fished around and found the scrap of paper I was looking for. I unfolded the scrap and there were the seven names and dates of their disappearances.

Tommy Crawford disappeared December 30, high school athlete

Brent Russell disappeared January 24, store manager

George Howe disappeared February 26, auto mechanic

George James disappeared March 27, bank loan officer

David York disappeared April 27, store owner

Travis Gordon disappeared June 26, electrician

Eric Saunders disappeared July 25, tow truck driver

Looking at the list I tried to connect the dots. I sat in my room and wondered how and if they were all connected.

I re-examined the list. What were the common factors? I paused, thinking.

They were all men. No. That was a lie.

There was a boy on the list. A black boy was on this list. He was the only black person on the list. I stopped there. This list wasn't a list of missing. It was a missing black boy and six missing white men. That distinction was significant.

There was a missing white man every month of the year, since the disappearance of Tommy Crawford.

The white men had all been snatched during the full moon. The last three had been found near water. That was interesting. I didn't see the connection.

I tried to figure out why there was no one missing in May. Could it be? I thought. Could it be that the reason there was no one missing in May is because it wasn't a white man missing?

I took my notebook from my backpack and wrote all my thoughts. Instantly, my mind reeled. I was electric. My ideas threatened to overwhelm me. I climbed to my feet.

I decided to test the MacBook. I checked and found it fully charged. I tapped a key, and the first error message came up. I tried to correct that error, only to open another error. Stymied by the string of error messages I paused. There had to be a remedy to the problem. The computer was a tool and in the right hands it was an incredible tool. Yet, after two hours trying to bypass the litany of error messages the realization finally began to dawn upon me. The technology that had created this MacBook in 2006 had long been outdated. The only way to salvage the MacBook was an update. Sadly, updating the nearly fifteen years of updates was not something I could do.

So, Bo and I went downstairs to find grandpa. Grandpa was in the kitchen making dinner.

"Grandpa that computer of yours doesn't work," I said.

"Maybe," he said from the stove without looking back. "I haven't turned it on in a while."

"Yeah, well, it needs to be updated," I said.

"Sounds like something I'm not interested in doing," he said.

I had to go back to the library and do some research. I went downstairs asked grandpa if he knew anyone that I could borrow a bike from. Grandpa Clark knew everyone on his block. He knew everyone on the two blocks around him.

"You need a bike?" Grandpa Clark asked.

I gave a weak nod.

"Well, go down to Nelson just down the street. He lives in the white house with a blue door. He's good people," Grandpa Clark said. "He was an avid cyclist. He did marathons, triathlons, and races and then one day decided to quit." Grandpa Clark shook his head. "He's a kook. He has all sorts of bikes that sit unused in his garage." He paused and smiled. "You go by there and be ready for a story. I'm sure he'll let you ride a bike. He might even have one that fits you perfectly."

Mister Nelson was in his sixties and in decent shape for his age. He was built like a human greyhound. He had long limbs and moved like an athlete. He was rail thin but there were cords of muscle beneath that slender frame. Nelson was wearing a T-shirt and shorts and flip flops.

In his garage were at least ten road bikes, time trial bikes, three mountain bikes and a black bike frame without a rear wheel. On the side of the garage was a toolkit and a standing mechanic's cart.

"You Clark's grandson?"

"Yes sir," I said.

"They said you didn't talk," Mister Nelson said, looking at me with his gray eyes.

"I talk," I said.

"Well, that may be, but they said you didn't talk," Mister Nelson said.

I smiled.

"So, you need a bike?"

I gave a small nod.

"You know how to ride?" Nelson asked.

"Yes sir," I said with a smile.

"Well, I'll loan you one of the mountain bikes. They are heavy and durable. They are almost bulletproof. Just don't leave it out on the street because people still steal here," Mister Nelson said.

He and I walked through the hanging bikes suspended from the garage rafters on hooks. Mister Nelson had a story for each bike. I listened to his stories, and he loaned me one of his mountain bikes. He adjusted the bike so that it rode comfortably.

I thanked Mister Nelson and after he gave me a Kryptonite lock and key and directed me to the safest bike route I rode to the library on his super bike. The ride was smooth and quick. The cars zipped by as if I wasn't there. I rode on the street most of the way. Mister Nelson said the cars would not hit me if they saw me.

I wheeled the mountain bike back to grandpa's house and tried my first wheelie. I was unsuccessful.

"Look at this, my grandkids are bikers," Grandpa Clark said with a chuckle seeing me wheel into the garage.

I parked the bike next to Bird's scooter.

"Okay, I got a real important question," I said at dinner.

"Shoot," said Mom.

"Okay, what would you do if you knew something or found something, and it was related to a crime? Would you take it to the police? Would you not take it? Wait, I forgot to add, that someone in your family might be involved in the crime," I said a little muddled.

"Let me unpack this," Mom said. "You found something."

"No, I didn't say I found anything," I said. "I said what if I found something."

"Okay, Zee, let's say what if you found something and it was related to a crime that someone in your family might be involved in," Mom said, looking at me curiously. "Am I getting this correctly."

I gave a weak nod.

"So, what I am leaning toward is telling the police," Mom said.

"Aw, mom," I said, disappointed.

"You had a different answer?" Mom asked.

"I don't know. I was hoping you said wait it out. Or, you said family first. I don't know," I said, suddenly confused.

"What did you find?" Bird asked.

"I said I might have found something," I said to Bird.

"The problem with might of finding something or finding something the police don't care. They see it as a crime. Think it's interfering with investigations," Grandpa Clark said.

"I shouldn't have asked," I decided.

"No, you should have asked. I want you to continue to ask the easy and the hard questions," Mom said. "You may not like the answers, but you know that we are going to answer you as best we can."

I gave a tiny nod.

Chapter 16.

The next morning, we ate scrambled eggs, southern fried apples, bacon, grits, and chicken and waffles. After taking Bo for a walk, I dressed for the library and took my backpack with me. Inside I made sure that I had my library card, a notebook, three pencils, an eraser, and a bag of gummy worms, for snacks.

"I'm going to the library and then ride around a bit," I said to Mom and Grandpa while Bird was upstairs dressing.

"Be careful," Mom said.

Arriving at the library I locked the mountain bike to the bike rack with the Kryptonite lock and entered. I greeted Miss Graham and went to the newspaper area. I took out my notebook and considered all the questions I needed answered.

I asked Miss Graham if she could help me find some information on the missing people. I gave her my list.

"Well, Zee, a lot of the information you want is on the Effingham Daily Record website," the librarian said. "I can show you how to get the information you are looking for quickly."

The librarian showed me how to do an informational search.

I came away with a ton of information. What was incredible was what the search produced. In minutes I had answers to questions I had not thought to ask.

After the library visit, I walked to the steps of the Effingham Police Department. I thought they might be able to help me. I also wanted to give them the watch I had found.

I was on my way into the police station when I saw Frankie Brooks standing on Fourth Street. He was dressed in a polo shirt and jeans. He was waiting for a bus and didn't seem to see me.

I turned around and climbed on the bike I had borrowed and followed the bus Frankie climbed aboard. I didn't have to ride very far, thankfully. Frankie climbed off the bus on Maple Street and walked up the street to the Effingham Performance Center.

I lagged behind and watched as Frankie walked to the loading dock of the center. There two men greeted Frankie like they were friends and talked. One of the two was a big, muscular guy wearing a baseball cap with a beard and mustache. The other was a tall and slender guy. Frankie and the two men talked seriously for a few minutes and then they said their goodbyes and Frankie left.

From a distance I watched as Frankie walked back down Maple Street to Jefferson Street to wait for another bus. I was about to follow Frankie when I saw Paris and Bird.

Paris seeing me waved.

I waved and walked my mountain bike toward the two girls.

"You got a bike?" Bird asked.

"Yeah," I said.

"I hope you didn't steal it," Paris said, joking.

"Naw," I said. "What are you doing down here?"

"Should ask you that?" Bird said.

"I wanted to see the Performance Center," I said, looking in that direction.

"Oh, really," Paris said with a smirk and shake of her head.

"I got a bike. I just ended up here," I amended my original statement.

"Which is it?" Paris asked.

"Don't lie," Bird said.

I shrugged. Bird stared at me. Paris smiled at the silence.

"Well, if you want to talk to Tommy's mother or his uncle, they are coming over later to see my mom," Paris said. "My mom said that it would be fine if you and Bird came by. You can talk to them then."

I smiled. I bobbed my head. The invite to meet Georgina Gibson and Joshua Pernell was unexpected.

"What time?" I asked.

"After two," Paris said.

It was a little before noon when I left Paris and Bird on Jefferson.

The ride back home was uneventful. When I arrived Mom and Grandpa Clark were sitting in the kitchen about to eat lunch.

Lunch was a light bit of food in the Clark household. For lunch we ate catfish, collard greens, mac 'n cheese and cornbread. For drinks Grandpa had sweet, iced tea. For a dessert we had banana pudding. While we ate Mom and Grandpa Clark talked about things.

I ate and thought of the hundred things I wanted to talk to Tommy Crawford's mother or his uncle about. I was formulating the order in which to ask the questions when my mother asked me a question.

"Zee? What are you doing the rest of the day?" Mom asked.

"I'm going over to Bliss Park and see Paris and Bird," I admitted.

"I'm glad Bird made some friends down here," Mom said. Grandpa agreed.

"Pop? You got plans?" Mom asked.

Grandpa Clark smiled. "Now that HAM-JAM is over, sweetie, all I have to do is wait for Thanksgiving and Christmas," Grandpa said.

Mom smiled.

I changed shirts, put on a pair of jeans, and left for Bliss Park a little before two o'clock. The ride up to Bliss Park was just about ten minutes from grandpa's house. I arrived at the park and as I did, rode past Frankie.

Frankie seeing me smiled, a good sign.

"Hey, Frankie," I said.

Frankie raised his chin in answer.

"I'm supposed to see Paris," I said.

Frankie bobbed his head and gestured behind me. I turned and on the opposite side of the street was a yellow and white house with a KIa Telluride parked in the driveway. On the curb was a GMC Yukon.

Walking toward the house with the two SUVs I saw Bird's scooter parked near the SUV in the driveway.

"You came," Paris said.

I smiled weakly. Paris and Bird were all smiles. Paris led me to the kitchen.

LaShay Brooks was in her kitchen when Paris led us into the room. In the very same kitchen sat a woman with short black curly hair dressed in a maroon jumper with black platform sandals on. Seated next to the short-haired woman was a dark man with a tight fade and well-trimmed mustache and beard. He was wearing a dark blue collared shirt and black jeans. Around his neck was a thick gold necklace. On his pinkie finger was a gold ring.

"Mama," Paris said, timidly. "You remember Zee? Bird's little brother?"

I smiled.

"He wanted to meet Tommy's mom and Tommy's uncle," Paris said.

Paris seemed, in front of her mother, like an average, obedient daughter.

I looked to Paris and Bird standing in the kitchen.

"So, Zee, you wanted to talk with Tommy's folks?" LaShay Brooks asked with a smug smile.

I raised and lowered my chin in answer.

"Use your words," LaShay Brooks advised.

"I do," I said, looking at Tommy's mom and uncle.

"What you want to talk about youngblood?" Tommy's uncle asked.

"I read how you went out to the ranch where Tommy was last seen and couldn't get in to search around," I began.

Tommy's uncle listened and did not seem like a patient man.

"Well, if he left that party there's only a couple of places he could be if they dumped his body," I said. "What I want is permission to go and look."

"Look?" Tommy's uncle asked, looking at me skeptically.

"Where?" Tommy's mother asked, her voice rising.

"Well, I think that on that road, if things went bad, the people would have wanted to get rid of the body as soon as possible," I said.

"The police told us that if things got violent the people would have gone where they felt comfortable to dump the body," Tommy's mother said.

"Maybe," I said. I looked at Tommy's uncle and then Tommy's mother. "If the attack was planned, I'd agree," I said. "But hear me out, if the people that found Tommy at the party decided to hurt him, then it wouldn't have been planned. They, whoever they were, then would have to find some place to get rid of him fast." I paused. "I think there's only a couple of places on that County Road where that made sense."

"So, who are you again?" Tommy's uncle asked.

I smiled.

LaShay Brooks, Georgina Gibson, Joshua Pernell sat in the kitchen and listened to my theory. There were holes but based on the information I had gleaned it seemed a reasonable theory. I was a little surprised that Joshua Pernell was suddenly interested in my kid theory. After laying out my theory of what had happened, I stopped and allowed them to ask me questions.

"How old are you?" Pernell asked.

"I'm twelve," I said.

"You done this kind of thing before?" Pernell asked, scratching his head.

LaShay Brooks smiled at the question. "Zion is a sort of amateur detective, according to his mama," she said. "He can find anything." She paused, thinking. "He's a big deal in his school and Chicago."

"Okay," Pernell said.

The conversation changed.

"Why would they want to hurt Tommy?" Georgina Gibson asked.

"Jealousy," I said with a shrug of my shoulders.

Paris and Bird agreed.

"Tommy thought he was bulletproof," I said and immediately regretted saying those words. "I mean, he thought being a star athlete and friends with whoever he went to the party with would be enough to protect him from the jealousy all around him."

Missus Gibson moved her head side to side. Her eyes welled up. LaShay Brooks reached out and consoled her friend.

"The question is: Where is Tommy?" I asked. "Give me a week, I'll find your son... and your nephew." I said looking at the weeping mother and resolute uncle.

"You know he's been missing for nearly seven months?" Pernell asked, skeptically. His lower lip quivered.

I nodded weakly. "If what I think is correct, he's still there," I said.

"What is it going to hurt?" LaShay Brooks asked, holding Georgina Gibson in her arms.

"What do you want from us?" Missus Gibson asked.

"Nothing," I said. "I just want the chance to help."

Chapter 17.

When I stepped out of the front door of Paris's house Bird and Paris jumped me. They seemed like they had lost their minds. They grabbed me, pushed me, and dragged me to the side of the house.

"What are you doing?" Bird asked, nearly screaming.

"Are you serious?" Paris said holding my arm.

"Can you back up any of this?" Bird asked, pulling me toward her.

"Zee, this is absolutely crazy," Paris said.

I didn't respond to the barrage of questions. I waited for the two to stop talking.

"Why didn't you tell me you think you know where Tommy is?" Bird asked.

"Do you really know where he is?" Paris almost screamed.

"You know this is serious?" Bird said, looking at me carefully.

Paris looked to Bird and back to me.

"Did you talk to mom about this?" Bird said, narrowing her eyes.

"You can't play with people's emotions," Paris said.

"How do you think you can find someone when no one else has?" Bird asked.

"Answer me," said Paris.

"Yeah," said Bird. "Answer us."

I pushed the two girls away from my face. They stepped back but did not release me. I held their wrists and tried to break their vice-like grips to no avail. I pushed against them but neither Paris nor Bird moved. I took a deep breath and let my hands drop to my sides.

"Okay," I said coming to grips with the fact that Paris and Bird were in control. "I am going to help Tommy's family find Tommy. I am serious. I have been trying to figure things out. I have done the research. I think I have a pretty strong belief in what I'm doing. This is not crazy. I'm not crazy. I didn't tell you or anybody that I know where Tommy is. I don't. I think I have a good idea of where he can be found. That is different," I said to Bird. "Again, I think I have a pretty good idea of where he is. I know that this is serious. I would never say something just to say it." I paused, recalling all the questions. "I didn't tell mom or grandpa about this. They got things to worry about of their own. Lastly, I understand what I'm doing. So, I'm not playing with anyone's emotions. Based on the location of that party there aren't that many places to get rid of a body. That, like I told Paris, people don't see me and that's an advantage." I reached up and removed Bird's hand and then Paris' hand. "Before the end of the week, I am pretty sure we find evidence of Tommy Crawford."

I stepped back and tried to smooth my crumpled T-shirt. I shook my head at the two girls. I took a deep breath and smiled.

"You sure?" Bird asked.

"I'm pretty sure," I said.

"Pretty sure?" Paris asked, curious.

"No one can be one hundred percent sure, unless they were there or did it," I said.

"Zion," Bird said, gaining my attention. "How come you didn't tell me about this?"

I smiled. The neighborhood beyond the Brooks home was quiet. There were no kids on the streets. I looked across the street toward the park. I would have imagined that at two or three in the afternoon there would be kids out playing or swinging on the swings, but there were no children playing.

"So, you think you know where Tommy is?" Paris asked, a little calmer than before.

I bobbed my head up and down.

"Seriously?" Paris asked.

I gave a smaller nod.

"You believe any of this?" Paris asked Bird.

"Well, he is a bit of a freak. He is our go to in the family to find things," Bird said.

"For real?" Paris asked.

"Yeah," Bird admitted. "It's kind of weird how he can figure out things. He helped me find all sorts of lost stuff."

"But this ain't looking for your lost keys or a purse," Paris said.

"I know, but he's freaky good," Bird said.

Paris smiled.

I edged away from Paris and Bird while they talked.

"So, you want to tell me how you are so certain?" Bird asked looking to the spot where they had cornered me. "Zee?" Bird said.

Bird looked up and she and Paris watched as I climbed on the bike and pedaled back toward Grandpa Clark's house.

"Zee! Come back here," Bird yelled.

"Let him go," Paris said. "He just better be as good as you said."

I pedaled down the street thinking. I had a lot to think about. I had a week to find Tommy Crawford.

I didn't need it. What I needed was a few days to convince Mom and Grandpa Clark that I knew what I was doing. When I arrived at grandpa's house Mom was just back from somewhere in the Toyota. She smiled seeing me riding up the driveway on the bike.

"How was your ride?" Mom asked.

"Good," I said.

"Can you help me with the groceries?" Mom asked.

I smiled broadly. I put the bike in the garage and returned to the car to retrieve a couple of grocery bags. I carried the groceries into the house and sat them in the kitchen as Bo appeared and circled me.

"Are there any more groceries in the car?" Grandpa asked.

"I got them," I said and walked back outside with Bo trailing. I was closing the car door when Bird arrived on her scooter. I watched as she rode the scooter past the Toyota and into the garage.

I waited for Bird. Bird appeared from the garage with a smug smile on her face. I knew that face. She felt that she had some juicy gossip that was going to expose someone. As she walked up to me, I knew that Bird was planning to steal my thunder and telling Mom and grandpa what I was doing for Tommy Crawford's family.

"You know I'm going to tell them," I said to Bird.

"Okay," Bird said as Bo and I walked up the back stairs and into the rear of grandpa's house.

On the second trip to the kitchen grandpa reappeared. He was dressed in Chicago Cubs T-shirt and dark trousers. He was wearing his Cubs baseball cap.

"Are the Cubs playing today?" I asked grandpa.

"They play every day," grandpa said with a smile. "During the season," he added.

I smiled at grandpa's joke and loitered in the kitchen as Bird watched, waiting for me to bring up the subject.

"What are we having for dinner?" I asked.

"Nothing too amazing," Grandpa Clark said. "Just going to have fried chicken, red beans and rice, candied sweet potatoes, and peach cobbler."

I smiled.

"You should go and clean up. Food should be ready in about an hour," grandpa said.

I exited the kitchen with Bo by my side. Bird watched with that mischievous smile on her face. We walked upstairs shoulder-to-shoulder. Bo followed obediently.

"What do you think Mom is going to say?" Bird asked.

I didn't answer.

On the second floor Bo and I walked to my bedroom. Bird went to her bedroom.

In my bedroom I sat at the desk and looked at the MacBook box. I wondered how much quicker I could have figured things out if the laptop wasn't so out of date and completely useless.

Bo nosed against me. I looked down at my mini lion of a dog and rubbed his head. Rubbing Bo's head meant that he would be glued to me as long as I showed him attention.

Sitting at the desk I looked at the chessboard I had brought from Chicago. I adjusted the chess pieces and pushed out the pawn over the white queen. It was a simple and basic move. Starting the game with d4 forced the other side to respond. c5 was the mainline for black, I knew. I thought about the mainlines to get my mind off the dinner and Bird's attempt to convince Mom and Grandpa that I was out of my depths.

I washed up and headed downstairs with Bo behind me. When I arrived downstairs Bird and Mom were setting up the table. I looked around and tried to help.

"Go help daddy bring out the food," Mom said.

I walked to the kitchen and grandpa handed me a bowl of cornbread and a bowl of string beans. I spun on my heels and returned to the dining room where we were eating that night. Placing the two bowls on the table Bird grabbed the cornbread and sat it in the middle of the table. Mom smiled and took the string beans from me.

"Get us some napkins," Mom said.

I gave a small nod. I returned to the kitchen and searched for some napkins.

"What are you looking for?" Grandpa Clark asked.

"Napkins." I said.

Grandpa smiled and opened a drawer and pointed to some cloth napkins stacked in the drawer. I grabbed a handful of napkins and started for the dining room.

"Take this out with you," Grandpa Clark said, pointing to the small pot of red beans and rice with a serving spoon. I gave a nod. I carried the small pot and napkins to the table.

"Put them at each plate," Mom said of the napkins.

I folded each napkin and put one by each plate.

"All right, everyone, let's sit down," Grandpa Clark said as he entered the dining room. Grandpa brought out the candied sweet potatoes were in a glass dish and the last part of dinner, and the main course was sweet tea fried chicken.

We all sat down. Grandpa sat at the head of the table. Bird and Mom sat on either side of Grandpa. Me, I sat to the left of mom. Bo, ever present, laid down at my feet.

"Who's going to pray over the meal?" Grandpa asked.

"Thank you, Lord Jesus, for the food we are about to receive. Thank you for our family. Thank you for the hands that made the meal. God bless everyone at the table. Thank you for the love we share and our open hearts. Let us always have a willingness to care for others. Amen," I said.

I looked up and found my mom smiling. Grandpa smiled as well. Bird smirked.

"That was nice," Mom said.

"Yeah, that was nice," Grandpa Clark said.

We ate and Bird waited for me to speak. I ate the string beans on my plate. The red beans and rice were delicious, but I didn't fill up on them. My favorite part of the meal was the candied sweet potatoes and fried chicken. I only ate two pieces of chicken before I felt stuffed.

"What did you do today, Bird?" Mom asked.

"I just hung out with Paris," Bird said. "Ask Zee what he did," Bird said, seeing her chance to put my plans on display.

"Anybody want anything else?" Grandpa Clark asked. Mom moved her head side to side as an answer. Bird had eaten string beans, red beans, and rice and one piece of fried chicken before pushing her plate away from her.

Grandpa climbed to his feet and retreated to the kitchen. He returned with dessert. The dessert was peach cobbler.

"Zee? What did you do today?" Mom asked.

"I didn't do too much," I said, looking at Bird out of the corner of my eye. Mom smiled. Bird grinned evilly.

"I rode my bike downtown," I said. "I went to the library. I rode around downtown and ran into Bird and Paris." I paused, watching Bird. She smiled like she was eating a pie.

"I came home and had lunch with you and grandpa," I continued. I paused. "I went to see Tommy Crawford's mom and uncle. I told them that I think I know where their son might be. They were surprised by that. They told me that it had been nearly seven months and no news."

Mom frowned.

Grandpa had given everyone a piece of peach cobbler and was sitting in his chair when he stopped and looked at me like I had grown another eye in the middle of my forehead.

"Wait. What?" Mom asked, puzzled.

Grandpa set his fork down and chewed his food silently, watching me at the dining room table like I was a stranger.

"Back up," Mom said. "You said what?"

"You know that Zee thinks he is some junior Sherlock Holmes or something," Bird said at dinner table.

I did not respond.

"Zee, you are twelve years old and no matter how smart you are you can't tell someone's mother that you can find their missing child after seven months," Mom said.

"Why not?" I asked.

"You can't give her that false hope," Grandpa said. "That ain't right."

"But what if I'm right?" I asked.

"What if you're wrong," Grandpa countered.

"I'm not," I said.

There was a deafening silence at the dining room table.

I sat and waited for the inevitable. I knew that there were
going to be a hundred questions, at least, to shake my confidence, or at
least attempt to shake my confidence.

Mom and Grandpa Clark asked a handful of questions. I was
surprised that the questions were remarkably similar to the questions
asked by Georgina Gibson and Joshua Pernell. I listened and answered
all their questions knowing that I would never be able to convince
them of my abilities in words alone. Yet, I tried.

"All I need is a few days," I said. "If I don't find some hard
evidence to prove that I am on the right track then I'll stop. I'll tell
them that I made a mistake and apologize."

Mom and Grandpa Clark did not respond immediately.

"Give me a chance," I said. "That's all I'm asking. Give me a
chance to prove to you and everyone that I'm right." I looked at the
two who were already on the fence about me attempting to prove that
I could find Tommy Crawford.

"Or wrong," Bird said.

"How long did you say it would take?" Mom asked.

"A week," I said. "Seven days."

"Mom, ask him to explain how he came up with his theory,"
Bird said, not trying to help.

"Mom," I said. Explaining all the thoughts in my head seemed
Herculean. I looked to Mom, and she did not immediately protect me.
I understood, deep down. She wanted me to prove myself as well. I
looked to grandpa and though he seemed mildly interested, he was not
my salvation.

"So, explain," Mom said.

"Okay," I said, hesitantly. I studied the dinner table and
looked at Bird, Mom, and grandpa. They would not understand my
thinking. I barely felt that I could explain my thinking clearly. I mean, I
understood how I connected things, but many times there were these
drastic leaps of logic. The information might be hiding, and I had seen
a snippet of that information. Seeing that sliver of detail, a meaningless
description, or having listened to someone talk or avoid a topic
triggered something in my thinking. In that thinking there were all
these tendrils that led me to my thoughts. I thought all this and
paused, puckering my lips, and preparing to speak.

"I just read the newspapers and realized that the things that they weren't saying was saying something to me. I don't know if that makes sense to anyone else. So, I just started connecting things." I paused. As I spoke, I was trying to understand how Frankie played in all this. In my head, the puzzle pieces that involved Frankie clicked together and for some reason I thought I should go and talk with my new cousin.

I felt hot. I wasn't sure if I was sweating, but I felt as if everyone at the table was staring at me.

Chapter 18.

The next day, which was partly cloudy and threatened to rain, I took Bo for a morning walk. We walked to the field. Bo did his business and I tried to focus on what needed to be done that day.

"Okay, Bo," I began, after taking Bo for a walk. "I'm going to be gone for a while. I should be back in a couple of hours. Mom and Bird are here. Grandpa Clark is here too. So, don't freak out."

After breakfast I did all my chores that mom and grandpa had for me. I cleaned up the kitchen and then headed to the Village Mall. I had promised Zada Gallamore that I would return after talking to Tommy Crawford's family.

I rode the mountain bike to the mall. I locked it up at one of the bike racks there.

"You back again?" The reporter asked with a smile.

"I said I would come back," I said.

"Yeah, I didn't think you were serious," Zada Gallamore said. "I heard you talked with Tommy's family."

"I did," I said. I studied Zada and took a breath. "Well, I only have a few questions," I said.

"Okay. Shoot," Zada Gallamore said.

We talked for an hour. In that hour I learned all that I needed to know about Tommy Crawford and his disappearance. Zada Gallamore had a police report of the last known description of Tommy. She also had a list of his personal items.

"Most of the details were withheld," Zada Gallamore said, concerned. "The belief was that whoever was behind the disappearance might try and sell his personal items later."

She told me, in her opinion, the most important thing in the police report was the location of the party ranch.

"It always irked me that they didn't have a complete list of people at the party or a suspect list because the party was filled with high school students."

"I don't get it," I said.

"I don't get it either," Zada said. "Suspects are suspects. I'm not sure if they interviewed anyone from the party. Or if they did," the reporter paused. "I'm not sure they wanted to solve the disappearance."

"Why?"

"Think there were some important people's kids at that party," Zada said.

After talking to Zada Gallamore, I returned to grandpa's house. The clouds overhead darkened and spit a few drops of rain. It was the sprinkling of raindrops that fell for a few minutes and after was forgotten.

When I walked in the house Bo, of course, acted like he had not seen me in years. Silly dog. Bo and I walked to the field. I decided to revisit the loose earth where I had found Frankie a few days before.

I found the mound and walked around what suddenly looked like a grave.

Bo shouldered me and made me aware that I was in the grass field that stretched from Eiche to Blohm. I swallowed, blinked, and tried to decide what to do.

Should I dig up what was under the loose soil? Should I go and tell grandpa? Mom? Bird?

I looked around. The gray skies darkened. No one was in the field or on the street as the rain threatened me and Bo. Well, I hoped no one was in the grass field with me and Bo that morning.

The idea of being so close to a possible grave gave me gooseflesh.

I ran from the possible grave with Bo barking and following. I ran and tried to think who the best person would be to help me with this very prickly situation.

As I ran grandpa's house grew bigger as I got closer, I wanted to connect the loose earth to Frankie. I wanted to make Frankie the full moon murderer. I wanted to have figured out the whole South-Central Illinois Werewolf swindle. My cousin, the werewolf sounded dramatic.

I ran and though I wanted to say that Frankie was the South-Central Illinois werewolf I knew I couldn't. He didn't fit the profile. He didn't work at the Effingham Performance Center. He was creepy and weird, but so was I. Creepy and weird didn't make you a serial killer.

So, when I reached the edge of Eiche I decided that Frankie, though creepy, was not the killer or the person snatching these men. My cousin was not the werewolf. Whoever was snatching these men had to be big enough to overpower full grown men. I stopped to catch my breath and with Bo by my side we crossed the street. We ran to the back of grandpa's house. I looked to the garage and seeing it closed, headed up the back stairs and into the rear of the house.

"Grandpa, I have something to tell you and you cannot freak out about," I said out of breath.

Grandpa was at the stove making lunch when I entered the kitchen. He turned wearing khaki trousers and a white T-shirt.

"What are you talking about Zee?"

"Grandpa, I know you were in the Army, and you'll have a calm response about what I'm going to tell you," I said.

Grandpa Clark looked at me concerned.

"What's going on?"

"I think there's a dead body in the field outside," I said, blurting it out louder than I wanted.

"What? Why would you say that?" Grandpa Clark asked, concerned.

I opened my mouth only to close it. I squeezed my lips together tightly. I looked at my grandpa and took a deep breath.

"I can show you better than I can tell you," I said.

Grandpa Clark looked seriously at me and turned back to the stove. He turned some dials off on the stove.

Bo nudged me, drawing my attention to him for a moment. I reached down and patted Bo on the head.

"Okay, show me," Grandpa Clark said.

I gave a slight nod and turned to walk out of the kitchen and to the back of the house. Grandpa Clark followed along with Bo.

We walked to the field, and I led grandpa and Bo back toward the loose soil that concealed a grave. As I got close to the location my stomach twisted. I was suddenly nervous.

What if this was a grave? What if there was a dead body under the loose soil? My head was swimming with those and a hundred other questions as I stopped and pointed to the grave.

Grandpa Clark stopped and looked at the loose dirt just a few feet from him. He slowly walked around the rectangular bit of loose earth. He bent down and touched the soil.

I stepped back. I didn't know what I expected but seeing my grandpa touching the dirt of a possible grave was not in my thought pattern.

Grandpa brushed some of the soil away with his hand. Nothing unusual appeared in the effort. Grandpa brushed more soil.

"What are you doing?" I asked.

"Well, you can't say this is a grave and not have something buried here," Grandpa Clark said.

I trembled a little. I swallowed and bent down to the dark loose soil and began to dig up the area in front of me.

Grandpa Clark was kneeling and digging as well. Bo seeing us digging in the dirt did his part.

After a few minutes, Grandpa Clark stopped.

"Zee," Grandpa said, his voice cold and serious. I looked up and Grandpa was waving me away from the loose soil. He climbed to his feet and there, by his foot, was an untied boot just poking out of the soil with a sock and foot inside. "Go inside and call 9-1-1. Think this is something that I am not capable of handling on my own."

I stumbled back seeing the boot and grandpa brushing the dirt from his hands. I was hypnotized by the sight of the untied boot, dark sock and foot knowing the boot was at the end of a person beneath the soil I was digging in seconds before.

"Go on now," Grandpa Clark said. "Tell your mom and sister to stay in the house until I come back inside."

I ran and Bo seeing me run pursued. Bo and I ran back to the house, and I found grandpa's phone in the kitchen and called the police.

Mom appeared while I was on the phone.

"Zee? What are you doing?" Mom asked, concerned.

"Hello," I said. "I am calling to report that my grandpa just found a dead body in the field by our house," I said.

"What?" Mom asked, stepping to the phone and me. I pointed and gestured to the window. Mom walked past me to the window and looked to see grandpa standing in the grass field.

I gave the police the address and told them my name.

"Can you hurry?" I asked.

"We'll have someone there as soon as possible," the police dispatcher responded.

I rung off.

"Mom," I said, standing in the doorway that led to the back of the house. "Grandpa told me to tell you and Bird to stay inside the house until he came back inside."

"Zee," Mom said, trying to remain calm. "What the hell is going on?"

"Bo and I saw this loose dirt and I walked around it and it looked like a grave and I told grandpa about it, and he went outside to check," I said all jittery. "He found a shoe with a foot attached to it. So, he told me to call 9-1-1 and tell you and Bird to stay inside."

Bird appeared rubbing her eyes dressed in her pink top and blue jeans.

"What's going on?" Bird asked.

Mom explained.

The Effingham Police arrived at grandpa's house thirty minutes after the call.

Mom opened the door and I walked to the front with Bo.

"There was a call about a possible dead body?" The police officer said.

I pushed to the side of my mother and smiled.

"I called," I said.

The police officer looked at me dressed like he was preparing to go to war. I noted the bulletproof vest, the radio, the tear gas, his short-sleeved shirt, and big biceps and yellow handled taser on one hip and the black handled pistol on the other. He was dressed in comfortable cargo pants with a half dozen oversized pockets above his combat boots.

"You called?"

"Yep," I said. "My grandfather and I found something in the field over there," I said. I pointed toward the field.

The police officer looked in the direction of the field and grandpa.

Bird pushed her way forward.

"I'll go and check it out," the police officer said.

I followed.

The police officer paused and when he did, I pushed past him and walked to the field ahead of him with Bo.

"So, what do we have here?" The police officer asked.

"Well, I was out here with my grandson and came upon this," Grandpa Clark said. "I poked around and found this." He pointed to the untied boot and foot inside.

The police officer called in the details.

"We'll need a crew to dig this spot up," the police officer said into his radio.

The police officer took a notepad from one of his pockets. He looked at the loose soil and the grave.

He took a preliminary report. A second police car arrived. The police officer who arrived opened his trunk and placed barriers around the loose soil. A third police car arrived on Eiche.

How many police were there in Effingham?

Grandpa and I stood around and, after the police officer who had shown up first was relieved by another thin white man with a mustache, we returned to the house.

I thought to give the police the watch face but hesitated. Grandpa pushed me toward his house, and I reluctantly complied. When we returned to the house Mom and Bird had a million questions. Bo was all riled up as well.

"Okay, everyone calm down," Grandpa Clark said with a seriousness that quieted everyone including Bo.

"Zee and Bo went out for a walk and found some loose dirt and he thought it might be something," Grandpa Clark said, sitting down at the kitchen table. "It was something."

"It was a body," I said. Mom and Bird looked at me. "A dead body."

Bird moved her head side to side.

"Yeah, there's a body out there and they think it might be others out there," Grandpa Clark said seriously.

"Are we safe?" Mom asked.

"Yeah, why wouldn't we be safe?" Grandpa asked.

"I don't know. In all the time I lived in Chicago I didn't wake up and find that there was a dead body just in the park across the street from us," Mom said smugly.

"We're fine," grandpa said. He took a deep breath. He looked around the kitchen. The pots and pans were where he had left them nearly two hours earlier. "Who's hungry?"

"How can you think about food now?"

Grandpa Clark climbed to his feet, walked to the kitchen sink, and washed his hands.

"Everyone has to eat," he said from the sink. "Good, bad or otherwise," grandpa said as he reached out and grabbed an apron and slipped it over his head. He reignited the flames under his pots and slowly increased the heat as he prepared to finish lunch.

On that weird day with the police just outside searching the field for any other bodies Grandpa Clark made slow-cooker breakfast hash with eggs. Grandpa chopped up some fresh fruit and made us all fruit cups to go with our brunch.

For the next seven hours there were more police on Eiche and in the field than I had seen in my entire life. The clouds overhead continued to threaten rain but only threatened.

The police searched the ground where I had found Frankie and after a slow and methodic unearthing found a man dressed in green trousers, a light green shirt, and those brown boots.

At the door, a police officer appeared.

"Can you tell me how you found the grave again?" The police officer asked.

"I was walking my dog and he found it. I saw it after him," I said.

"I thought you said that you found it Mister Clark?" The police officer asked, curious.

"I did find it," grandpa said.

The police officer looked at Grandpa Clark without saying anything.

"Is there a problem?" Grandpa Clark asked.

"No," the officer said. "Just want to be thorough," he said.

"So, just so I am clear," the officer said, slowly, checking his notes. "Who found the body?"

"I did," Grandpa Clark said.

"Okay, so your grandson found the grave?" The police officer asked.

I gave a weak nod.

"Yes," Grandpa Clark said. Grandpa looked at the officer with his notepad writing down notes. "Is there anything else?"

"No, that will be all for now," the officer said.

Chapter 19.

Two days later the white Yukon pulled in front of Grandpa Clark's house, I knew that Joshua Pernell, Frankie, and Paris would be waiting. Pernell had arranged the first meeting. None of them were aware of my discovery in the field next to grandpa's house.

"Mom? Grandpa? They are here," I said, heading to the front door with Bo on my heels.

I stopped at the door and waited for one or both adults to appear.

Bird, Mom, and Grandpa Clark met me at the front door.

"Take Bo to the backyard," Mom said as Bird and Grandpa Clark watched.

I dutifully took Bo to the backyard.

"Okay, you behave while I'm gone. Wish me luck," I said to Bo. "I won't need it, but it's just a saying."

Bo licked my face. I gave the furry lion dog a hug. Bo licked my face again. I climbed to my feet. Bo nosed against me. I did not look at him. Instead, I walked to the back stairs.

"Stay," I said, and Bo stopped at the bottom of the stairs to the back of the house. I left Bo in the backyard.

Returning to the house I wiped Bo's spit off my face with the back of my hand. I looked around the kitchen and grabbed an apple for later. I put the apple in my windbreaker pocket and headed for the front of the house.

"Okay, Zee," Mom said, concerned. "I am letting you do this but, as we agreed, if you can't find any evidence then I will pull you off this."

Great, I thought. More pressure. Find Tommy Crawford. Don't get Tommy's mother too hopeful. Make sure that Tommy's uncle doesn't run out of patience. Prove to everyone that I know what I am talking about.

I gave a small nod.

"Bird is going with you," Mom added. "I don't know these people. Your grandpa knows Paris and Frankie, but the uncle is a complete stranger."

I didn't argue. There was no point.

Bird was standing on the curb in front of the SUV with Paris talking when I waved goodbye to Mom and grandpa.

"You ready?" Paris asked.

I tried to smile.

"Where to?" Joshua Pernell asked once I climbed in and got comfortable in the seat behind Frankie.

"County Road 1525 East," I said from the rear passenger seat next to the window.

Frankie looked back and had to crane his neck to see me.

I lifted my chin just a little to Frankie. He tipped his chin to me and disappeared behind the front seat headrest.

"Right," Joshua Pernell said and pulled the Yukon away from the curb.

The Yukon rolled through the streets of Effingham and in minutes found the State Road 45 and beelined for Douglas County.

Paris and Bird were seated to my right, talking and giggling. They acted like they were on some school field trip. They were dressed like they were going to just hang out and not search for Tommy Crawford. I, on the other hand, was dressed in jeans, closed toed comfortable shoes, a T-shirt and windbreaker.

"You coming along to help search?" I asked.

Paris knitted her forehead. Bird smirked.

"What is with the chain-link fence?" Paris asked as we drove away from grandpa's house.

Bird told her the details. Everyone in the SUV quieted as Bird told them that grandpa had found a dead body in the field.

"You know," Paris said. "I thought for a long time that you were kidding, and that Bird was going to call me and tell me to call the whole thing off. But I never got that call." She looked at me, waiting for me to respond. "Now, you finding dead bodies in fields? What? Are you like incredibly lucky?"

I smiled. Paris in her own way was trying to be nice.

"Do you really think you're going to find Tommy?" Bird asked.

I gave a deep nod.

"What makes you think so?" Paris asked.

Bird leaned forward.

"It's kind of simple," I began and stopped. "You were there when I explained it to her mom and the others," I said. "I still believe that whoever hurt Tommy did it on accident if that's possible. You know? Like when you hit someone too hard?"

"Yeah," Paris said. "You explained that already," she noted.

"Well, if that happened and they, whoever they were," I said, more to myself than to Paris. "Then they were in trouble. They had to get rid of a hurt Tommy. They had to hide him even if they didn't kill him," I said.

"Hide him?"

I gave a small nod.

"So, where would they hide him?"

I smiled. "That's where the winnowing comes in," I said.

"Winnowing? What's that?"

"It's when you start to take things away until there's only one choice," I said. "I read it in a book. So, I have to get rid of the places where he could be seen first. My belief is that Tommy left the party and then things happened. So, that helps me figure out where he could be," I said.

Paris looked at me and smiled. Bird, who was leaning forward to hear me, leaned back, and looked out the rear passenger window and watched the world go by.

Pernell drove to 2000th Avenue which changed into County Road 1525 East after a turn.

"Where to?" Pernell asked.

"Well, you know where the party was. Let's go there," I said.

"We have been there already," the driver said.

"I know, but not with me," I said.

"The little man thinks he knows more than you or the cops," Frankie said from the front passenger seat.

I didn't respond. There was no need to. I wasn't fighting with Frankie, Pernell, or Paris. I was trying to see my theory through to a logical conclusion. The idea of someone being lost was an impossibility in my mind. People did not disappear. They ran away for whatever reason. If you looked hard enough and turned over enough stones, you could find the runaways. It would be incredibly hard, but not impossible. The ones that were kidnapped or abducted had not disappeared. They had been taken and if knowing the slavers habits

145

and routines that too was not impossible to unravel. In my head, the idea of someone missing needed to be looked at not as to where they might be, but what was the reason of the disappearance.

Pernell drove the Yukon down the two-lane road to the spot where the high school party had been held two days before the start of the new year. He pulled off the road and put the SUV in park.

I looked across the road at the fence that barred entry into the ranch house that had been rented for the party. I scanned the road in both directions from the back seat of the Yukon and fixated on the mailbox attached to the three barred fence chained and secured to the stone fence posts.

"Now what?"

"Can we drive up to the next road? If it too far we have to turn around and come back here," I said.

"You don't want to get out?"

"No," I said.

"Okay," Pernell said.

"Are you sure about this?" Bird asked in a whisper, leaning over Paris.

I gave a weak nod and after less than two minutes driving, we found ourselves at the end of County Road 1525 East and at East 2100th Avenue. Pernell looked back and into the rearview mirror.

"What now?"

"Turn around," I said. Then I had a thought. "No. Turn to the left." If my thinking was correct, we would not have far to go.

Pernell turned the Yukon onto East 2100th Avenue. Less than one hundred yards I asked him to pull off the road. Everyone in the SUV looked at me curiously.

I opened my door and climbed out and onto the quiet road. Behind me I heard the SUV doors open and the others exit.

"Where are you going?" Bird asked.

"There's a creek here," I said. I had copied the map of Green Creek based on the descriptions and details given to me by Zada Gallamore and knew that the Henry Creek ran near the party ranch.

I pushed into the bushes along the shoulder of the two-lane road and found myself just a foot from the four-foot-wide Henry Creek.

"This is a great place to hide a body," I said as Pernell then Frankie arrived at my side. I was kneeling along the bank and studying the water's current.

"What do we do?" Frankie asked.

"The hard part," I said and began to walk down the bank slowly, methodically, with the current looking for Tommy Crawford or his remains.

Chapter 20.

From nine to noon Pernell and Frankie helped search for Tommy Crawford. Paris and Bird stumbled around and screamed when they found stuff that was not Tommy Crawford. Of the two, Paris seemed the more serious. Bird took a bunch of pictures on her cellphone.

"You sure about this kid?" Pernell asked as I knelt by the bank of the creek looking at anything that should not be there.

I looked at Joshua Pernell and understood that he wanted me to be right and at the same time hoped that today I was wrong and that he would not find his nephew. It was an understandable paradox. I understood that Pernell wanted to have some closure, but simultaneously, dreaded the inevitable and all that came with that closure.

We stopped for lunch. In three hours, we had searched two hundred yards of the creek.

"You think we're on the right track?"

"My sister is giving you until the end of the week," Pernell said. "That means I am giving you until the end of the week to help us find Tommy."

I ate lunch and found everyone's eyes on me. They wanted me to crack or break and surrender. Perhaps, I thought, they wanted me to fail. It was easier to accept failure than success I imagined if you are used to broken promises. I understood. I sympathized with the four sitting and eating with me, but I did not see how my thinking was flawed or could disappoint.

So, even though they needed me to reassure them I did not. There was no point. We were here. Proof was the reassurance I hoped for and nothing less.

Finishing my sandwich and washing it down with a juice box mom had packed away for me I was ready to continue the search.

"Are you ready?"

After lunch, Paris and Bird headed back to the Yukon. They were useless anyway.

By one o'clock the sun was unbearable, and Pernell and Frankie took shelter in the shade of the trees along the bank of the

Henry Creek. Despite the heat I pushed on and about three hundred yards from where we started, I found the first of half a dozen personal items of Tommy Crawford.

The first item I stumbled upon was his muddied rubber wrist band that read: Black Lives Matter. A few feet away from the rubber wrist band was another distinct bracelet, this one made of rope and metal. We found three more rubber wrist bands, all of which, according to the police report, belonged to Tommy Crawford.

The discovery of the wrist bands inspired Pernell and Frankie and less than an hour later they found one of his shoes on the opposite side of the bank. Frankie had crossed the bank with a belief that he might have better luck there.

In a pile of bushes Pernell was the first to discover Tommy's baseball cap. Frankie and I moved down the creek and there lodged beneath a rock ledge were the visible skull and bones of a body.

Pernell called his family and then the police.

Tommy's mother and her family were parking on the side of the road by the time the first police car arrived. The family members gathered on the side of the road and most had their phones out and filming. They were crying, hugging, and consoling one another.

Immediately, the Effingham Police tried to take control of the situation as the family members tried to document where Tommy Crawford, or the body and skeletal remains lay.

The second and third Effingham Police car arrived along with one Douglas County Sheriff SUV nearly forty minutes after Pernell's call.

"Back up," said one of the Effingham Police officers to the crowd of family members.

"Who made the call about the dead body?" One of the police officers asked.

Pernell stepped forward to the thin police officer in charge and in front of me and Frankie.

"I called," Pernell said, emotional. "I came down here and begged you to help find Tommy and you did nothing."

The police officer frowned. He looked at Pernell confused.

One of the men near Pernell reached out and restrained him.

"You could have helped find my nephew, but you sat on your fat ass and did nothing," Pernell said.

The police officer took a step back.

"Whoa," the police officer said "This is my first time here. I don't know what you are talking about."

"We found our boy, no thanks to you and Effingham Police," the family member said.

"Hey, I don't know what you're talking about, but need you to calm down, just a little," the officer said. "We're here. You called. What's going on?"

Pernell was too emotional to talk.

One of the family members stepped forward who I did not know and explained that the body of their nephew was on the Henry Creek bank, just four hundred yards from the road.

"He found the body?"

The family member closed his eyes. Pernell turned around with tears in his eyes.

"You had a chance to find Tommy and you did nothing," Pernell said, his voice choked with emotion.

The police officer looked in the direction of the brush and back to Pernell and the two family members.

"We'll check it out," the police officer said.

"Like hell you will," Pernell said. "We ain't going to let you go down there and tell us that the skeleton we found isn't Tommy," he said, blinking back tears. "We going with you."

"This is a criminal investigation now," the police officer said, as an explanation. "We need to keep the crime scene as pristine as possible."

"Pristine? Seven months after the fact?" Someone asked with a derisive laugh.

Two of the Effingham officers holding back the family stood and watched as Kenner, the thin Effingham police officer, and one of the Douglas Sheriff deputies walked into the brush on the side of the road with Pernell and one of the family members.

While the two officers went into the brush two more of the Douglas County Sheriff deputies pulled up to the already crowded road. They talked with the Effingham police and the three began roping off a section of the road.

I stood on the side of the road and watched. Paris and Bird were watching as well.

"You know that this is a big deal?"

I bobbed my head slowly.

The family members were on the banks of the creek watching the police and deputies. A camera crew from somewhere appeared and suddenly things got ramped up.

One of the police officers called in the details.

"We'll need a crew here," the police officer said into his radio.

The police officer took a notepad from one of his pockets. He took a preliminary report. A third Effingham police car arrived. The police officer who arrived opened his trunk and placed cones along the side of the road.

How many police were there in Effingham?

I stood with Bird and, after the police officer who had shown up first was relieved by another white man with a mustache, we returned to the SUV.

"You can't cover this up," someone said to the police. "We got this all on video."

"We want to know if this is Tommy," someone else said.

The police officers tried to keep the twenty family members calm and behind the makeshift barriers.

With all the people, cameras, and police the discovery of the skeletal remains of what Tommy Crawford's family believed had to be their family member there were tense moments as the police waited for the coroner to arrive. The police from Effingham doubled in size and became rigid in their directions of the small crowd to allow the police to do their jobs.

"Do your job?" Someone asked. "We wanted you to do your job in December and January, not when some little boy figured out where Tommy was in July."

"Do your job," someone chanted. The voices grew louder to the police.

When the coroner arrived, there were half a dozen Sheriff deputies on site, pushing the families back two hundred yards from the crime scene. 2100th Avenue had been blocked off in both directions and the only way to get around was down County Road 1525 East.

The Effingham Daily Record reporters appeared wearing matching windbreakers with PRESS emblazoned on the chest and back. I had not met any of the reporters from the Effingham Daily

Record but seeing two men wearing baseball caps that were embroidered with EDR I had to wonder if either of the two was John Bell, Henry Riley, or William Scoggins.

The chief investigator a curly-haired man in his forties with a thin mustache and jowls wearing a bulletproof vest under his suit jacket, questioned Pernell. I was briefly spoken to, but when he realized my age, I was dismissed.

Zada Gallamore was in the crowd. She waved and smiled. I detoured to the reporter.

"So, is it true?" Zada Gallamore asked with a big smile on her face. "Did they find Tommy Crawford."

I nodded slowly.

"Did you find Tommy Crawford?"

I smiled.

"Zion, how did you find someone that has been missing for nearly seven months?" Zada asked fumbling in her bag for her phone and camera.

Bird and Paris seeing me talking to Zada Gallamore gravitated toward me, curious.

"Who are you?"

I made quick introductions.

"Zada gave me some important information to help me find Tommy Crawford," I said to Bird and Paris.

"She did?" Asked Zada with a grin.

"You know Zee wouldn't have been able to figure things out without me and Paris," Bird said. "We introduced him to Tommy's mother and uncle."

"That's true," Paris said with a toothy grin.

"Maybe, when I am done here, I can talk to you two?"

"Okay," Bird said.

The two let me finish my interview, but not without interruption.

"So, Zion, tell me how all this happened," Zada said sticking the phone in my face.

"Well, you know most of it already," I began. "The only thing that you don't know is that after you gave me the information about the party, I started thinking that whoever hurt Tommy Crawford didn't plan on it."

"How did you come to that conclusion?"

"Well, it was a party. Right? No one goes to a party to fight, usually. So, Tommy shows up at the party and whoever decides to beat him up. But before they can beat him up, they take him for a ride. Someone said that Tommy left the party with people he didn't come with. So, somewhere outside of the party things get out of hand. Tommy gets hurt but bad. Now, the people that hurt Tommy have a problem. They have to get rid of Tommy so no one can blame them." I paused. "The question was where could they toss Tommy so no one would find him immediately? I looked at two possibilities. I also knew that the Henry Creek ran behind the house where the party was that night. So, I figured it out."

Zada smiled broadly and after took half a dozen pictures for the paper.

"Thanks Zion," Gallamore said.

I gave a tiny nod and was getting ready to leave when two men walked up.

"Gallamore," one of the Effingham Daily Record reporters said, seeing me being interviewed.

"Riley," Zada said with a professional nod.

"Who do we have here?"

Henry Riley was a thirty something with a crew cut haircut, square jaw, and bent nose of someone that might have been a boxer once. He was average height and weight and dressed in khaki trousers and a light blue collared shirt. In his blockish hands was his phone.

"No one you would be interested in," Zada Gallamore said.

"Let me decide that," Riley said.

The man beside him, smirking at Zada, had a scar across his clean-shaven chin. He was taller than Riley and had long black curly hair. His face was crescent shaped and ending in a slightly pointy chin. He had dark eyes, a pronounced nose, and thin lips beneath his mop of hair.

"Hi kid," Riley said with a fake smile. "What are you doing here?"

Paris and Bird seeing the two reporters stepped in and stopped the reporters questioning.

By the time Bird and I were dropped back at grandpa's house it was nearly six o'clock.

Chapter 21.

A day later, after walking Bo and seeing the new fencing around the recently dug up grave, the Effingham Daily Record had a front-page story on the discovery in the grassy field between Eiche and Blohm. I sat in the kitchen and read the article while grandpa made breakfast.

The article was interesting and if I hadn't been the one to discover the grave, I would have believed the story the reporter told. Thankfully, I was there, and I could distinguish fact from fiction.

The headline read: *Officers Find Body in Grassy Field.* The story read: *Thursday morning the Effingham Police Department were informed of possible activities in a grassy field in the southside of Effingham. A veteran officer went to investigate and came upon a gruesome discovery in the grassy fields between Eiche and Blohm. Police officers were called. They investigated the field and discovered the remains of a still unnamed man buried in a shallow grave where there was some illegally dumped trash.*

"We come here every so often because of trash complaints," Officer Tatum, one of the investigators, said.

The Effingham Police Office has decided to do a thorough sweep of the field as it may be the home to more bodies. At the height of the investigation there were no less than a dozen men and women scowering the grassy field for evidence.

"This field is out of the way and with no cameras," Officer Brown said. "We will be keeping an eye out on this and other key spots as we continue the investigation."

The police force is dedicated to finding the culprit or culprits behind this string of disappearances.

At present there are three missing persons cases still open.

As of the writing of this report there has yet to be any identification of the individual.

"Grandpa, did you read the newspaper?"

Grandpa Clark only smiled.

"They didn't interview you or me," I said.

"The paper ain't written for us," Grandpa Clark said.

"What do you mean?" I asked.

Grandpa didn't respond.

I didn't push. It seemed as if the newspaper didn't care for the real story.

Two weeks after the discovery of the dead body in the grassy field was the Harvest Moon Festival but the festival was nearly overshadowed by the finding of two more missing people. The Thursday of the first week after the police pulled David York out of the ground a FedEx truck driver stumbled onto another dead body near Cipps Lake.

The Effingham Police were called, and the body was pulled from the reeds of the lake. The body was identified as Travis Gordon.

In the Effingham Daily Record, the headline read: *Cipps Lake Discovery.* The story read: *The 51 days (about 2 months) of wondering where Walmart cashier Travis Gordon disappeared to has been solved, to a certain extent. Yesterday, Effingham Police Department spokesperson, Jonathan Shaw, reported that a FedEx employee was on break and hitting golf balls near the lake. He went to retrieve his golf balls near the lake and there in the reeds he saw a hand. He investigated.*

"I thought it was a prank," Roger Everett said.

It was not a prank. Everett contacted his supervisor and then called 9-1-1. The police were sent to investigate. The police dragged the bloated body to land and after a cursory examination it was taken to the county coroner. At the coroner, the body was identified as Travis Gordon from dental records.

Of course, there is speculation as to the cause of Gordon's death as his disappearance occurred during a full moon. When he disappeared, many believed the cashier at the Super Walmart might have become a victim of the South-Central Werewolf.

A week later, on the Wednesday before the Harvest Moon Festival, there was a second body found. There was a front-page story of the finding of the local mechanic by a couple of kids in the Little Wabash River.

Eric Saunders's body was found in the Little Wabash River by Linda and Nancy L., both minors, before sunset on Friday. Saunders was reported to be missing for 21 days (about 3 weeks). The Effingham mechanic disappeared and was reported missing three days after not showing up for work or answering phone calls from family or friends.

"He was a normal guy. He was not someone that didn't show up to work," Terry Hollis, a mechanic and co-worker, said.

The discovery of the remains of Saunders on the Little Wabash River does not answer all the questions of Saunders disappearance but instead opens more questions. There is a police investigation into the death and mutilation of Saunders body. Unfortunately, there was no CCTV in the area where the body was dumped.

There are many that want to suggest that the South-Central Werewolf is to blame for this death as Saunders body was badly decomposed and ripped apart. Some doing the investigation suggested that his body could have been ripped apart by animals.

No one I knew seemed to care about the discovery of the dead missing people. They, grandpa, Mom, Bird, and everyone I knew or ran into, were more interested in the upcoming Harvest Moon Festival.

Me, I was more concerned about the whereabouts of Tommy Crawford.

"So, are we going to the Harvest Moon Festival?" Bird asked, on the front porch. Bo was sitting on the porch with his head on the chair near me, listening.

"It's the last fling of the summer," I said.

"Before we go back to Chicago," Bird said.

"We're going back to Chicago?" I asked, surprised.

"Yeah, I think so," Bird said.

"How do you know?" I asked my sister.

"Mom had a couple of interviews and a couple of offers," Bird said. "They're all in Chicago."

Grandpa Clark climbed onto the front porch dressed in his Chicago Cubs baseball cap, T-shirt, and khaki pants. On his feet were his work boots.

"What are you two up to?" Grandpa Clark asked seeing us sitting on the front porch.

Bo stood up and padded to Grandpa Clark. Bo shouldered grandpa. Grandpa Clark looked down and gave Bo a much-needed rub. Bo shouldered grandpa and the big man patted Bo on the head as he sat on the wall of the front porch.

"Grandpa did you know that Mom got a job?"

"I heard," he said. He looked at Bird. "Did she make a decision?"

"I think she is going to work with the advertising firm," Bird said, timidly. "At least, that was the last thing she told me."

"How come everyone knows but me?"

Grandpa Clark shrugged his thick shoulders.

"When does she start working?"

Bird shrugged her shoulders.

"When are we going back home?"

"After the festival," Bird said. "I do know that."

I shook my head.

The next morning, I woke up, feed Bo, took Bo for a walk and as per usual walked on the field. Thinking about what Bird had said.

A few days before the Harvest Moon Festival Bird and I walked outside. The weather was still nice. We were sitting outside in the driveway with Bird sitting under the steering wheel of grandpa's Jeep and with Bo laying in the rear seat with his head on my lap. I was looking up and at the dark sky. The lightning bugs were flicking on and off to the left and right of us.

I was still smarting with the realization that the Effingham Police did not talk to grandpa or me after that day when I called them about finding the dead body. I wanted to figure out who was behind the disappearances, but it seemed that only I cared.

"You know there was a dead body in the field that grandpa and I found?" I asked Bird.

Bird gave a weak nod.

"Doesn't that mean anything?" I asked.

Bird shrugged her shoulders.

"We're leaving here in a few days, Zee," Bird said. "All the crazy small-town drama we're leaving behind." She looked back at me. "None of this will matter next week."

"It will matter to some," I said.

Bird did not respond.

I looked into the night sky, thinking.

"You know that the Harvest Moon Festival is a big deal for this backwater town," Bird said letting the seat back so that she could see the stars better.

"You think they will have it now?" I asked.

"Why wouldn't they have it?" Bird asked, looking back at me.

"You know the missing people?" I said. "The person who snatched the people is still out there."

Bird scoffed.

"You don't think there is someone snatching people?"

Bird moved her head side to side. "I think someone by themselves is a target," Bird said.

"Where is Paris?" I asked.

"She got grounded," Bird said with a smirk. "She got a boyfriend, and her mother wasn't having him sneaking around her house without her permission."

I shrugged at the explanation. None of that mattered to me. All I really heard was that Paris couldn't hang out with Bird and so she chose to hang out with me.

We sat and listened to the radio playing music from U of I in grandpa's Jeep.

"You know that the Harvest Moon Festival is during a full moon? Right?" I asked.

"So?"

I paused.

"No one believes that crap you and Frankie are talking about," Bird said, suddenly angry.

"But, he knows," I said, surprised at Bird's anger.

"Frankie doesn't know anything. He's got you all mixed up in the stupid idea of a conspiracy. No one believes that Zee. There ain't no werewolf going to show up and snatch someone because it's a full moon."

I looked at Bird, troubled.

"He's ridiculous," Bird said. "I get you. You don't know any better," Bird said, dismissing me. "But Frankie is graduating and he's going to have to get a job or go to school or both," Bird said frustrated.

For the next few days, I stayed around Grandpa Clark's house. I was a bit of an Effingham celebrity. Well, I was a local black Effingham celebrity, if that makes any sense. The small black population of Effingham could not stop gushing over me.

When I went to church with Grandpa Clark and the family the pastor took time to recognize me and my family and helping the Crawford family find peace in the return of Tommy.

It was at the end of the church service that a woman and man approached Mom, Bird, and grandpa. They were in their thirties or maybe early forties. The woman was wearing a wide brimmed Sunday hat. She was the color of chestnuts and just a little taller than me. The woman was dressed in a dark blue dress with matching flats.

The man beside her was a head taller than her and dark as a pecan. He was not incredibly muscular, dressed in a chestnut brown suit with a brown tie. He looked incredibly serious.

Grandpa Clark stepped in between the couple, Mom, and Bird.

"How can I help you?"

"Mister Clark," the man said, looking at grandpa sincerely. The man spoke quietly with grandpa and because Mom and Bird were shielding me, I was not able to hear the conversation. I watched as the two men talked and looked back toward me. I knew that the conversation had to do with me and since I had never seen the two before it had to be about me finding Tommy Crawford.

"Zee, this is John and Vera Wright," Grandpa Clark said, as we stood on the sidewalk in front of the church. Church members passed by on their way to the parking lot. The pastor was the last to exit the church as I met the Wrights.

The Wrights told me about their missing son.

I listened to the story.

"Solomon was a good kid," John Wright said.

"He is a good kid," Missus Wright said, correcting her husband.

"Yeah, yeah," he smiled. "He's just been missing for so long that I don't know what to think," John Wright said. "He's been missing since May and..."

"We heard about how you found Tommy Crawford," Vera Wright said, with a small smile. "We want you to help us find Solomon."

I opened my mouth to speak.

"We'll pay," John Wright said. "We don't have much. But we know that you might be our last hope."

"We wouldn't ask for money," Mom said.

I looked at my mom and grandpa. It seemed as if they had decided for me what was my next summer activity. Bird smiled and moved her head side to side.

"So, you going to make some bold prediction on this one?" Bird asked with a smile.

I did not make any predictions. Instead, I thought about the information the Wrights had given me and asked after we returned to grandpa's house could I be excused.

"What? You don't want to hang out with us for a little bit?"

"I do, but suddenly I have to try and find someone's son that has been missing for the last three months," I said.

Mom smiled at my intensity.

"Grandpa is it okay to look through some of your papers in the garage?"

"Sure," Grandpa Clark said. "Just put them back when you're finished. They make good kindling for the barbecue."

I headed to the garage with Bo in tow. When I entered the garage and found the stack of newspapers stacked three feet off the ground I smirked at grandpa's handiwork. He read the Effingham Daily Record every day and at the end of the week walked the weeks' worth of news to the garage. Doing some quick math in my head, I knew I had to go back at least ninety newspapers to find May. Not knowing the exact day Solomon disappeared I was hoping that the Effingham Daily Record would be a good jumping off point.

So, I carefully peeled off ten newspapers and then another ten. I worked my way to about two feet of newspapers by my side when I came upon the first May issues of the local newspapers. I skimmed the month of May reported by the Effingham Daily Record.

Bo sniffed around the garage and after a while returned to my side and laid at my feet while I searched for information on Solomon Wright. Since I was skimming the Effingham Daily Record, I knew that if there was going to be any news about the disappearance of Solomon Wright it would be on the front page or in the Local News section. As I searched, I also focused on the South Central Illinois Werewolf stories. Knowing that the disappearances were somehow connected.

The last week of May I read there was a full moon but there was no mention of anyone missing. I stopped digging and paused, thinking.

The newspaper printed information that had happened, I reasoned. So, the odds of the newspaper having reported something that happened in May were slim to none. It was more likely that a story of a missing person from May being reported in June.

I retrieved the last few papers on the stack and read through them looking for pertinent information. In the first week of June there on the front page the newspaper mentioned a report of a missing boy in West Cedar.

The West Cedar area finds itself not immune to the disappearances in Effingham. It was reported that a teenager who was last seen in West Cedar is missing. The last known location of the missing boy as of the writing of this article was near the McDonald's and Phillips gas station off S. Banker Street.

I started restacking the newspapers when Bo climbed to his feet and looked toward the open garage door.

Bird appeared at the door with a smile. Behind her I noticed that it was already getting dark outside.

"What time is it?"

"Almost dinner," Bird said.

I picked up another handful of newspapers to replace them on grandpa's stack.

"So, you like it here?"

I looked at Bird, confused.

"I mean, here you are a big deal," Bird said.

I stopped with a handful of newspapers in hand and looked at my sister uncertain. I waited. Bird had a real question behind her first question. I knew.

"This place is small," Bird said.

I listened.

"I mean, you can't say anything to anyone without it being repeated and told to the wrong people," Bird said.

I listened trying to decipher what my sister was not saying.

"You know if we were in Chicago and I told Freddy that I thought someone was cute, she wouldn't go and blab it the person," Bird said.

I frowned, confused. Who had Bird told she liked? No. There was only one person she could tell, I reasoned. The bigger question was who did Bird think was cute?

"I think that being down here there just aren't a bunch of choices," Bird said. "I mean, the choices are limited. You know?"

I looked at Bird and gave a tiny nod as if I knew what she was talking about.

"I think this is a great place for someone your age," Bird said. "I mean, this is great for young kids. It's safe. There's not a lot to do to get in trouble with." Bird moved her head side to side. "Down here, you get to be a kid."

I wondered if Bird thought Frankie was cute? Or was it Donny? Perhaps, I thought, my sister thought Trey was cute.

"I bet you can walk anywhere around here, and no one is going to bother you. I mean, there can't be gangs down here. I can't imagine there's drugs down here," Bird said. She picked up a newspaper, looked at the front page, and placed it on the stack of papers I was replacing.

It seemed like Bird was paying Effingham a compliment, but her tone was just the opposite.

"It's still small potatoes down here," Bird said. "I can't wait to get back to Chicago."

I placed the newspapers in my hand on the stack. I listened not sure what to say.

"This place is full of small-town drama," Bird said. "I know that you're doing good and helping, but down here there's always going to be more and more drama."

"Why?" I finally said.

"It is how it is down here. Everything that is small is bigger," Bird said. "The insults that are normal everyday insults anywhere else end up being the cause of a family feud," Bird said.

"A family feud," I said, confused.

"People are thick here and thin skinned at the same time down here and more than comfortable killing you rather than trying to talk to you," Bird said.

"What?"

"They act all simple and plain and think that they are helping, but only get in the way," Bird said.

I was confused.

"In Chicago people don't get involved," Bird said, frustrated. "Down here, in the cornfields, they think they are helping, but a lot of times their helping is hurting."

Helping? Hurting? Bird was talking about Paris and her. Paris had told Frankie, Donny, or Trey that Bird thought he was cute. That was a problem. Bird didn't like them knowing how she felt.

Bird looked at me.

"But grandpa lives down here," I said. "He ain't like that."

"Grandpa is old. Old people don't count. They get old and they start acting like they can say anything," Bird said. "I am amazed that grandpa can cook and care for himself."

"He's not that old," I said.

Bird sulked.

I continued to restack the newspapers.

"It ain't all bad down here," I said. "I mean, look at Paris and them," I said. "They'll be our friends for life."

Bird smiled.

"They will always remember this summer," I said.

"So will we, but for different reasons," Bird said.

"Why?"

"I don't know," Bird said. "We've had a helluva summer. It definitely was better than I thought it was going to be when we left Chicago."

I gave a weak nod.

Bird looked at me with her dark eyes and stopped.

"What?"

"I just wish that there was something I could do to help."

"You can," I said. I smiled at Bird.

"What?"

"Well, according to my research Solomon Waters lived in West Cedar," I said.

"Okay," Bird said.

"Can you give me a ride down to the McDonald's in West Cedar?"

"Where's West Cedar?"

Chapter 22.

After dinner Bird and I rode her scooter down South Banker Street looking for West Cedar. We rode past the Dairy Queen and the Village Mall as it started to get really dark. We rode to West Poplar Drive and a few minutes later rode past Elm Avenue.

"This is pretty far," Bird said as we continued down South Banker Street.

"We should be pretty close," I said holding onto Bird with all my strength.

One hundred yards from Elm Avenue off to the right sat the familiar arches of McDonalds. Bird expertly slowed and exited South Banker and drove toward the Phillips 66 gas station. On the other side of the gas station sat the McDonalds.

There were four cars parked at the Phillips 66 gas station getting gas. A van was parked near the entrance to the gas station store. At the door were two guys talking.

Bird parked the scooter in the McDonald's parking lot and let me climb off before she did. Once off the scooter, I stretched, feeling tense. My arms felt like every muscle was knotted. I shook my arms out.

"Now, what?"

"Well, I need to look around and see if anything jumps out to me," I said. I noted the gas station and the ease of getting on South Banker Street. If someone had unintentionally hurt Solomon, then he would not be too hard to find. The area around the McDonalds and the gas station were well lit.

"I'm going to use the bathroom," Bird said.

I gave a quick nod.

Bird walked into the McDonalds.

I walked around the McDonalds and stopped finding some crudely made and weathered missing fliers for Solomon Wright. I stopped and looked at the picture of the dusky boy with the gentle eyes staring back at me. Wright was one of those pretty boys with wavy hair that everyone liked.

I continued my walk around the McDonalds noting the empty field directly opposite of the fast-food restaurant. On the far end of the empty field was a fire house. I walked back toward Bird's scooter seeing that there was an ATM machine on the West Jaycee Avenue side of the McDonalds.

On the way back to Bird and the scooter I saw a knot of kids around my age near a corner. I walked slowly toward them. Seeing me, the boys looked up and watched me approach.

"Hey," I said as I got close to the three boys.

They were all dressed in T-shirts, jeans, and sneakers. One was dark and had a cubic zirconia earring in his ear. One was a pointy chinned boy who had a tight fade. The third boy was sandy colored and had big ears that looked like they wanted to pull away from his head.

They looked a little skittish as I approached. I looked back to see Bird come out of the McDonalds. The boys studied me and looked a little shifty, but nothing to get nervous about.

"What you want?" Asked the dark boy with the cubic zirconia earring.

"You know Solomon?"

"Why you asking?" Asked the boy with the tight fade.

"He's a friend of my family," I said, trying to sound casual about it. "I'm here for a couple of days and trying to find out what happened to him."

The three boys looked at each other and then me.

"How you know him?" Asked the sandy colored boy with big ears.

"I just said. He's a friend of my family," I said, trying to sound casual.

The boy with the big ears shook his head. "We don't know you," the sandy colored boy with the big ears said.

"So," I said. "All I wanted to know is if any of you knew Solomon? He disappeared a few months ago."

The dark boy with the earring looked at me like he wanted to spit. I looked at him as he studied me.

"We don't know you, man," the boy said, looking at his two friends.

"I ain't ask you to know me. All I want to know is what you know about Solomon," I said, watching the three boys near the corner.

"You a cop or something?"

"What? Are you crazy? I'm twelve," I said.

"I don't know," the boy with the big ears said, with a shake of his head. "I don't want to get involved."

"I didn't ask anything about you," I said, looking at the boy with the ears that stuck out. "I just wanted to know what happened to Solomon."

"I'm out," The boy with the big ears said. He turned and walked away from the others back toward South Banker Street.

"I heard he disappeared a couple of months ago," I said to the dark boy with the earring. "I just wanted to know what happened. Who was he hanging with?" I paused and looked at the boy with the tight fade. "I'm just looking for any information to give to the family."

"What you think, Joey? You think he think he a cop or something?" The dark boy with the earring asked grinning smugly.

"Maybe," Joey grinned.

"Naw," I said. "Just a friend of the family. Nothing more." I paused and looked at Joey, the boy with the pointy chin and tight fade.

"All I know is that he disappeared like you said a couple of months ago," Joey said. "What you know Willie?"

"Don't know much more than that," Willie, the boy with the earring, said.

"Kind of surprised no one is looking for him," said Joey.

"Right," said Willie.

"He was supposed to be close with that white girl," Willie said.

"White girl?" I asked, casually.

"You know, the mayor's daughter," Willie said.

"Yeah, I heard he was hooked up with her for a minute, then it ended, and he disappeared," Joey said.

"You saw her down here?"

"She would come down here once in a while," Willie said with a shake of his head and laugh. "Remember she drove that ragtop?"

"Yeah, a Benzo," Joey said.

I listened and wanted to scream.

"When was the last time you saw her down here?"

"The last time Solomon was around," Willie said.

"Thanks," I said. I walked back to the McDonalds.

"You get anything?" Bird asked.

I gave a quick nod.

"Let's go. I'll tell you later," I said.

Bird smiled. She climbed back on the scooter and started the engine. I climbed on the back of the scooter, and we rode away from the Southwest end of Effingham.

"Thanks," I said.

The ride back to grandpa's was uneventful, but Bird seemed to enjoy racing the scooter as fast as humanly possible.

When we arrived back at grandpa's, Mom and grandpa were sitting in the kitchen talking.

"How was the scooter?" Grandpa Clark asked.

"Good, gramps," Bird said. "It's running like a top."

I laughed.

"What?"

"Tops don't run," I said, with a guilty smile.

"It's a figure of speech," Bird said.

I shook my head, not understanding the figure of speech.

"I'm glad you're enjoying yourself," Mom said to Bird. She paused. She looked at me. "Being here has really been good for you."

I gave a quick nod.

Bird and Mom talked.

I headed upstairs with Bo on my heels.

In my room, I had a lot of information.

Bo climbed onto the bed and laid on my bed watching me.

About ten minutes later Bird appeared at my doorway. She walked to the edge of my desk and tapped me on the shoulder. She sat down on the corner of the bed. Bo seeing Bird edged to her. She scratched his ear and Bo was glued to her from that moment.

"What's up squirt?" Bird asked. "You were supposed to tell me what you found out down there at McDonalds."

"I know," I said. "I was thinking," I said, looking at Bird scratching Bo's ear "You know he'll be your friend forever, now," I said with a chuckle seeing Bo content.

Bird smiled. "So, what did you find out? Talking to those boys," Bird asked.

167

I rubbed at my eyes, thinking what to tell Bird.

"So?" Bird asked, looking at me.

"Think that Amber James is somehow connected with Tommy and Solomon," I said, excited.

"What? How? Why?" Bird asked.

"Think she was involved with Tommy Crawford and her father, or the Klan, got upset and needed to teach him and her a lesson," I said. I was formulating a theory. I had all the pieces I just needed to arrange them correctly. "I guess at the party one of the boys saw a chance. This part I'm not certain of, but it seems like they were trying to teach Amber a lesson."

"Why?"

"I don't know but when I got a chance to read the police report Amber James was at that party,"

"Shut your mouth," Bird said.

"I guess after disappearing Tommy that night, the lesson didn't stick. She went to Solomon and the same thing happened to him." I paused, thinking. "The way I see it she was being too nice with him, and someone didn't want her around either of them. So, they made Solomon disappear."

"How you know?" Bird asked.

"I don't. I just have pieces," I said.

"You know where he is Zee?" Bird asked.

I shook my head.

"But you have an idea?"

"The problem is that Tommy seemed to be a lesson gone too far," I said. "Solomon seemed more intentional. You saw the place where he disappeared or was last seen?"

Bird pouted, thinking.

"Too well lit," I said. "No one is going to snatch someone, and no one see it," I said.

"So?"

"So, they made him disappear." I spoke.

"Who is they?" Bird asked.

"I'm not one hundred percent certain," I said. "I have my suspicions."

"Who?" Bird asked in my bedroom.

I shook my head.

"You know you can trust me?" Bird asked.

"You know that anyone that lies to you usually says that they can be trusted?" I asked.

Bird moved her head side to side.

"You can trust me," Bird said. She looked at me from the corner of the bed with Bo's head on her lap. "Okay," Bird said, pulling Bo's ear playfully. "I mean, you can tell me anything."

"So," I said, but suddenly too tired to argue with my sister.

"So, if you want to bounce ideas off me then I'm all ears," Bird said.

I smiled at my sister.

"You want to tell me what you're thinking?"

"No," I said. "I need time to figure out if what I'm thinking makes sense or if it is what I want it to be."

"Well, trust your gut," Bird said, moving Bo's head and climbing to her feet to leave.

"Why would I trust my gut?" I asked.

Bird moved her head side to side.

"How you never hear that before?"

"I have heard that before," I said. "I just never understood it."

"It means trust your first thoughts," Bird said. "They are usually right."

"That's not true," I said.

Bird moved her head side to side and walked out of my bedroom and into the hallway.

For what seemed forever I sat at my desk thinking. I found my iPod and headphones and listened to my created playlist of songs that I had meticulously culled together into two hours of nonstop hip hop beats.

I checked the time and knew that I needed to go to bed, but I could not climb up from the chair at the desk. My mind pinballed from thought to thought. I was trying to decide where Solomon Wright was. I was trying to determine if what the boys I met near West Cedar were believable. They had no reason to lie. They didn't know me from Adam.

My hopes were that Monday I would go to the library and do a little research before heading to the Village Mall and talking with

Zada Gallamore. But, that Sunday night after following up a lead my mind would not shut off.

I laid in bed and could not sleep. I tossed and turned in bed.

Bo hearing me climbed to his feet and placed his head on the bed.

"I can't sleep," I said. "Sorry, boy."

I climbed out of bed and dressed in my pajamas walked Bo downstairs. Usually, the kitchen was lighted, I thought. Grandpa was usually in the kitchen and at the stove when I came downstairs. I walked Bo to the rear of the house and opened the kitchen door and let Bo out and into the backyard.

I walked outside and sat on the back porch in the darkness. The garage sat there, closed and quiet. It was late or early that Monday morning. Effingham, at that time of hour, was quiet and still. Somewhere in the backyard darkness Bo was relieving himself. I could hear him moving in the darkness below, but I did not descend the stairs or look too hard for Bo that morning.

Instead, I sat on the back porch struggling with where Solomon Wright was and if he was even in Effingham. If Zada Gallamore was correct and the police report was accurate the last place Solomon Wright had been seen did not make much sense. It was too open, too public. The location did not make any sense.

So, sitting on the steps to the back porch and waiting for Bo to return I switched gears and found myself thinking of the six men who had disappeared in Effingham. It was an exercise that helped me clear the mental palette. I could not turn my brain off. Once I was grappling with a problem my brain worked ceaselessly at trying to unknot the knotty puzzle in my head.

It was during moments when I was not thinking about the problem directly that my mind unlocked or unknotted situations that seemed impossible at the time. Bo appeared and he and I returned to the interior of grandpa's house.

"Okay, let's go back upstairs," I said.

Bo found the stairs and climbed quickly up the flight of stairs and turned automatically to the left and headed to my bedroom. I followed.

A yawn escaped my mouth. Inside the room, tired and preparing for bed, I decided to check something before I forgot. Bo sat and watched me as I retrieved my backpack. I sat at my desk.

Bo tilted his head, confused.

"I'm just looking for something," I said to Bo. I opened my backpack and fished around inside. I rummaged through the backpack and was surprised at the number of things I had tossed inside. There was a roll of duct tape, a pocketknife, a roll of quarters, a nail clipper, a stack of post-it notes and several Sharpie markers. Also, in the backpack was the events calendar, I looked over the year and saw that the disappearances related to the events on the calendar. I removed the Effingham calendar that I had taken from the library the first time I visited the two-story building.

Opening the event calendar. I looked at December on the calendar.

December 30 there had been just a couple of events that day. According to the calendar there was a Monastery Museum Tour. The Monastery Museum Tours were during the day. They rarely did tours at night. The other event was a musical performance at the Effingham Performance Center that started around eight o'clock.

January 24 there was a performance at the Effingham Performance Center with jazz musicians. The concert was scheduled for eight o'clock.

February 26 there was a dance performance at the Effingham Performance Center.

March 27 there was another performance at the Effingham Performance Center and a show called: Spring Sounds.

April 27 there was a Monastery Museum Tour and the same day a cultural event at the Effingham Performance Center.

May 26-27 there was Summer Series live concert downtown and a Farmer's Market as well as a Monastery Museum Tour and that night a performance at the Effingham Performance Center.

June 26 there was the annual Race to the Cross and Monastery Museum Tour. That night there was a jazz show at the Effingham Performance Center.

July 25 the calendar pointed out that in the morning there was the Farmer's Market, followed by HAM-JAM and that night there was a performance at the Effingham Performance Center.

August 27 was a Monastery Museum Tour and then the Harvest Moon Festival and there was a night event at the Effingham Performance Center.

I had connected the dots. At least, I felt like there was a connection between the men and their disappearances.

Chapter 23.

The last ten days of August was special in Effingham. It was during this time that the Harvest Moon Festival happened. It was a big deal in the Crossroads. It began officially on Friday and concluded the following week on a Sunday. There were all these smaller events and attractions throughout the ten-day event. There was a dance. There was a silent auction. There was a ceremonial parade. There were nightly costume parties. Each night there was a running of the corn maze for money.

For ten days, Effingham collectively held their breaths and whatever was going on was put on hold for the Harvest Moon festival. There were banners announcing up and down Banker Street the festival. At diners there were special sandwiches and meals named after the festival. At stores there were Harvest Moon sales.

Now, not everyone was excited about the festival. Bird, for some reason, was unimpressed about the festival.

"There's going to be a Ferris wheel there," Grandpa Clark said.

"You go to the festival?" Bird asked shocked by grandpa talking about the festival.

"I go every now and then," Grandpa Clark said. "They have some good music there."

"You know that this is going to be another lame thing in Effingham," Bird said.

I didn't agree with Bird but kept my opinions to myself at that moment. I had done a little research and found out that the Ferris wheel would have been one of the bigger draws at an event like the Harvest Festival, or the dunk tank, or the hall of mirrors, but it was the annual creation of two corn mazes that was the festivals biggest draw. The corn mazes, according to grandpa, had lines that had to be monitored by security to keep people from cutting and line jumping.

"There's an adult sized corn maze that stretches the length of an entire football field," Grandpa Clark said. "It's a doozy."

I tried to figure out why Bird was not excited about the Harvest Moon Festival. It did not take too much time. Since being in

South Central, Illinois Bird had become fast friends with Paris and her friends. It was Paris' friend, Trey, that Bird seemed to be interested in.

Trey was a little odd. He, the first time I met him, was okay. Trey was kind of funny and silly, but nothing special. But for some reason he and Bird seemed to like each other. I did not attempt to understand the whys and where's of Bird's attraction to Trey.

The Friday night we showed up was the first night of the ten day festival and also the first night of the running of the maze.

The Harvest Moon Festival was a big production. The event took place off South Banker Street on unincorporated land beside the recycling center. The land was behind the Effingham Community School Superintendent offices. It was cordoned off and a parking lot was marked off. The entry was located just behind the offices of the superintendent.

"Meet us here or we'll leave you," Mom said reminding us to meet up at grandpa's Jeep no later than ten o'clock. The festival ended every night at eleven o'clock.

I checked my watch and figured that we had about four hours to be back at the Jeep.

People lined up for their chance to run the maze. The contest was to determine who could record the shortest time in and out of the maze. The record, that night was a jaw dropping thirty minutes and twenty-one seconds.

As Bird and I stopped and looked at the line for the maze I was not too surprised to find people in all sorts of costumes. There were princesses walking around the festival alongside of muscular men in Freddy Kruger and Michael Meyers masks. I knew that the Effingham Police were ensuring that no one in those costumes was carrying any weapons.

The first Friday night the full moon was peeking from behind some low hanging clouds. Bird and I walked around and checked out the food vendors and the carnival before we found Paris and her crew.

I tagged along with the group. A few minutes of walking I reached out to Paris.

"Yeah," Paris said, looking at me.

"You know Solomon Wright?"

Paris stopped and looked at me, seriously.

"Why you asking?" Paris asked, serious.

"Were you friends with him?"

"I suppose," Paris said.

"Did you know that Solomon was seeing Amber James?"

Paris hardened her face. In so doing, she gave away her emotions.

"You and Amber are friends?"

"We know each other," Paris said. "We were Pee Wee cheerleaders together. I've known her since we were kids."

"I think that Amber James is mixed up with Solomon's and Tommy Crawford's disappearance," I said.

"What you mean, mixed up?" Paris asked.

"Well, I think that she was being friendly with Tommy and Solomon and that got them snatched up," I said.

Paris took a step toward me. Her hand was balled into a fist.

Bird stepped in between me and Paris.

"What are you trying to say?"

Donny and Trey appeared with hotdogs and sodas.

"She has been dipping her toes in forbidden waters," Bird said.

"That's not true," Paris said.

"She was at the party where Tommy Crawford disappeared," I said.

"What's that mean?" Paris asked, turning from Bird to me. "There were a bunch of people at that party."

"Yeah," I said. "But there are too many people that said that Amber liked Tommy Crawford. It was a high school thing maybe?" I paused not knowing what else to say to Paris.

"Maybe she was just curious?"

"It didn't mean anything," Paris said. "Tommy was this star athlete. He was going to play football at Notre Dame and Amber thought he was cute. It was harmless fun."

"Not down here," Bird said.

"Yeah, Amber is a big deal down here," Bird said. "She's the mayor's daughter. The great white hope. She can't be seen liking some black boy who everyone knows from running up and down a football field," Bird said with a shake of her head.

"It's not like that," Paris said.

"What's it like?"

"Amber can't help that she's the mayor's daughter. We are friends. Well, we were friends," Paris said.

"So, your opinion is suspect," I said.

"What does that mean?"

"It means that your opinion may not be the best," Bird said.

We were standing in the middle of the festival. People moved around us, but no one seemed to notice or pay attention to our conversation. The costumes were interesting. There was a cowboy with cowboy hat walking past as the three of us talked.

"Listen," Paris said to Bird, frowning. "Don't nobody talk about Amber but me. She's my friend."

Bird raised her hands in surrender.

"Now, how you come up with this stuff about Amber?"

I explained what I had deduced.

Paris, Trey, and Donny listened. I looked at Bird and she just pouted.

"Okay, let's find the snowflake and see what she knows about all this," Paris said after my explanation and for the next hour we walked around the festival looking for Amber James.

I tried to imagine what was going to happen if Paris found Amber.

"You know this is not going to end well," Bird said to me as we walked, searching for the mayor's daughter.

"We're leaving behind all the crazy small-town drama," I said, trying to repeat what Bird had said. "None of this will matter next week." I smiled.

Bird smirked.

Amber James and the Barbies were standing at the entry to the adult cornfield maze when Paris confronted them. The four Effingham beauties were together with four cornfed boys dressed in blue jeans and cowboy boots. The one who was standing closest to Amber James was wearing a cowboy hat and had a thin nose and lips. The one next to the cowboy hat was wearing a St. Louis Cardinals baseball cap had a pointy chin. The third one had his thick arm around the waist of one of the Barbies and was wearing a Kangol golf cap. The fourth boy attached to a Barbie had long blonde hair that he managed with a hairband. The tall blonde boy was wearing a number twenty-one baseball jersey from Effingham High School.

Everyone, except Paris, paused seeing Amber and the Barbies with their boyfriends. Paris marched toward Amber James and through the Barbies and the boyfriends.

The boy in the cowboy hat stepped forward and reached out a hand to stop Paris. From behind Paris stepped Donny, who deflected the boy's hand and body six feet to the left. Donny had not punched the cowboy, only gently shoved him out of Paris's way.

The thin nosed boy turned ready to do battle.

Donny smiled at the boy's belief in himself. Donny closed the distance between himself and the upset cowboy and in half a dozen punches turned his back on the boy. The boy, no longer wearing a cowboy hat or a threat, crumpled to the ground holding his stomach like he had been shot.

The second boy, wearing the St. Louis Cardinals baseball cap, stepped forward menacingly. Donny smiled. Donny squared up with the second boy. The second boy swung first but Donny was not someone to play with. Donny seemed a seasoned fighter. He did not hurry. He did not rush. He waited for the second boy to swing again before hitting him with a fierce punch in the side. Three good shots put him on his toes. The fourth punch put St. Louis on his back.

Paris grabbed Amber James by her blouse front and drew back a fist. Bird reached out and held Paris' hand, to stop her.

"Tell me you didn't have anything to do with Tommy and Solomon's disappearance," Paris said in a hiss.

Trey and Bird were by Paris's side, watching the Barbies and the one boyfriend who had not attacked. The Barbies stepped forward Donny appeared. The Barbies seeing Donny stopped in their tracks.

"What are you talking about?" Amber asked, trying to break Paris's grip.

"What? You got all friendly with Tommy and Solomon and what?" Paris was screaming. "Tommy and Solomon disappeared because of it?"

Amber looked at Paris confused.

"What are you talking about?"

"What? Daddy didn't want anyone to know that his little sweetheart had a black boyfriend?" Paris asked.

"What? Stop it, Paris," Amber said.

"Your daddy find out?" Paris asked, fuming. "He tell someone to talk to Tommy at the party?"

"No," Amber said. "It wasn't like that."

"What was it like?" Paris asked.

Paris let Amber go.

"I heard about Tommy later," Paris said.

"What do you mean?"

"They said that they were just going to talk with Tommy," Amber said. "I swear to God that I didn't know that anything bad had happened until later."

"Later? Later?" Paris repeated. "You mean you knew something had happened to Tommy?"

Amber lowered her eyes.

"What about Solomon?"

"My dad doesn't like me being friendly with anyone except the boys he approves of," Amber said.

Paris looked at Amber wide eyed.

"What?"

"He doesn't care if we are friends," Amber said to Paris. "He just doesn't want me to have any boyfriends."

"Black boyfriends," Bird said for emphasis.

Amber pouted.

"What are you saying?" Paris asked, not wanting to believe what Amber was saying.

Amber moved her head side to side.

"Where is he?" Paris asked, pointedly.

Amber shrugged, looking wildly toward the Barbies.

"Where is he Amber?" Paris reached out for Amber's blouse again.

"I don't know," Amber said.

I stood there with all the others and shook my head.

"I don't know," Amber said and started to cry.

That was it. Everyone knew. Well, everyone I knew that mattered knew.

Chapter 24.

A few days later, after the dust had settled and Amber James and Paris had ended their on again off again friendship, I took Bo for a walk. Bird was sitting in grandpa's Jeep under the steering wheel.

"You okay?"

Bo, ever curious, stopped and looked at Bird.

"No, but it doesn't matter," Bird said.

I stood trying to figure out why Bird was pouting. Looking at my sister behind the steering wheel she looked upset. It wasn't even eight o'clock in the morning.

Bird had been upset for a few days. I imagined that it had something to do with Paris.

"It's not your fault," I began and stopped.

Bird glowered at me. I smiled and walked away silently with Bo.

For some reason I could not fathom Bird was upset about the whole Paris and Amber James break-up. Maybe, I thought, Paris blamed Bird for me figuring out that Amber liked Tommy Crawford a little more than she did. Was that it?

Bo bounced down the street and I shook the idea of ever understanding high school girls from my head. It would be easier to find a needle in a haystack I mused.

As Bo and I walked down Eiche Avenue I was surprised that the fencing was still up around the field just across the street from Grandpa Clark's house. I stopped and noted the porta potty inside the chain-link fencing and a gate opened at the end of the field closest to the street. There were two security guards on duty there now. They were dressed in dark blue polo shirts and dark blue tactical pants. They had radios and around their waists, handcuffs and a yellow handled taser.

One of the two security guards was leaning on the chain-link fence watching as Bo and I walked out of the rear of grandpa's house. I lifted my chin, as was the custom in South Central, Illinois, and the security guard raised his chin and grinned.

Bo and I walked down Eiche Avenue and for the first time since I had been in Effingham the neighbors on the street waved at me and raised their chins. Some smiled.

"You Clark's grandson?" A dark woman asked from her front porch. I paused and tried to get a good look at the owner of the dry and rattly old voice. On the porch, near the front door, sat a woman with sagging skin that signaled her long life on earth.

I gave a quick nod.

"Tell Clark that Juanita says hi," the woman said.

I gave another quick nod and continued walking down Eiche toward Banker Street.

"Heard you discovered a rat's nest in Effingham," one of the neighbors sitting on the porch said.

I only smiled as Bo sniffed a bush and tinkled.

"Come on Bo," I said, heading toward Banker Street.

A pot-bellied man wearing a print short-sleeved shirt and khaki shorts was near his car as Bo and I passed.

He, like Juanita earlier, said hello.

"Tell Clark that Sidney Garvin said, 'Hey' for me," Mister Garvin said.

It was a weird feeling to find the usual neighbors that I walked past on Eiche Avenue were suddenly engaging with me and Bo and aware of my comings and goings.

We walked to Banker Street and turned around.

On the way back to grandpa's house more neighbors said hello or asked me to tell Grandpa Clark hello.

Back at grandpa's I relayed all the messages from the neighbors.

"What? Did you talk to everyone?" Grandpa Clark asked with a crooked smile.

"No, they just seemed to want to make sure you knew they were thinking about you," I said.

"I think they wanted you to know Zee that they knew what you did for Tommy Crawford's family," Grandpa Clark said.

I frowned. I did not understand.

"But," I began.

Grandpa Clark raised a hand. I stopped.

I had read the Effingham Daily Record and there was no mention of me in the paper after the police identified the remains of Tommy Crawford.

There had only been one article written by Henry Riley and Walter Scoggins about Tommy Crawford. I had read it several times and could almost repeat it word-for-word.

After an exhaustive search and incredible police resources the remains of Thomas Crawford were found in Green Creek. Effingham Police were alerted to the possible location and with the assistance of the Durham County Sheriff Office found and retrieve the skeletal remains of the high school teenager who had been missing for nearly seven months.

We walked to the kitchen and grandpa sat at the table thinking.

"Grandpa, how did they know?" I asked, returning to the neighbors.

"I don't know," Grandpa Clark said at the kitchen table, sipping his coffee. "This is a small town, and we celebrate small victories, even if the bigger papers try to pretend like we aren't doing anything."

I looked at Grandpa Clark and smiled.

"So, me and your mom are thinking about going to the Harvest Moon Festival this week since you will be heading back to Chicago Saturday," Grandpa Clark said, changing the subject. "My treat."

I smiled. I chuckled at the idea of paying for the Harvest Moon Festival. All summer I had never spent my own money. There never was a need. I stayed around grandpa and if we got hungry then he bought us something to eat. If I needed something, grandpa always seemed to know.

Bird, on the other hand, would ask for money from mom or grandpa. They never denied Bird. She never asked for crazy amounts of money. Bird just wanted walking around money, at least that was what grandpa called Bird's requests.

"I'll go," I said. "I hope this time it will be better than the last time."

"It has to be," Grandpa Clark said with a smile.

That Tuesday, four days before we were scheduled to return to Chicago, Bird and I returned to the Harvest Moon Festival with

Mom and grandpa. It had been a tumultuous seven days. Bird was mad about something, and no one could figure it out.

I decided that it had something to do with Paris or Trey, but I was not one hundred percent certain. When mom told us to meet her and grandpa at the entrance at ten o'clock, before they went to explore the festival, I felt like that night seemed to be electric.

"What's going on with you?"

"What do you mean?" Bird asked.

"You are being a little more annoying than normal," I said.

"I guess that this small town is getting to me," Bird said. "I am just so tired of the small-town drama. Everything is a big deal down here when it really isn't."

I listened confused.

"You know that we're leaving Saturday," Bird said. "We are shaking this small-town dust off our shoes and heading back to Chicago."

"You feeling sad?" I asked, making a sad face.

Bird balled her hand into a fist. She swung out and barely missed hitting me. I dodged her punch and laughed skipping to the right.

"You're too predictable," I said. I smiled and found Bird trying to corner me.

"Bird? What are you doing?" Paris asked. "I thought you agreed that no one got to give Zion a real beat down except me first and then you or... us together?"

Bird turned around and smiled at Paris. Paris, dressed in a cartoon T-shirt midriff that showed off her flat stomach and skirt with basketball sneakers.

"What? Why?" I said to Paris. "I don't deserve a beat down."

"Shut up, squirt," Paris said, becoming serious. "You messed up something I had... for as long as I can remember."

"That wasn't my fault," I said.

Bird stepped in.

"Paris, we agreed," Bird said to Paris.

Paris closed her mouth and pouted.

"What?" I said to Bird, looking out the corner of my eye at Paris. "Does she think I went looking for a reason to break-up her friendship with Amber?"

"End it," Bird said. "We're not talking about that anymore."

I stood there, next to my sister, confused.

"We going to let all that go," Bird said. "We come here for a little fun... before we go back to Chicago." Bird smiled at Paris and then me. Paris smiled back. I smiled at the two, still confused.

Behind her appeared a werewolf costumed Frankie and Donny. Trey appeared behind the two werewolves smiling from ear-to-ear.

"Hey, Bird," Trey smiled awkwardly.

I switched my focus from Bird and Trey to Frankie. He was dressed in jeans, black sneakers, the rubber werewolf mask with pointy ears and furry face, high school varsity athlete jacket and red plaid collared lumber jack shirt. On his hands were a pair of furry paws with claws.

Donny was dressed identically.

I frowned at the exactness of the two outfits.

"What gives?" I asked. "Why are you both wearing the exact same thing?"

"This is the Michael Jackson Thriller werewolf," Frankie said, removing his werewolf head. Donny seeing Frankie take off his head only shook his head and stood like a werewolf statue.

"Take off your mask Donny," Bird said.

"He won't," Trey said. "He's trying to enjoy the whole werewolf thing." Trey paused. "He's in character for the night." Trey shook his head. "He's going to make a bunch of classic werewolf poses and get everyone to take pictures with him to boost his 'gram." Trey laughed. "It's genius."

Bird rolled her eyes at Donny and Trey.

"Are you thinking of going in now?" Paris asked.

"No," Bird said. "The lines too long."

"Right, we should come back," Paris said.

"The line usually gets smaller when there is a band on stage," Trey said.

Paris gave a small nod. Frankie and the werewolf beside him gave a small nod as well.

"Okay, fine," Bird said. "What do you want to do until the next band is on?"

"We can ride the Ferris wheel? Or go and have one of these boys show us how strong they are?" Paris said with a mischievous smile.

With that everyone, including me, made our way toward the midway, where the carnival games were set up under two rows of brightly lit stalls with stuffed bears, cars, watches, and jewelry for anyone willing to toss a ring on a milk bottle, bust a balloon with a dart, or knock down three fuzzy clowns to win a prize.

I stopped at what looked like a simple game where multi-colored rubber ducks floated in a metal tub of water and moved in groups of ten or twenty around the interior of that tub. The ducks were pushed along by some unseen motor that kept the water moving. Behind the tub were fifty goldfish bowls with a single goldfish swimming inside of each bowl. All I had to do was give two dollars to the carney and pull a duck. Each duck had a prize on its underside.

Scanning the prizes behind the tub, beyond the goldfish, there were stuffed animals, stuffed dolls, five nice looking watches and three cell phones.

I looked around the stall and saw that the tub of ducks sat on the end of the aisle and afforded three opportunities to grab the duck that seemed the right duck.

"Two dollars give you a chance to walk away with a cellphone worth six hundred dollars," the barker said, looking at me. "You can't beat that deal with a stick."

I smiled at the barker.

I thought long and hard about trying my luck, but at that exact moment I saw Frankie sit on a bench just off the midway.

"I'll give you two ducks for two bucks," the barker said, seeing me lose interest. "That is a once in a lifetime deal for you right here and right now."

I shook my head and turned on my heels and went to talk to Frankie.

I looked around and noticed that Paris, Donny, and Trey had disappeared. They were probably heading back to the maze or some of the rides.

"Can I talk to you?" I asked Frankie, smiling seeing his strange cat-like head with yellow eyes, whiskers, and pointy cat-like ears next to him.

"Sure," Frankie said. "About what?"

"Well, I found something, and I wanted to know what you think," I said.

"Sure, kid," Frankie said after he pouted and gave a tiny nod. Frankie was dressed in his werewolf costume, minus the strange cat-like head with yellow eyes, whiskers, and pointy cat-like ears. People, in and out of costume, were walking past at the Effingham Harvest Moon Festival. Some headed to the midway. Some heading to the bandstand. Others, I was sure, were heading to the corn maze. There were a lot of werewolves' costumes at the festival. It seemed an extremely popular costume choice.

"So, Michael Jackson wore this?" I asked, pointing to the cat-like head.

"No," Frankie answered. "It was a part of his Thriller video."

I shook my head. I had heard a few Michael Jackson songs, but I liked more edgy stuff like Drake and Little Weezy. I looked down at the bench and considered sitting down beside Frankie. I decided against sitting down.

"Can I talk to you?" I questioned.

"Sure," Frankie said. "About what?"

"Well, you know I found something in the field the other day where you were standing," I announced aloud.

"Okay," Frankie said after he pouted and bobbed his head.

I stood, not sure if I wanted to sit next to the sketchy brother of Paris Brooks.

"Well, I wanted to know what you know about what I found?"

"What you trying to say? You think I am mixed up in that?" Frankie asked, looking at me smugly. "If that is what you think then you got your wires crossed."

"Well," I began, cagily. I was watching Frankie. I was trying to figure if he was someone I could trust, like grandpa said. He was the wildcard in all of this. He was also the one that seemed to know the most about all of the disappearances. "What were you doing there that day?"

Frankie had his werewolf head by his side. I remained standing, watching him.

"Why?" Frankie asked, curious. He looked at me unsure. "Why you asking?"

"Well, it sort of makes sense that I would ask. Right?" I replied. "I mean I ain't saying you did or didn't do something, but I thought you might have a theory as to why that body was there."

"Well, it's funny you say it like that," Frankie said. "I do have a theory. Now, no one will hear me out, but I have a theory."

I smiled. I was not surprised by Frankie's belief that he knew something no one else might. Grandpa said that he was one of those martyrs.

"Okay, I was there because someone told me that something was in that field." Frankie paused. "But I didn't have anything to do with what you discovered. I went by to see if what I had been told was true or not."

"Who told you?"

Frankie did not answer. Instead, he continued on with his unexplained theory.

"So, if my theory is correct there is someone or someone's grabbing these people. Now, there could be a bunch of reasons, but I have to lean on the tried-and-true cause; jealousy."

"Who is jealous of these guys?" I asked.

"Or were these guys jealous of the someone picking them off?" Frankie asked.

I shook my head. Frankie's theory had too many holes to be believable.

"Okay, so you think it's jealousy?" I asked.

"Yes," Frankie said. "I think that's the reason there has been a missing person in Effingham every month all year," Frankie concluded.

"A flimsy reason," I replied.

"Hear me out," Frankie said. "At first, I thought the disappearances were just for publicity. You know? I mean we're in the armpit of Illinois and they are always trying to make it a place to visit. So, at first, I thought the whole werewolf thing was made up, for the thrill seekers. You know?"

I listened. I had learned not speaking much usually got more information than interrupting.

"Then, I started to think," Frankie said. "The mayor doesn't want bad publicity. He wants people to come down here and spend money." Frankie paused, thinking. "I think there's a reason, a pattern," Frankie said. "The men, most of them aren't the nicest."

"What do you mean?" I asked.

Frankie leaned forward. He almost climbed off the bench as he leaned forward.

"South-Central Illinois is not the most friendly place for people that are melanated," Frankie said, looking at me knowingly.

I frowned, uncertain.

"You know, no one wants to be labeled a racist nowadays," Frankie said. "So, they have traded in their white hoods for baseball caps and what aboutisms. They are still dangerous."

Just then there was a ruckus in the festival and Frankie stood up to see what was going on.

While I watched the people move from one side of the festival to the other Frankie slipped on his werewolf mask.

"Frankie?" I uttered aloud looking for him. He had disappeared in the surge of people. In his stead there were easily twenty people looking back frightened. Some of the people were costumed, some not in the midway. Behind them there were screams and shouts in the distance. A mummy ran by followed by a group of little green men. Two dozen people flooded into the festival midway.

"What 's going on?" I said to a girl in a costume.

"There was a fight," a girl dressed as the Black Panther said as she ran by looking for somewhere to hide.

"Someone had a gun," another person said wearing a Cardinals T-shirt and jeans.

I looked in the direction the crowd had run from. There were a handful of people, slower and older running to the Midway and looking over their shoulder as they did. I looked back where Frankie had been sitting before the crowd surge.

Three minions were standing where Frankie had been. Captain America, well someone dressed up as the first Avenger, stood on the bench behind the minions. Two Batman costumed kids ran past me, bumping me and nearly knocking me over.

There was a bunch of people suddenly in the midway. I looked for Frankie, Donny, Trey or anyone else, but everyone I knew at the festival had gone. I looked around and thought I should head back to the corn maze when Frankie appeared. Frankie, wearing his werewolf mask now, was at the head of the festival midway leading back to the darkened passage that led to the festival entrance.

I walked toward Frankie. He gestured and waved toward me. I grinned and closed the distance between Frankie and myself. Within arm's reach of the Michael Jackson inspired werewolf I stopped.

"Is everything okay?" I asked. "I mean, no gun or anything?"

Frankie bobbed his werewolf head.

I looked at my costumed cousin and frowned. Something seemed off with Frankie. I studied Frankie, confused.

"So, you think you have an idea of who's behind the disappearances?" I questioned, cautiously.

Frankie did not speak. Instead, he gestured and walked me away from the suddenly crowded Midway.

"Frankie? Where are we going?"

Frankie pushed me along a little roughly. I looked back and for the first time I felt that I was in danger.

"Frankie? What is wrong with you?" I questioned, trying to keep things light.

That was when Frankie lunged at me. He actually tried to grab me with those fake furry paws.

I dodged him and ran. I ran and thought that Frankie was trying to hurt me.

I ran into the darkness where the other section of the festival was situated. It was maybe one hundred yards away from the midway, but with a crazed Frankie chasing it seemed like a hundred miles.

Chapter 25.

The first attraction that I came to was the hall of mirrors. For half a second I thought about running past the painted smiling clown beckoning anyone to enter the hall through its mouth, but with Frankie closing in, it seemed my only solution.

My plan was to go in the hall and lose Frankie inside. If that worked, I was going to escape the attraction and find grandpa or Mom and tell them that Frankie was insane and trying to hurt me.

So, I ran inside the quiet hall of mirrors, surprised that no one was outside to take tickets or explain the rules of the attraction. Inside the hall of mirrors, a flash went off as I slid forward and into the first hall. I was immediately confronted by dozens of me, dressed in a red cartoon T-shirt, green cargo shorts and gym shoes. My hair was a little longer than usual, but I still had my part cut into the left side of my head level with the crown of my head. The scar on my chin I had received jumping off my bed when I was eight seemed bigger in the giant reflection.

I was sweating. My eyes looked bigger than normal. I wiped at my sweaty nose and tried to think. I had a plan. Now, I had to work my way through the hall of mirrors without Frankie catching me and find grandpa or Mom. Simple.

Frankie appeared in the mirror reflections behind me, and I ran forward and away from Frankie. I had little choice. I moved deeper into the maze of mirrors. My heart was beating in my ears as I weaved through the reflections of me looking for the exit. Behind me Frankie still wearing his werewolf costume and mask pursued.

Entering the reversal hall, I slowed. I thought quickly, the hall could be used to my advantage. I reached out and moved along the side of the hall and stopped. I turned to wait for Frankie even though every fiber in my body told me just to run.

"Frankie? What did I say that got you all crazy? I mean, I know that South-Central Illinois isn't the most friendly place," I said, looking down the hall and seeing Frankie's reflection appearing at the top of the hall. His reflection was immediately next to my reflection even though we were one hundred feet apart.

Frankie had a knife in one of his paws and seeing my reflection next to his, he stabbed at the glass viciously.

I backed away alarmed. Frankie really was trying to hurt me. The idea of being beaten up was one thing, but the idea of being stabbed or killed was something that made me shiver unexpectedly.

I needed time to think. I was in another part of the hall of mirrors that elongated my reflection. I was suddenly eight feet tall. Or my reflection was eight feet tall.

I moved through the hall where my reflection stretched and to a dark section of the hall. The mirrors were lighted and only the mirrors. The reflections were magnified.

I hid in the darkness and tried to think if there was a way to avoid Frankie and double back to the entrance to escape.

Frankie appeared holding the knife in his furry paw.

From the darkness I noticed something that seemed odd. Had Frankie changed his shoes? I could have sworn that he was wearing black sneakers. I pressed myself against the wall in the darkness and held my breath as the costumed Frankie holding a knife moved through the dark section of the hall of mirrors. Frankie turned the corner and disappeared from the dark hallway.

I forced myself to move. I ran back to the elongated mirror section of the hall of mirrors and then down the reverse hallway. I looked back only for a moment and slammed into my own reflection. I fell on my butt with the impact. I climbed to my feet and made my way back to the entrance of the attraction.

Once outside, I ran headlong toward the section of the festival with people. The sound of laughter and music was a relief to hear as I reached the border of people milling around in front of the corn maze. Looking back, I was relieved not to see Frankie following. I pushed through the crowd looking for a friendly face.

The first person I saw was Mom. I pushed people aside with all my might to close the distance between my mom and myself. My mom seeing me smiled and immediately realized that there was something wrong.

"What's going on?" Mom asked, hugging me to her.

I explained.

Grandpa appeared. Bird and Paris, along with Donny appeared as well.

"Your brother is a psycho," I said seeing Paris.

"What happened?"

I explained, before I finished Trey walked up with Frankie.

"Keep him away from me," I almost screamed.

Grandpa Clark seeing Frankie stepped between him and me.

"What's going on?"

Mom and Paris explained.

"That wasn't me," Frankie said. "I was with Trey."

Trey agreed.

Frankie had a hotdog in his furry paw and a drink in the other. His cat-like werewolf head was under his arm. I looked down and he was wearing black sneakers.

All around us streamed costumed children in superhero outfits. Skeletons bounced by. A football player and a baseball player walked past as Frankie and Trey tried to convince everyone that they were nowhere close to the hall of mirrors or me.

"He was with you? For how long?"

"Well, at least for the last thirty or forty minutes," Trey said. "We walked around a little bit. Then we got on the Pirate Ship. It took a while to get on, but it was fun."

"Okay, what did you do after the ride?"

"We just walked around," Trey said.

"Did Frankie ever leave you?"

"No," Trey said.

"Okay," Bird and Mom said.

Grandpa was watching Frankie.

"I don't think he was in the hall of mirrors," Grandpa Clark said. "He was just as surprised as anyone hearing about us thinking he tried to hurt Zee."

"Yeah," Mom said. "Trey says that he and Frankie were together for at least the last thirty minutes." She paused. "That would have been when Zee was being chased."

Bird and Paris pushed me from under the watchful eyes of Mom and Grandpa Clark. Once away from the adults the two girls peppered me with questions.

"Why do you think someone was trying to knife you?" Paris asked.

"Did you do something?" Bird asked.

I smiled and shook my head.

"Seriously, did you do something or say something stupid?" Bird asked, looking at me seriously.

"Did you notice anything odd about him?" Paris asked.

I smirked.

"Think Zee," Bird said. "Why would someone be trying to knife you?"

I shook my head.

"He was wearing different shoes," I said.

"So? There's someone else dressed like Frankie and Donny here?" Paris asked, confused. "At the festival?"

I gave a frightened nod.

Frankie slowly made his way to me and the girls. Trey and Donny followed.

"You know I wouldn't hurt you? Zee?" Frankie asked.

I studied Frankie and Donny and realized what I had noted and registered in the hall of mirrors. The Frankie that was in the hall of mirrors was wearing a black T-shirt under his plaid shirt. He wore everything else that Frankie and Donny were wearing, and they all had the weird cat-like costume head with whiskers.

I pointed at Frankie.

"Hey," I said to Grandpa Clark. "I think it can't be too many people wearing this costume. All we need to do is round up the cat heads that are the same size as Frankie and Donny."

Grandpa chuckled.

"There's easily a thousand people out here tonight," Mom said. "There's no way to round up anyone. We ain't the cops."

I bobbed my head and looked to Paris and Bird. The two grinned and looked to Frankie and Trey. Donny, silent and in character stood acting like a werewolf statue.

"So, why did fake Frankie try to knife you?"

"I don't know," I said, unsure. "I think I must have said something or done something to get on the wrong side of someone."

"That is what you do every day," Bird said as the group stepped away from Mom and grandpa.

"Okay, this is the plan," Paris said. "We're going to find this faker and figure out what is going on."

"Word," said Trey.

"Okay, so, I want Donny with us," Paris said. "We need someone that is willing to throw hands if need be."

"The only thing is you have to take pictures of people taking pictures of Donny if you take him with you," Trey said.

"Deal," Paris said. She fished out her cellphone and took a picture of herself and Donny.

"Satisfied?" Paris asked the werewolf Donny. Donny dipped his chin.

"That means Trey and Frankie better take care of Zion," Bird said, looking at the two boys.

"Okay, meet back here, at the maze, in an hour," Paris said, and she and Bird headed off looking for the fake Frankie dressed up like him and Donny. Donny followed behind the two girls clawing in the air like he was a werewolf.

"Okay, let's hit it," Trey said, looking around the festival crowd.

"You know that wasn't me? Right?" Frankie asked as we walked in the opposite direction of Paris, Bird, and Donny.

"I guess," I said as we walked through the crowd looking for the impostor Frankie werewolf. "But I don't know how you left me?"

"I thought you left me," Frankie said, walking beside me. "Remember when there was that big rush of people?"

I recalled that moment.

"Well, I slipped on my costume, I was thinking that Donny had a good idea," Frankie said with a chuckle. "I posed and a couple of people took pictures with me. I took a couple of more pictures. When I was done you were gone. I looked around and then headed back toward the rides, thinking that was where you were headed."

I shook my head at how I had almost been killed because I hadn't asked something.

Trey and Frankie moved through the crowd looking for the impostor werewolf. I looked occasionally not sure what I was going to do if I saw another Michael Jackson cathead werewolf.

"I want to stomp this punk," Trey fumed.

Frankie was leading the way, moving slowly through the crowd of costumed and uncustomed people at the festival. He was not a very big person, but bigger than Trey or me. Dressed in his werewolf outfit, minus the cat-like head, I looked down and smiled at his black sneakers.

"Where did you get that outfit?" I asked.

"There's a store on Banker that sells a bunch of werewolf costumes," Frankie said. "They have all types of werewolf costumes." He paused, scanning the crowd.

"Yeah, the werewolf is a big seller down here," Trey said. "People love the legend."

"There are a bunch of different types of werewolves and costumes to choose from," Frankie said.

I shook my head at the idea of a store filled with werewolf costumes of various types. The idea was a little hard to imagine. Looking at Frankie I reluctantly surrendered to the idea.

"So, what video is Michael Jackson dressed like a cat?"

"He's a werewolf," Trey said.

"Thriller," Frankie said. "It's a classic."

"You never seen it?" Trey asked, dressed in a baseball undershirt with blue sleeves, shorts, and basketball sneakers.

I shook my head.

"You should check it out," Frankie said.

I smiled.

"So, what are we going to do if we find this perpetrator?" Trey asked.

"When we find him, we grab him and get the police involved," Frankie said. "I mean, he tried to knife Zee."

"Yeah, we beat him up a bit before the police arrive," Trey said. "Give him a taste of Effingham South justice."

"Whatever that is," Frankie said with a chuckle.

"We got this," Trey said.

"Yeah, I want to find this faker trying to make me look all sketchy," Frankie said.

I had a thought, but before I could completely formulate it Trey grabbed Frankie.

"Hey," Trey said, pointing toward a cat-like werewolf head in the crowd. The cat-like head was standing in front of the Tilt-A-Whirl ride in line.

Trey and Frankie beelined toward the possible Frankie impostor. Frankie dropped his cat-like costume head.

"Remember, he was wearing a black T-shirt and church shoes under his costume," I said. "Be careful," I said, as a warning. "He had a knife."

"Got it," Trey said.

"Bum rush him if he has a black T-shirt on," Frankie said, speeding up.

Trey and Frankie were nearly at full speed when the cat-like werewolf costumed person was spooked.

The cat-like werewolf seeing Frankie and Trey closing in stepped back and out of line. Before they could reach him, he turned and ran back and into the crowd of people waiting to get on the Ferris wheel. He bumped into a couple of men who tried to grab him. He changed direction only to knock over a woman and boy not paying attention near the end of the line.

I tried to keep up, carrying the cat-like head and seeing the impostor Frankie turning and running.

Another woman screamed as Trey and Frankie chased the fleeing werewolf.

"He's got a knife!" I screamed and suddenly the crowd separated and two of the Effingham Police officers who had been standing by one of the rides were in motion. The officers surveyed the situation and ran toward the three running for the exit.

Trey and Frankie were fast. They were much faster than me or the police. The werewolf they were chasing was no slouch. He skidded to a stop and tried to hurdle the tables where the people paid to enter. He nearly cleared the table, but his back foot dragged across the top and he went head over heels to the ground. By the time he recovered Trey and Frankie had ahold of him. Frankie had one wrist and Trey held the other tightly.

Frankie and Trey restrained the struggling werewolf and would not let him escape.

"We got him," Trey crowed.

"Yeah, we did," Frankie said with a smile. He reached out and pulled at his costume. He grabbed his black T-shirt and looked down and smiled at the dress shoes. "Look at this."

I caught up to the three as the two policemen arrived. The two policemen were talking into their radios.

The police officers arriving pulled their guns and aimed at Frankie and Trey. I opened my mouth, stunned.

"Let him go," the police officer said, aiming at Frankie.

Frankie and Trey released the costumed man. The man climbed to his feet and looked to make a quick exit.

The third police officer, who was outside the festival stepped forward and placed a hand on the jumpy man's shoulder.

"No one's going anywhere," the police officer said to the costumed man.

"Okay," the police officer said with his gun leveled on Frankie. "What's going on?"

I stepped forward cautiously and raised my hands as I got closer to the gun toting police officer.

"He has a knife. He tried to stab me," I said.

"That's a big accusation, kid," the police officer said. "Even for someone as small as you." He holstered his gun. His partner holstered his gun as well.

"Let's see who this is," the police officer holding the costumed man said. He pulled the mask off and there in front of Frankie, Trey and I was someone I had seen days before at the KCBS Cookout.

He was one of the mayor's men.

"Cushman? What are you doing dressed up?" The third police officer who had unmasked him asked.

"Is the mayor here?" The second police officer asked, looking around the crowd.

"James? What's going on?" The first officer near me asked with a smile.

"I thought it would be fun to just let my hair down," James Cushman said, nervously.

"Did you chase this boy?" The second police officer asked Cushman.

"No," James lied. "I was just enjoying myself. Not bothering anyone. I was about to get on a ride when these two thugs came running at me," James continued to lie. "There were two of them coming at me and I wasn't sure what was going on. Maybe they were on drugs? I didn't know. So, I began running."

The police officers listened, sympathetically.

"Wait," I said. "If he didn't chase me then he wouldn't be in the hall of mirrors. Right?" I quickly added. "And he wouldn't have a knife, like I said."

"That makes sense," one of the police officers said.

The police officer detaining James did a quick search and found a six-inch knife hidden in the werewolf's high school jacket.

"What are you doing with this?" The police officer asked holding the knife in his gloved hand.

James for the first time did not have a ready answer. The police officer with the knife pulled out of plastic bag and dropped the knife inside. He scribbled something on the front of the bag and slipped it into one of the pockets of his tactical pants.

"I remember that there was a flash when I entered the hall of mirrors. I think if someone goes there, they will find a picture of me and the werewolf, dressed like he is now," I said.

The police officer, I was talking to, directed his partner to send someone to the hall of mirrors and retrieve the last hour of pictures.

Mom and Grandpa Clark appeared, seeing all the people watching the police activities with Frankie, Trey and me with the white man named: James. Grandpa Clark did not listen to the police officers trying to keep people back. He bulled past the police officers and when they tried to stop him, he looked at them as if they were insignificant.

"That's my grandson there," he said.

The police officer watched silently as Grandpa Clark and mom pushed through and to my side.

"What have you gotten yourself into?" Grandpa Clark asked with a shake of his head.

"That guy tried to stab me," I said, pointing to James, the mayor's man.

Grandpa frowned at my words.

"What? Have you lost your mind? You see that he is just a kid?" Grandpa Clark said through gritted teeth. He stepped forward menacingly. One of the police officers stepped in front of grandpa to stop his progress.

"Easy," the officer said. "No one knows what exactly happened," the dark-haired police officer dressed for military combat said, raising a hand.

"If Zion said some stranger tried to stab him then I believe him," grandpa said.

Mom, now beside me, reached out and hugged me tightly.

"That is just an awful thing for anyone to do," Mom said, frustrated and on the verge of tears. "He's just a child. What could he have done to be threatened by you?"

By the time Mom had spoken, there were easily thirty people trying to get a glimpse of the happenings. There were police, security, as well as carnival employees, the two owners of the traveling carnival and Paris and Bird watching the activities.

The police determined that there was a need to investigate what had happened in the hall of mirrors, but they were not certain of the crime committed.

"How you not know if there was a crime committed?" Someone in the crowd crowed.

"This little boy was nearly killed by that full-grown man," another person said.

"With a knife," Trey said, pointing to the knife.

"We are going to get all the information and warn Mister Cushman not to bother your son or talk to him," the police officer said.

"That is not acceptable," Mom said. "I want someone here to make some real decisions."

"I am making real decisions," the police officer said holding his notebook and pen in hand.

"No, you are not," Mom said. "You are allowing someone that intended to harm my son, to threaten to kill someone, to go and threaten someone else tonight. And the worst part is that you are telling him that even though he was caught to just be aware that people are watching," Mom said.

"It's not like that," the police officer said.

"It's exactly like that," Mom said angrily.

"Listen, this is the procedure," the police officer said. "What we have is your son's word versus Cushman's word."

Mom seemed frustrated. Grandpa Clark scanned the crowd for someone.

All around the police officers people were talking and pointing at people.

A few minutes later a carnival worker appeared with twenty pictures from the last hour of the attraction.

"I was taking a break," the carney said. "No one was supposed to be in there." He frowned. "I saw the werewolf leave but didn't think too much about it."

He handed the pictures to the police officer.

"These are the pictures that were taken while I was on break," the carney said. "It's like the kid said. There's a picture of him running into the hall of mirrors and then the werewolf."

He lifted to the two pictures up to the be seen by the police, onlookers, as well as Frankie, Trey, and me.

"We'll take your statements," the police officer said. Looking at Frankie and Trey, he turned to me. "You said that he tried to stab you?"

"Yes," I said. "I was by the midway and he called me over and pretended to be my friend. He was dressed just like him."

The police officer took notes and recorded my statement.

"Did you do anything to antagonize him? Talk to him?"

"No," I said. "He just attacked me and tried to grab me. I ran and he chased me."

"To the hall of mirrors?"

"Right," I said. "Inside I tried to hide, and he pulled a knife and tried to stab me."

The police officer listened and took his notes.

"Okay, is that it?"

I twisted my lips, unsure. "Do you need me to tell you what I saw when Frankie and Trey saw him?" I asked.

"No, I think I have enough," the police officer said.

"So, what happens now?" Mom asked.

"Well, we have all the information we need. I have to write up a report on this. I will have a case number for you before we release you. You can call the department tomorrow and someone will be assigned to follow up on this matter." The police officer explained.

"Will he go to jail?" Mom asked.

"Not tonight," the police officer said. "The detectives will investigate and one way or another we will make a determination of the next steps."

"Next steps?" Mom asked, skeptically.

"Yes ma'am," the police officer said. "If he is arrested for aggravated assault or not."

"He had a knife," Mom said. "He could have killed Zion."

"I understand that, but he didn't," the police officer said a matter of fact. "Thankfully, your son got away without being harmed. Now, it is up to us to follow up."

Nearly an hour later the police officer returned to our family group.

"Here's your case number," the police officer said.

It was nearly ten o'clock when we finally left the Effingham Harvest Moon Festival.

Chapter 26.

The Effingham Police Department assigned two detectives to my case. They appeared on Wednesday. Three days before our return to Chicago. When the two detectives showed up, we were packing for Chicago.

"I'm Lucy Garvin, I have been assigned to your case," the woman said handing Mom a business card. "This is my partner." Lucy Garvin was dressed in a gray blazer, button front ruffled blouse, and dark blue trousers. She was a blonde-haired woman with small eyes and lots of lines around her throat. She had a crooked nose and thin lips.

"I'm William Jenkins," the big man with the woman said, showing his badge. "We have a few questions that we need to ask Zion." Jenkins was broad shouldered and heavy browed. Beneath his eyes were nearly slit-like eyes. He possessed a high forehead and long nose above his thin lips.

I was sitting in the living room with Bo, Bird, Mom, and Grandpa looking at the odd couple in grandpa's house. They both were armed and wearing bulletproof vests under their blazers.

"You want something to drink?" Grandpa Clark asked the two detectives sitting in the living room.

"No, we're fine," Lucy Garvin said with a momentary smile.

"We just have a couple of questions," William Jenkins said, pulling out a small notepad.

"What is your question?" Mom asked.

"Well, the first question we have is why do you think James Cushman, a member of the mayor's office, would attack you?" Lucy Garvin asked me.

I did not know. So, I did not answer.

"You know that we only came down for the summer and that Zion doesn't even know this crazy man," Mom said.

"Did you talk to him before you and he went into the hall of mirrors?" Garvin asked.

I tried to think. I had to recall the conversation we had.

"I asked him what he had been talking about, before the crowd ran to the midway," I said.

"You said that there were a bunch of people that came to the midway and that was when you lost contact with Frankie," Jenkins said.

I gave a little nod.

"Is that when you first saw Mister Cushman?" Garvin asked.

"I didn't know he was Cushman," I said.

"Okay," William Jenkins said, nodding. "What happened before you went to the hall of mirrors?"

"I thought he was Frankie. So, I asked him why he said that Effingham was not the most friendly place to live. That was the last thing I said before he tried to grab me and chase me," I said.

"Okay," Lucy Garvin said.

"One last question," William Jenkins said. "Had you ever met or talked to Cushman before the festival?"

"No," I said.

"Okay, thank you," Jenkins said.

Garvin smiled and put away her notes and prepared to stand up.

"So, what's happening with this Cushman?" Mom asked.

"We received the photos from the hall of mirrors and his possession of a knife is troubling," William Jenkins said.

"We have a good case against him for aggravated assault," Garvin said.

"We have not arrested him yet," Jenkins said.

"Why not?" Mom asked.

"He works for the mayor," Jenkins said.

"So? What? No justice for normal people not working for the mayor?" Mom asked, looking at Jenkins and then Garvin.

"No. It's not like that. It just is a little more delicate," Garvin said.

"He committed a crime," Mom said.

"Yes," Jenkins said.

"Shouldn't he be arrested?" Mom asked the detectives.

"Well, yes," Jenkins said.

"But he's not arrested or in jail?" Mom pointed out.

"We are doing all that we can," Jenkins said. "The DA has to make the final decision on the arrest."

"So, if you have friends in high places you don't have to worry about the law touching you?"

"No," Jenkins said.

"Yes," Mom said. She had climbed to her feet and was at the front door. She opened the door. "Good day."

The detectives stepped out of grandpa's front door and Mom turned and looked at Bird and me.

"If there is anything--"

Mom shut the door on the detectives.

"That was rude," grandpa said to his daughter.

"Rude? Pop, what is rude is the belief in a system that has never been built to protect us," Mom said.

"I don't believe that," Grandpa Clark said climbing to his feet and shoving his hands into his pants pockets.

"Believe it or not, you know that man is not going to spend a day in jail, even though he could have killed Zion," Mom said, her voice choked with emotion.

Bird was immediately beside Mom. I climbed to my feet. Bo seeing me on my feet climbed to his feet as well.

"We can't live like this," Mom said. "We can't."

"Live like what?" Grandpa asked.

"Not being seen or heard or valued," Mom said. She was angry and upset. "This is the reality of living in any small-town." She paused. "I just expected things to improve."

The rest of the day there was a weird tension in grandpa's house.

After a surprising quiet lunch Bird and I went down to the park to shoot baskets. Well, Bird shot baskets. Bo and I hid in the shade and tried to understand what had happened earlier.

"You think that what Mom said is true?"

"What do you mean?"

"That the mayor's man isn't going to go to jail," I said.

"Well, Mom has been around longer than you or me," Bird said. "She has a good understanding of how things work." Bird paused. "But so do you and me." Bird smirked. She paused. "Not all the criminals go to jail."

I gave a tiny nod. Then I rethought my acceptance of what Bird was saying.

"He could have killed me," I said.

Bird raised and lowered her chin and shrugged her shoulders.

"The rules aren't the same for everyone," my sister said.

Grandpa walked out of the back of the house and went to tinker on things in his garage.

For two hours he sat and cleaned his tools and rearranged them in his toolbox. During that time, he slipped on a pair of coveralls that were hanging on a nail by a cabinet.

I sat and tried to understand what was so broken about Effingham.

"Grandpa," I began.

"Yeah, Zee," Grandpa Clark said, looking up from organizing some tools.

"You love mom?"

Grandpa chuckled.

"Then why are you and her fighting?"

"We're not fighting, Zee," Grandpa Clark said. "We are not seeing eye-to-eye."

"It sounds like fighting," I said.

"Naw," Grandpa Clark said. "Sometimes adults disagree. No biggie."

"Okay," I said.

Grandpa Clark walked around his garage and took a box from a cabinet and unboxed a shiny piece of equipment. He walked it to the Speedster and disappeared under the Porsche for almost an hour.

When he climbed up from beneath the car, he found a shop rag and wiped his hands. Grandpa Clark wiped his coveralls off and smiled seeing me and Bo still in the garage.

"I'm going inside to make dinner," he said and before I could respond he had stripped off his coveralls. He headed back into the house leaving me and Bo in the garage.

In the garage, with grandpa gone, I decided to snoop around. The first thing I did was sit in grandpa's fix it project. The Speedster was a sleek machine. At some point grandpa had found a passenger door. The interior was just so nice. Everything about the convertible looked incredible.

Twisting the steering wheel, I noticed that the car had a key in the ignition. I smiled. The Speedster had all four wheels, both doors, the two seats and a stick shift. The dashboard was missing something that I did not recognize.

I wanted to start the engine and hear the roar of the Porsche engine, but I did not twist the key. Bo appeared and sniffed at the interior of the car and tried to climb inside. The interior was not incredibly big and as Bo tried to climb in over me, I decided that it would not be a good idea to have him on the black and red leather interior of grandpa's prize.

When I walked into the kitchen grandpa was in the kitchen. He was at the stove and cooking.

"Go and get cleaned up," Grandpa said.

"You think you'll be able to drive your car anytime soon?"

Grandpa looked at me, curiously. I smiled and stared back at my grandfather. He was dressed as he was earlier in the garage, except he had an apron tied around his waist that read: While I Have This Apron On I'M Boss (Any Questions?).

"Food going to be ready," Grandpa checked the clock. "In about an hour."

I raised and lowered my chin and headed upstairs.

On the way to my bedroom, I poked my head into Bird's bedroom. She was lying on her bed looking at her cellphone.

"You okay?"

"Sure," Bird said, turning over and watching me and Bo enter the room.

"Grandpa said that dinner will be ready in an hour," I said.

"Okay," Bird said, sitting up in her bed.

I hesitated. Bird seemed to be struggling with something.

"You know. I'm kind of looking forward to leaving this place," Bird said. "I mean, there's all the crazy small-town drama. I'm sort of looking forward to the straightforward love, hate, and backstabbing of Chicago."

I grinned knowingly. Then I decided to say something. "You know that there are some good things about a small town."

"Like what?"

"It's quiet," I said with a smile. "I think that the people, good or bad, are nicer," I said. "They are really your friends if they become your friends."

"You mean loyal?"

"Yeah," I said.

Bird looked at me and Bo. Of course, Bo had walked to Bird's bed and laid his head on the edge of it, looking for a scratch or pet.

"I don't know," Bird said. "Maybe, some of them."

I smiled and shook my head at Bird's comment. I turned on my heels and exited my sister's bedroom. Bo followed. We walked down the hall just a few feet and entered my bedroom.

There were a dozen boxes with all my personal belongings in them. The only thing I did not pack was my toothbrush, underwear, jeans, a couple of T-shirts and my shoes and socks.

I washed up for dinner and before mom or grandpa could call me downstairs, I headed down. I helped set the dinner table. Bird appeared and she helped me finish arranging things for our last dinner in Effingham.

Grandpa, the greatest cook in the family, made a simple meal but in his hands it was incredible. The first course was a salad of lettuce, tomatoes, cucumbers and diced hard boiled eggs. There were buttermilk biscuits served with green beans, baked beans, and fried chicken.

While we ate grandpa sat and made small talk with Bird about returning to Chicago and playing basketball. I was a little surprised that grandpa took any interest in Bird's athletic ability. He had never mentioned it while we were in Effingham.

"You know," Grandpa Clark said eating a drumstick. "I might come up and catch a couple of your games this year if you send me the schedule."

"What? I thought you hated Chicago," Bird said.

"I never said that," grandpa said, with a piece of chicken in his hand.

I was about to remind Bird what grandpa said when mom spoke.

"Pop, I want you to come back to Chicago with us," Mom said at dinner.

"Why?"

"It's not safe down here," Mom said.

"It's safer than Chicago," grandpa said.

"Oh, really? I can't recall the last time there was a body found buried in Garfield Park or two boys go missing and the police not do a thorough search for them," Mom said.

"That was just bad policing," Grandpa Clark said. "There's bad eggs in every basket."

Mom grimaced at grandpa's words. "I hate when you do that," Mom said.

"Hate?" Grandpa Clark asked, tilting his head toward mom.

"I hate when you try to give the oppressors excuses for their oppression," Mom clarified.

Grandpa Clark sat silently, thinking about what Mom had said.

"They don't care about us here or anywhere particularly pop," Mom said, suddenly exhausted. "I'm tired. I just want to be able to believe when Zion or Bird go out they will come home alive and unharmed." She looked from grandpa to Bird and me. "I just don't want to add you to the list of family that I have to worry about coming home safely every night."

Mom was not crying but it looked like she was seconds from having tears fall. She looked to Bird.

"Go outside," Mom said to me and Bird.

"But we aren't through with dinner," I said, pointing to the dessert in the kitchen. Grandpa had made banana pudding. It was my favorite.

Bird reached out and grabbed my hand. We walked to the back porch and out of the door with Bo trailing.

"Where are we going?" I asked, looking at the banana pudding and unable to have any.

"I don't know," Bird said once in the backyard. Bo was following obediently. Bird opened the gate and Bo trotted out and onto the driveway.

I looked to the darkened garage.

"We can go for a ride on the scooter," Bird said.

I looked at Bird and thought how my sister drove on her scooter. I shook my head in answer.

"We can sit on the front porch," Bird said, looking around and heading to the front of grandpa's house.

I gave a nod.

The front porch was safer than a ride on the back of the scooter with Bird the Speed Demon.

Once on the porch and seated I broached a subject I had been struggling with to Bird.

"Bird, I found something in the field when I found the body," I said.

Bird listened in the darkness of the front porch.

"Okay," she said, finally.

"Well, I am wondering what I should do with it?"

"Is it money?" Bird asked.

"No."

"What is it?" Bird asked, suddenly annoyed.

"A broken watch," I said.

"Why don't you just throw it away?"

"I found it when I found the dead body," I said as an answer.

Bird frowned at my words. "Let me see it," Bird said.

I had carried it since the late afternoon, when Mom had told me the detectives were coming to ask me a few questions. In my mind, I had thought I would give them the broken watch and let them piece together what they could of the mystery of the man in the field, but the meeting and interview had gone in another direction. So, I was stuck with a broken watch of a dead man in my pocket.

Fishing the watch out of my pocket I handed Bird a plastic baggie with the watch inside.

"It's all dirty," Bird said, examining the watch in the baggie. "There's some writing on it."

I gave a tiny grin. I let her discover what I already knew. It was nice to watch Bird's discovery process.

"To David, From Your Biggest Fan, Reita," Bird read. "Who is David? Who is Reita?"

Bird looked at me with her dark eyes and studied me. She did not say anything immediately. Instead, she seemed to be weighing an idea in her mind.

"So, this is one of the white guys that went missing?"

I bobbed my head.

"Hmmm," Bird hummed. "So, what is more important is who is Reita? Such a weird way to spell someone's name. It's like it was supposed to be Rita but then it wasn't. You know?"

I gave my sister a little smile but did not know what Bird was talking about exactly. I concentrated as Bird tried to figure out the name of the woman that had given David York the watch. All I knew for certain was that it was Wednesday, and we were leaving Saturday.

72 hours (about 3 days), I figured. Three days to figure out who Reita was and if there was any connection or connection to those names beyond the Effingham Performance Center. I paused. I wondered for a long moment if I should share my thoughts about the performance center.

There was no need to share something that I had no way to prove. The idea of burdening my sister with my hundreds of theories seemed cruel. Only I needed to deal with the many knots of the mystery of Effingham and it's missing six.

"I think I'm going to the library in the morning," I said to Bird.

"Why?"

"I need to check a few things," I said. "I think I'm going to the mall too."

"Well, I should probably go with you to make sure no one tries to kill you," Bird said.

"Okay, but I am going to ride my bike there," I said. "I don't like riding on the scooter."

"Come on," Bird said.

"I'm serious," I said. I thought about the information I was now looking for and wondered if the library or Zada Gallamore would be able to unravel the truth hidden in the inscription on the back of a broken watch.

"What are you thinking?"

"I am thinking that whoever this David is had some girl that liked him a lot," Bird said. "She liked him so much that she gave him a watch."

"I don't get it,"

"Maybe they were high school sweethearts or something," Bird said. "I don't know. All I know is that this Reita gave David a watch and he liked it enough to hold onto it."

I looked at my sister curiously, not knowing if what Bird said was true of not.

"Should I give it to the police?"

"Hell yeah," Bird said. "You don't want them finding it on you and then blaming you for someone's murder."

I was surprised by Bird's response. For some reason, I thought she would have said no to handing something over to the police.

"Before you hand it over though," Bird said, with an evil grin. "We need to find out who Reita is. Once you find that out, we can put the watch in the mail and mail it to one of the detectives if you like."

That was more like the Bird I knew.

A few minutes later mom called us back inside the house.

We returned to the house, and I found myself looking at the uneaten banana pudding.

"Is everything okay?"

Mom gave us a tired nod.

Bird looked at me and held my gaze for a moment. Without saying anything she wanted me to remain quiet. I looked to the banana pudding and then back to my sister and reluctantly gave her a frustrated nod.

We walked back into the dining room and there was grandpa sitting where he had been earlier. He had his arms crossed in front of his chest. Upon seeing us enter the dining room he smiled.

"You still hungry?"

I silently bobbed my head up and down.

Grandpa Clark climbed to his feet and went into the kitchen. He returned shortly with plates and forks and the banana pudding. I smiled.

Chapter 27.

That Thursday when I woke up Bo was already up and wagging his tail. I slipped on my flip flops and he and I walked downstairs. Bo knew the morning routine. He bounced down the flight of stairs to the main floor of Grandpa Clark's house and headed toward the kitchen only to pause. The black tongued Chow turned around and walked back toward me as I continued to walk slowly toward the kitchen. Bo hearing noise in the kitchen spun around and entered ahead of me.

"Good morning grandpa," I said.

"Morning Zee," Grandpa Clark said from the kitchen stove. He was already making breakfast.

I continued walking through the kitchen with Bo beside me. We exited the kitchen and then the rear of the house as I grabbed Bo's leash. We walked down a dozen steps to the gate. Bo waited for me to attach his leash and open the gate. When I did, he bounded out and onto the driveway where grandpa's Jeep sat and behind it mom's Toyota Rav4.

I paused and studied the sky. The sun was up, and the sky was blue for as far as I could see. I looked to the left and was not surprised to see the street, Eiche Avenue, and across the two-lanes of the street the now chain-link fence. Bo walked to the far side of the Jeep, and I followed looking at the fencing that separated the vacant field that stretched from Eiche Avenue to Blohm Avenue.

Bo did his business. We walked to the bottom of the driveway with Bo sniffing the grass. To the left of us was a small shack inside the fencing. The shack was not very big and looked like one of those sheds where they store tools. It had a couple of windows and a door. I had no idea what was inside. All I knew was there were two security guards patrolling the outside the fencing. They had hats and jackets that said: Security on them. Since the fencing had been put up neither of the guards had said one word to me.

Bo and I walked down Eiche Avenue toward Banker Street. Bo sniffed and stopped and investigated every tree, bush and rock that was in the grass along the avenue. I walked on the sidewalk and smiled and waved to the neighbors out that early.

At Banker Street Bo and I turned around and returned to grandpa's house.

"Miss Juanita told me to tell you: Hey," I said as Bo went to his water dish and lapped up some water.

Grandpa Clark gave a wistful smile at the stove.

"Go tell Bird and your mom that breakfast is nearly ready," Grandpa Clark said over his shoulder.

I smiled at the idea of eating grandpa's food. I left the kitchen and a few minutes later Bo climbed the stairs behind me. I knocked on my mother's bedroom door.

"Come in," I heard.

"Breakfast is almost ready," I told my mom.

Mom was dressed in a gray T-shirt with a red outline of a heart on the front of it. She was wearing jeans and sandals.

"Thank you, sweetheart," mom said with a smile.

I spun around and headed to the opposite end of the hallway. Bird's door was closed. I stopped and knocked on the door.

"Yes," Bird said from behind the closed door.

"Breakfast is almost ready," I said and walked into my room.

Dressed in my pajamas I quickly grabbed the clothes I was going to wear for the day. I found a cartoon T-shirt with Speed Racer on the front, cartoon underwear, a pair of shorts, some NBA socks, and my most comfortable sneakers. I headed to the bathroom and cleaned up. I brushed my teeth and under the watchful eye of Bo put on some deodorant.

"Okay?" I asked.

Bo looked at me and tilted his lion-like head.

"I'll take that as a yes," I said and exited the bathroom dressed for the day. Once out of the bathroom I grabbed my backpack and headed downstairs.

For breakfast that Thursday Grandpa Clark whipped up French toast with strawberries and blueberries, hash browns, and scrambled eggs. We had milk, orange, and apple juice for drinks that breakfast.

"Mom, I'm going to the library," I said. "Is that okay?"

"Think you should have asked me first," Mom said and smiled.

I gave an awkward smile.

"Mom? Can I go to the library after breakfast?"

"Sure," Mom said with a chuckle.

"Can I go too?" Bird asked.

"Yes," Mom said.

"Dad, what do you have planned?"

"Not much," Grandpa Clark said. "I will probably putter around. I am supposed to go by the VFW later, around one, but beyond that not much," grandpa said.

"I need to make a few phone calls to arrange things for our return," Mom said.

"We're going to be in the same apartment?"

"No," Mom said. "We are in the same apartment house, but we should be a couple of floors higher. This time we should have a view of the park."

"Really?" Bird asked, surprised.

"That's what the realtor said," Mom said.

I climbed up from the table, went to the kitchen, and began stacking the plates near the sink. A few minutes later, Bird showed up. We cleaned the kitchen and put the leftovers away. When I finished, I went to the garage and pulled the bike out.

When I rode up to the two-story dark building that looked more like a factory than a library. Bird was already there. She had parked her scooter and locked it to the bike stand. I climbed off the bike and locked it to the bike stand with the kryptonite lock Mister Nelson had given me.

Stephanie Graham was in the Effingham Public Library when I arrived. She was at her desk talking to Bird when I entered.

"Zion? We were just talking about you," Miss Graham said.

I gave a clumsy smile.

"I didn't know that you were so observant," the librarian said. "I cannot believe that after seven months you figured out what people who are paid to find people couldn't do."

I listened uncomfortably. I tried to think of a way to leave Miss Graham without being rude.

"I played a significant role in helping," Bird said.

"I didn't know that," Miss Graham said.

"Yeah, I helped Zee in his investigations," Bird said.

I smiled at my sister.

"I'm going to look at some newspapers," I said. "If that is okay?"

Miss Graham and Bird stood at the reference desk as I excused myself.

I looked through the newspapers and found no mention of anyone named: Reita. I went to the library computer and typed in the name. The only names that came up were for an Indian physician and some anime character. Neither made sense in Effingham.

Returning to the librarian and Bird.

"Zion, I did not know that Bernadette helped you in the investigation," Miss Graham said with a smile.

I looked at Bird and smiled.

"Well, I didn't help that much," Bird said.

I didn't care if Bird tried to take credit for finding Tommy Crawford's body. I had other things on my mind.

"Do you have the high school yearbooks for the local high school here?"

"We have the last twenty years in reference," Miss Graham said, turning serious. "You know which year you are looking for?"

I did a quick calculation.

"Can I see the last fifteen years?"

"Are you sure?"

"Actually, can I see the last sixteen years?"

"Sure thing," Miss Graham said, turning around in her chair and climbing to her feet. She walked to a shelf with ESHS yearbooks. They were large. She took out the first four and walked them to me.

I looked around and found an empty table close to the reference desk. I took the first four yearbooks to the empty table as Miss Graham went to get the second set of four yearbooks. The sixteen yearbooks sat on the table in stacks of four.

Bird gravitated to the table.

"What can I do?"

"Well, you can look and see if there's a Reita in any of these books," I said.

I opened the first book and flipped to the end of the book, looking for the list of names of all students.

"This could take all day," Bird complained.

"No," I said. "The yearbook has a list of all the students in the rear of the book and page numbers of where they are featured. Just look for her name."

Bird sat down and she and I rooted through the Effingham Senior High School yearbooks for the last sixteen years.

"Why are we looking for the last sixteen years?"

"Well, four years to graduate from high school," I said. "Hopefully, David York graduated from high school in the last sixteen years. He was only thirty-one when he disappeared.

Bird fell silent.

"Did you find something?"

"Yeah," Bird said. "I found David York."

"Okay, good," I said, looking at Bird. "Look for Reita."

I was on my sixth book and smiling at a familiar face of a first year Zada Gallamore. She was all smiles and big eyes on the page. She was a part of the high school newspaper. Of course, she was, I chuckled.

Bird cleared her throat to get my attention.

"I just found a Reita Carr," Bird said.

"You sure?"

"I'm looking right at her," Bird said, lifting the yearbook. "She was on the Pep Squad and the Secretary for her class."

I put down the yearbooks I was looking at and climbed to my feet. I circled the table to get a look at Reita Carr. She was a dark girl with big eyes, straight nose, big lips, and smile with finger thick black braids of hair that fell to her rounded shoulders.

"Okay," Bird said. "What now?"

"Well, we try to find her, I suppose."

"You suppose?"

"Just figured that once we knew who she was we could talk to her," I said.

"How do we do that?"

"Well, Effingham ain't that big," I said. "Maybe, you can ask Miss Graham if she knows her?"

"Me?"

"Yeah," I said. "Why not?" I grabbed four of the yearbooks and walked them back to the desk where we had gotten them earlier.

"Help me put these back," I said.

"No," Bird said. "I have to go and talk to the Miss Graham."

I grabbed the next stack of yearbooks and returned them to the reference desk while Bird went to talk to the librarian. I watched the two talk as I gathered the last of the yearbooks and returned them to the desk.

Bird gestured to me, and I walked to the reference desk with my backpack over my shoulders.

"Zion, you won't believe this," Bird said with a smile, looking to me and back to the librarian. "Miss Carr works at the Village Mall."

"Reita is a couple of years older than me," the librarian said. "I went to school with her brother, Al. He was always cracking jokes and not paying attention in class," the librarian mused. "I think he works at one of the tow companies, now."

I smiled.

"Well, she works at one of the stores in the mall," Miss Graham said. "I haven't talked to her in a while."

I listened and waited.

"Miss Graham," I pronounced aloud. "Do you or your husband know anyone who works at the Phillps 66 gas station by the McDonalds?"

Bird looked at me, curious.

Miss Graham pursed her lips, thinking.

"I didn't want to be a bother," I said. "I just thought you or he might--"

"I think Darryl knows the owner," Miss Graham said, raising a hand and stopping me. "Why?"

"I just wanted to see if they had a copy of a video tape," I said.

"Can you give me five minutes?" Miss Graham asked. "I'll text Darryl. He'll know who you should talk to."

I smiled and walked away from the librarian's desk. Bird followed.

"What gives?"

"I was thinking that either McDonalds or the gas station might have a camera outside recording things happening around their business." I paused, looking at my sister. "What if they captured the moment that Solomon got taken?"

"What about McDonalds?" Bird asked. "Who do you think we need to talk to about their video tapes?"

I shrugged my shoulders.

Miss Graham called us over and with a smile gave us a name for the gas station.

"Well, thanks you for all your help," I said and headed for the library exit.

Bird followed behind.

"Where to now?"

"The mall," I said.

"Not the gas station?"

"Not yet," I said.

"See you there," Bird said, unlocking the scooter. "Where do you want to meet?"

"Well, let's meet at the food court," I said. I had a detour to make once I got to the mall and needed a little extra time. I unlocked my bike from the bike stand.

"Are you going by grandpa's?"

"No," Bird said.

"Okay," I said. "It may take me a little longer to get down there than you."

"I know," Bird said. "I'll wait. You want something to eat?"

"Can you get me a hotdog and a lemonade?"

"Got it," Bird said. "Hurry up and move those little legs of yours before your hotdog gets cold." Bird climbed on her scooter and turned on the engine. "See you in a bit."

With that Bird took off down the street.

I rode down the side streets avoiding traffic and traffic lights. Riding down South Park Street was a pretty direct shot to grandpa's house. The biggest street was National Road. I had to wait for a couple of trucks to pass before crossing. I rode past Bliss Park and Paris and Frankie's house on my way toward grandpa's house.

When I reached South Park Street and Eiche Avenue I was one block away from grandpa's house. If I had turned left and rode a few minutes I would have been with mom, grandpa, and Bo, but I didn't turn left. I just rode another six blocks and then saw the Village Mall.

I rode to the rear of the mall and locked my bike in a bike rack.

Now the Village Mall was a dozen small stores cobbled together with a Village Mall theater. There was a Resale Shop that seemed to be the anchor store of the mall for some reason. There was an insurance agency that sat in its own building. The Gallamore Fashion store though was inside the mall with the twelve other stores.

I walked into the Gallamore store with the giant red arrow pointing to the entrance and like before the three mannequins were in the window dressed in religious sweats that read: Chosen. On the mannequins' heads were baseball caps with the same branding.

The small store had not changed since my last visit. There was a main aisle that led to the rear of the store where an older woman wearing cat eyeglasses was sitting behind a sewing machine. On either side of the main aisle were rounders with T-shirts and sweatsuits on them.

As I entered the audible bell rang from inside the store to announce my arrival in Gallamore Fashions.

"How can I help you?" Asked Zada Gallamore. She had big brown eyes in her beechwood brown face with a slightly upturned nose above her full lips. Zada was wearing a green Chosen sweatshirt and blue jeans.

"Hi," I said. "Do you have a minute to talk?"

"Sure. What's up?"

I looked back at the woman sitting at the sewing machine.

"That's my mom," Zada Gallamore said. "What do you need?"

I pursed my lips.

"Do you know a Reita Carr?"

"Reita?"

I blinked and lowered my chin.

"Why?"

"I'm not sure but I think she might be involved in the disappearances," I said.

"How?"

I did not respond.

Zada frowned. "Are you sure the person you are looking for is Reita?" The Effingham Defender reporter asked.

"Yep," I said.

Zada paused thinking.

"Who is she?" I asked.

"We went to school together," Zada Gallamore said. "She was a year or two older than me."

I raised and lowered my chin.

"She is cool people," Zada said.

I knew that Zada was stalling for a reason. I just could not put my finger on it. I figured that it had something to do with high school. So, I waited.

"She was one of those people that moves to the beat of a different drummer," Zada said. "You know what I mean? I mean, she was a spark plug. She would come in the room, and everyone would get quiet waiting for Reita to say something." Zada paused. "She had all this potential and then she screwed around and found out that Effingham is the crossroads for a reason."

"What does that mean?"

"She thought she could play with the devil and not pay a cost," said Zada.

"The devil?"

"Yeah, down here the devil is real," Zada said.

Like werewolves? I wanted to ask. I smiled.

"You think I'm talking about werewolves and vampires? I'm not," Zada said. "This place is the crossroads. The devils have been using this town as a junction point. The first devils appeared here just after the emancipation. They were the original night riders. They used Effingham as a meeting place. Then the second version of the devils appeared. They used the same tactics as the first but targeted vocal black activists. The third and current devils erected that cross. It is a silent symbol of their agenda."

I frowned, confused as to how all this had to do with Reita Carr.

"She thought that being here and being attracted in someone was enough," Zada said.

I shook my head, still confused.

"She graduated from high school and thought she had a cush job working at one of the banks, but that job fell through. She applied for another and another job. No one hired her even though she was more than qualified."

I raised and lowered my chin, understanding the problem.

"She now works down at the As Seen On TV store," Zada said. "She's incredibly smart but they continue to punish her for thinking that deviltry didn't matter down here."

"Thank you," I said.

"Sure," Zada Gallamore said. "If you need anything else just ask."

"You wouldn't know the owner of the McDonalds in West Cedar?"

Zada Gallamore looked at me curiously.

"Should I ask why?"

"No," I said.

"Okay, I won't, but if anything comes of this, I want the scoop," Zada said. She walked to the rear of the store and returned with a backpack. She opened the backpack and retrieved a leather notebook. She also fished out a pen and index card. Zada Gallamore leafed through the notebook and finding what she was looking for scribbled down some information. She handed the index card to me.

"Good luck," Zada said with big smile on her face.

"Thanks," I said and left the Gallamore Fashion store and headed to the food court and Bird.

Bird was sitting at a table with my hotdog and lemonade next to her. She had a hotdog and Coke in front of her. Her hotdog had relish, onions, and mustard on it. Mine was garnished exactly the same as my sister's.

I sat down and looked at Bird. She stared at me.

"Thanks," I said.

"You're welcome," Bird responded and took a bit of her hotdog.

"How long you been here?"

"Not too long," Bird said. "I walked around the stores and tried to find Reita before buying our lunch."

"Did you find her?"

Bird gave a sly wink at me as she ate her hotdog and sipped her Coke.

"She's in the As Seen On TV store," Bird breathed in between bites of her hotdog.

I smiled and ate my hotdog. It was good, but it did not taste like the Chicago hotdogs for some reason. Chicago hotdogs just tasted different, I thought.

After we finished eating Bird threw away her trash and I did the same.

"You ready?"

I grinned at the possibilities.

We entered the As Seen On TV store.

Chapter 28.

Reita Carr was a short dark woman with shoulder length hair that had big hips. She was dressed in a dark blue blouse with a button front and khaki trousers. On her feet were blue and white sneakers. In her earlobes were gold hoop earrings.

"What do we do?"

I shrugged.

Bird looked at the woman we had come to talk to from two aisles away. She was straightening a display and placing some kitchen accessories in a particular order. Nervously, I picked up a box that held a slicer of some kind and pretended to be examining it.

"Well, we didn't come all the way down here to look at her," Bird said.

"I know, but I don't know what to ask her," I said. "I mean, I know that they went to school together. But I need to know why she gave him the watch."

Bird took a breath, stepped from the aisle, and walked to Reita Carr, who was still arranging a display on a shelf.

I stayed in the aisle and pretended to be looking at the slicer. All the while I watched as Bird spoke to Reita Carr. The two talked. Reita Carr smiled and the two pantomimed fifty feet away. She was maybe a few inches shorter than Bird.

Bird waved me over as she talked to Reita Carr. I stepped from behind the aisle and made my way toward Reita Carr, the woman who had given David York a watch.

"Zion, this is Reita Carr," Bird said. "Reita this is my brother Zion."

I looked at Reita and smiled.

"Zion has a couple of questions to ask you. Nothing too serious," Bird said with a smile.

I looked the short dark woman with big deer-like eyes.

"You know David York? The guy that went missing?" I asked with a feeble smile.

Reita Carr looked at me a little surprised. She smiled, but the smile had no happiness behind it. She frowned and then behind her eyes I saw her soften, just a little.

"I did," Reita answered.

"Well, I suppose I have to ask," I said knowing the question I needed an answer to first. "Do you know where he is?"

"No," Reita Carr said.

"Had to ask," I said. I fished out the broken watch still in the plastic bag. "Can you tell me about this?"

Reita Carr hesitated. She looked toward the front of the store and two people dressed in the same uniform as her.

"Can we talk about this during my break?" She asked, looking left and right in the quiet store.

"When's that?" Bird asked.

"In about ten minutes," Reita said.

Bird and I walked out of the store and sat on the bench just a few doors down from the As Seen On TV store.

"Think she knows anything?" Bird asked.

"It doesn't matter what she knows," I answered. "If she feels trapped, she'll lie. Everyone lies. I lie. You lie. Mom lies. Everyone lies." I paused. "None of that matters," I said to Bird. "What matters is what she tells us."

"How do you mean?" Bird inquired.

Reita stepped out of the store and gestured for us to follow. We walked just outside of the mall. We stood on a sidewalk that ran the length of the building that housed the mall. In front of us was the parking lot.

"So, I gave David that watch and that was the beginning of the end for me," Reita said.

"How do you mean?"

"They locked me out of opportunities," Reita said. She moved her head side to side. "I should be the manager of this mall, but they only give me a job that barely pays the bill, like a handout."

"What happened?"

"I made a mistake," Reita said with a shrug of her shoulders. "I got ahead of myself. I thought that down here things had changed." She paused. "I mean we have indoor plumbing. They de-segregated the schools. There are black firemen in the fire department. I think there's even a black doctor at the hospital."

"So, you liked David York," Bird said.

Reita frowned again and hesitated.

"We met in high school. In high school he was so different. He was confident and knew what he wanted to do. He told me he was going to play pro baseball," Reita said with a smile. "He went to St. Louis and tried out. It didn't work out. I felt bad for him. You know that was his dream."

I studied Reita Carr.

"He came back to Effingham broken. He didn't want to be a store manager. So, I gave him the watch. No big deal. But down here it became a big deal."

Bird elbowed me with Reita's words. I gave my sister a weak smile.

"When did you give him the watch?"

"Last year," Reita said. Reita stopped. "No, maybe in March or April."

"Was David mixed up with the Klan?" Bird asked.

Reita Carr paused. It looked like she wanted to run, but she bit her lower lip and continued.

"Like I said, in high school he was different. He liked me. He told me about his family foolishness," Reita replied.

"You were dating a Klansman?" Bird asked, but not to Reita Carr.

"It's not like that," Reita said. She moved her head side to side. "These people all have skeletons in their closets. David grew up with his family and their thinking but when he met me, he knew what he had been taught, but it didn't make sense."

"But he was a Klansman," Bird said.

I looked to Bird.

Bird moved her head side to side, uncomprehending.

"It's possible to change," Reita said.

"So, were you seeing David this year?" I quizzed Reita.

Reita reluctantly bobbed her head up and down.

"Damn," Bird said. "That is just too crazy," Bird said. "You might as well have laid in the middle of a busy street or freeway and expected the cars to slow down and not hit you."

Reita Carr looked at Bird and looked down to the sidewalk.

"So, you know, there's no such thing as one Klansman," Bird said.

Reita did not reply.

"Did you know his friends?" Bird asked. "Because you know they were Klansmen too."

I placed a hand on Bird's arm to silence her.

"You didn't think dating a Klansman was going to have consequences?" Bird asked, raising her hands in surrender.

"I don't know what I was thinking," Reita responded. "I mean, I knew there was no future with David or me, but I held onto... hope." She moved her head side to side, tears welling up in her eyes and angry all of a sudden. "I know how it sounds."

Bird looked at me.

I gave my sister a slight bob of my head.

"Thanks," Bird said.

"Thank you," I said. I thought quickly and before Reita could leave, I raised my hand. "Can I ask you one more question?"

Reita Carr looked at me, hurt, angry and guilty and all the other feelings that had to be swirling about her at that moment and paused.

"Have you heard any of these names?" I rattled off the five names of the missing men.

"They were all David's friends," Reita Carr said.

"One last question," I said with a weak smile. "Does anyone else know that you were with David York this year or that you knew his friends?"

Reita put her hand to her mouth and walked back into the Village Mall shaken.

Bird and I stood just on the outside of the mall and looked at each other.

"Holy shit, Zee," Bird said, reaching out and grabbing me by the shoulders and shaking me like I was a vending machine holding her selection hostage. "What do you think?"

"Well, it seems like someone did not like David York messing with Reita Carr," Bird said.

"Yeah," Bird said, listening to me and frowning at my conclusion. "That is what I was thinking."

I smiled at my sister.

"That's not what you were thinking," I said to Bird. "What were you thinking?"

"I was thinking that being down here is straight up crazy if Klansmen think they can have a black girlfriend," Bird said. "They hate us and Jews and just about everyone that isn't a part of their Nazi agenda," Bird said with a shake of her head.

"Why do they hate--" I began only to stop. I didn't want to know what some hate group believed. They were a hate group. In the declaration of the group, they were hateful. "Never mind."

"So, what now?" Bird asked.

"Well, it's Thursday and we have a little less than thirty-two hours before we head back to Chicago," I said. "I don't know anyone that can unravel this mess and figure out who is behind all the Klansmen disappearances." I paused. "I don't know if there needs to be a period at the end of this case." I said. "You and Frankie said that the Klan is filled with bad people."

Bird nodded.

"So, let's go to the gas station and see if we can look at some videos," I said.

"You going to ride on the scooter?"

I nodded.

The ride to the Phillips 66 gas station was a nerve-wracking experience. It wasn't that Bird was incredibly dangerous. It was that Bird thought that cars and trucks respected her on the road.

She rode in the slow lane and cars honked their horns for the ten second delays the slower scooter caused them. Some cars roared past, opening up their engines as if they were on a racetrack and passing us was for the win. Trucks seemed oblivious to our presence.

I clutched Bird. I tried to close my eyes as I rode but that only amplified the noises and kicked my dark imagination into overdrive. I watched as cars sped up and slowed down misjudging how fast or slow the scooter Bird rode was.

Thankfully, we arrived at the Phillips 66 gas station unharmed. We had only ridden six blocks and though the distance was not extremely far I felt as if I had traveled ten times as far and suffered three hundred times as many close calls.

"So, what now?"

"Well, we rely on the goodness in people's hearts," I said.

"That never works," Bird said.

"We'll see," I said and walked into the gas station.

The gas station was a box. Closest to the door was a locked box where the cashier sat behind bulletproof glass with a small opening to pass through money or cigarettes. There was a locked and reinforced door at the end of the box to entry or exit. There were two rows of various candies, treats and roadside essentials. In the rear of the store was a cooler where there were twenty brands of beers, sodas, and energy drinks.

When we walked in there was a couple of women at the cashier paying for something.

I waited patiently and when the women left approached the cashier.

"I was told to ask for Ben Hensley," I voiced aloud. "Is he here?"

The cashier looked at me and then Bird, curiously.

"Why you looking for Ben?"

"I want to see some of your video tapes for a particular night," I said.

"Yeah, we only keep our tapes for a week then we record over them," the cashier said.

That was disappointing news.

I bobbed my head and spun around to Bird.

Bird frowned.

We exited the gas station and stood just outside the store.

"What now?"

I pointed to the McDonalds.

What I learned talking to Nettie May Holloway, the store manager of the McDonalds, was that the fast-food restaurant I had seen all my life was a franchise. This particular franchise was owned by a rich man named Max Carpenter. Carpenter owned four McDonalds in South Central Illinois. He rarely came into the Effingham store. Nettie May Holloway was working to buyout the present owner of this McDonalds.

Nettie May Holloway was more than willing to allow us to look through the videos captured by the cameras. She walked us back to her small office and there, in the office just off the kitchen, were boxes and boxes of tapes, receipts, employee manuals and procedural manuals needed to operate the franchise. Amid all those boxes sat a small desk with two monitors on them. One monitor was displaying the various views of the interior of the restaurant and the drive thru window.

"We monitor only these key locations," Nettie May Holloway said. "Now, you might be able to see a little of the outside but not much."

We thanked Nettie May Holloway for her help and exited the McDonalds.

Chapter 29.

After breakfast and cleaning up the kitchen one last time, Bird and I walked down to the park so she could shoot baskets. It was not extremely hot, and Bird seemed unconcerned about the heat once we arrived at the park. I carried the frozen refreshments. There were two Gatorades. There were four frozen waters. Mom had sliced up two oranges. In the backpack I carried I also had Bo's snacks and collapsible water bowl. It was bulky but not too heavy.

Frankie and Donny appeared at the park where Bird was shooting baskets. I was sitting in the shade with Bo.

Donny sat next to me and Bo.

Bo sniffed Donny and after a few minutes forget about him. My dog sat in the shade and watched Bird and Frankie shooting baskets.

After a game of twenty-one that Bird won she and Frankie sat down and rested.

"You are good for a girl,"

"You are okay for a boy," Bird responded with a smile. Bird was sipping a Gatorade.

"I could have played on the high school basketball team," Frankie said.

"Don't get started," Bird said.

Frankie fell silent and sipped at the bottle of water I offered him.

Donny and I sat in the shade and listened to Frankie and Bird talking. I gave Bo some water in his collapsible bowl. He lapped it up greedily.

The sun was high above our heads and playing was over suddenly, but no one moved.

"So, what do you think happened to Solomon?" Frankie finally asked once he finished his water.

Bird moved her head side to side.

"No ideas?" Frankie asked.

"Well, I think that if all the information is correct that Solomon could be anywhere," I said. "I also think that like Tommy Crawford, Solomon disappeared because of Amber James."

"You think we're ever going to find him?" Bird asked.

I moved my head side to side.

"Why?"

I tried to explain that where Solomon was last reported being seen was a well-lit place. It was close to a road that led out of town. Once out of town the I-57 was just twenty minutes away and that led to anywhere. Not to mention Hull Cemetery was not that far away.

"It just doesn't look like there is going to be a body to find," I said. I paused. "I suppose there could be a deathbed confession, but I don't think those really happen. They seem made up."

'Have you told the Wrights yet?"

"I'm supposed to talk to them tonight," I said.

Bird climbed to her feet and stepped out and onto the court again.

"How long is she going to be out there?"

"I don't know," I said with a shrug. "Maybe another hour."

Frankie climbed to his feet. He tipped his chin to Donny. Donny climbed to his feet as well.

"We're out," Frankie said. He looked at Bird and waved to her while she was chasing down her basketball.

"Later Bird," Frankie yelled as he and Donny walked up the street and toward grandpa's house.

Donny waved goodbye.

Bo and I watched as Frankie and Donny walked up Park Avenue and slowly disappeared.

Less than an hour later Bird, Bo and I walked back up Park Avenue toward Eiche Avenue and grandpa's house.

"No Trey or Paris," I said as we walked.

Bird, dribbling her basketball, looked at me but did not respond.

"What was going on with you and Trey?"

Bird continued dribbling.

"Are you and Paris still talking?"

Bird gave a small nod as she continued dribbling the basketball.

"I'm the one that usually is quiet, and you are talking," I said with Bo by my side. "This is a little weird."

"Zee, sometimes talking doesn't solve things," Bird said.

We turned onto Eiche Avenue. We were just two blocks from grandpa's house.

As we got close to grandpa's house Bird caught the basketball and walked without dribbling.

"Do you know if the Wrights are coming over or are you going over there?"

"I think they're coming over," I said, but I wasn't certain.

When we entered the house grandpa was in the kitchen. Mom was sitting in the living room on the couch. She was on the phone talking.

"Grandpa," I said to get Grandpa Clark's attention.

He turned and looked at me with one of his novelty aprons on.

"Are the Wrights coming by?" Bird asked.

"Yes," he said. "You and Zee go and get washed up. Need you to change out of your stinky clothes. We got guests coming over in a couple of hours."

I smiled at the idea.

Mom appeared in the kitchen.

"You guys stink," she said, wrinkling her nose. Mom hugged both Bird and me. "I think you need to give Bo a bath before we leave tomorrow."

I looked at Bo who was padding around the kitchen in the middle of all the action. Bo looked at me and mom and tilted his head.

"I think you have a bath coming tonight," I said to Bo.

"Not tonight," Mom said. "Now."

I nodded.

"We have furniture coming in Saturday afternoon," Mom said to Bird and grandpa.

"You ready for a bath?" I asked my lion of a dog.

Bo looked at me talking and did not seem too concerned about anything I was saying. As a Chow Bo did not shrink from water. He liked water. Giving him a bath meant that I ended up taking a bath.

"Well, I can give him a bath now," I said to mom. "But you know that means I'll end up taking one as well."

"Then, after, you need to take a shower," mom said.

I smiled. Bird was already exiting the kitchen. Grandpa Clark continued cooking.

"Go out back and hose him down and then go wash up," mom said.

I grabbed the essentials and walked Bo out to the backyard of grandpa's house. Bo ran down the stairs thinking that we were going for a walk. I had two towels over my shoulder and had grabbed some shampoo and a bucket and instead of going to the gate, headed to the garden hose.

Bo studied me and followed. He watched as I squirted shampoo into the bucket and pulled out a rag, I would use to rub the shampoo into his fur. Bo backed up.

"Come here," I said putting the towels out of the splash zone.

Bo turned as I lifted the garden hose and shot him playfully with a blast of water. Bo ran and hid behind the pear tree in the center of the backyard.

"Come here, silly," I said. I sprayed more water at my silly dog. I sat down and waited.

Bo slowly approached. I squeezed the trigger of the garden hose just enough to let a trickle of water come out of the nozzle. Again, I knew that Bo loved water. So, I just waited. In a few moments, Bo was completely wet and soaped up.

"Okay," I said to Bo. 'Let's wash all this soap off you."

Bo tried to help. He stood and gave himself a big shake. The shampoo flew everywhere. I was covered in the shampoo.

"Bo, you are ridiculous," I said as I rinsed my dog clean of the shampoo. As I finished rinsing him Bo again gave himself another big shake. I grabbed a towel and gave the lion dog and big rub to remove most of the water.

The whole ordeal took about thirty minutes, but at the end Bo was clean and mostly dry. Me, on the other hand, found myself dripping wet.

Before Bo could get dirty, I commanded my dog into the house. I followed and immediately headed upstairs to take a shower. Bo followed.

While I showered Bo tried to dry himself and explore the second floor. I finished my shower and put on another T-shirt and a pair of jeans. I pulled on my sneakers.

Bo appeared at my bedroom door. I smiled. Bo's hair was still wet and laid close to his body. For the first time since we had been in Effingham Bo looked like a non-fluffy dog.

"You look so strange Bo," I said. "It's like you got a haircut."

An hour later the Wrights appeared. Like before they seemed weighed down with the uncertainty of where their son was at that moment. Missus Wright was wearing a pillbox hat when she came over to grandpa's house that evening. She was dressed in a blue large checked dress with blue suede flats.

Mister Wright stood beside his wife as dark as a pecan. He was dressed in dark brown suit, with a white collared shirt, and a brown tie. He looked miserable. Though I knew the couple were much younger than our mom the weight of the stress made them look ten years older.

For dinner, Grandpa Clark made cornbread, macaroni and cheese, collard greens, sweet potatoes, and fried chicken. The Wright ate at our dining room table and though they were cordial seemed to know the news I was going to deliver was bad. They ate and as we, at the table, ate blackberry cobbler mom spoke.

"Zion and Bird and I returning to Chicago Saturday," mom said with a weak smile. "We invited you here, tonight, to let Zion tell you what he has discovered."

John Wright looked as if he had not slept in weeks. His wife, dressed in lavender colored blouse and dark slacks, too seemed on the verge of exhaustion.

"Zion?"

"Well, I do not have good news," I said. "I checked and talked to people and if the evidence that I discovered is true then there is no telling where he is."

"What do you mean?"

I detailed as best I could what I pieced together. I did not go too deep in detail. They did not need to know who I had talked to or when. The parents of Solomon Wright just wanted to know if they could expect to see their son again.

"I have to say that I doubt he will return anytime soon," I concluded.

"Thank you for trying," Mister Wright said, his eyes lowered.

"Yes, thank you," Missus Wright said as well, her voice strained.

"Sorry we don't have brighter news for you," Mom said, sympathetically.

The Wrights left that night dejected.

I talked with Bird later about Solomon Wright.

We were in Bird's room. Her room looked like mine except with about ten more boxes. She sat on her bed. I sat on the floor with Bo's head in my lap.

"What do you think?" I asked my sister.

"What do you mean?" Bird asked, uncertain.

"I mean, what should I do now?"

Bird looked at me, confused.

"I have parts of two mysteries in my head," I said, playing with Bo's ear nervously. "I want to tell someone. Maybe they can solve either one with the information I have."

"There's no point," Bird said.

"There's always a point," I said.

"No, sometimes, the only justice we get is in the dark when no one is watching," Bird said.

"What?"

"I mean, no one is going to shed a tear for the missing Klansmen," Bird said.

I closed my eyes to Bird. I shook my head at my sister's words. "But they all have families and friends," I pointed out.

"Bad families and bad friends that would hurt you if they could get away with it and not be punished," Bird said. She frowned.

I wasn't sure if I agreed or disagreed with Bird.

"You helped Tommy Crawford's family," Bird said, reminding me of something good that happened that summer.

I nodded.

"You helped the Wrights too," Bird said. "They wouldn't have even known the stuff you found out without you." Bird paused, thinking. "They understand that this place is not fair for everyone. You need to understand that too."

"But--"

"No, Zee, this is the hard truth," Bird said. "There are people you will meet who hate and dislike you for no other reason than you look different than them. It's not your fault. It's not anything you can do to change that." Bird pouted. "They have the problem. They are twisted up with hate and meanness and that's on them."

"But--"

"We don't wish bad on anyone," Bird said, raising her hand to stop me. "But we aren't going to go out of our way to help those that would try and hurt us."

"That doesn't sound right," I said.

Bird shrugged her shoulders.

"All I know is that the information you know about the missing Klansmen ain't going to do anyone any good if you share it," Bird said. "Think of it this way," Bird said, pausing. "If you knew that there was a sick and dangerous dog in the neighborhood that threatened to hurt and maybe kill, would you try to save it? Or would you kill it and save the neighborhood?"

*　　*　　*　　*　　*

That Friday night I went to bed thinking about what Bird had said. Some of what she said made sense. Some, though, did not. I thought about the sick dog. Was there no other option? Was there a cure? If there wasn't a cure, could it just be isolated?

I understood what Bird was saying. I did. I knew there were evil and mean people that disliked me even though I had never done anything to them. I knew that. But I couldn't live my life like the mean and evil people.

If I only cared about the people I thought were deserving, then wasn't I just as bad as the mean and evil people who only cared or thought about being friendly to their friends?

That night Bo woke up and found me at my desk. He climbed to his feet as I wrote three of five letters. I had found five envelopes and addressed them.

Bo yawned and I gave him a pat on the head.

"I'm going back to bed in a minute Bo. Go lay down," I said to my loyal companion.

Bo slowly padded back to his spot next to the bed and laid down on his doggie bed.

In a few minutes I finished the third letter. I looked at the two last envelopes on the desk and placed a hand on them. I flipped the two last envelopes over in my hand and placed them back on the desk, undisturbed. My plan, if I had a plan, was to finish the other two letters in the morning.

I crawled back into bed and thought that writing the letters would ease my uncertainty over what I would do next. I slept for a few hours. When the sun rose, I found myself sitting up and ready to write.

Saturday morning, when I woke up, before I walked Bo for the last time in Effingham, I got up and finished the last two letters. Bo stretched and padded around to my desk while I finished the last two letters.

After finishing the letters I took Bo for a walk. When we returned to the kitchen grandpa was sitting and reading the Effingham Daily Record.

"You're up early," Grandpa Clark said from behind his paper.

"Lot of things to do," I said.

Grandpa continued to read the paper.

"Hey, grandpa," I said at the door to the living room. "You think Mister Nelson is up yet?"

Grandpa Clark folded down his paper. He looked at his clock above the door and then back to me.

"He is an early riser," grandpa said. "Give him another thirty before he is up and running around."

"I need to return the bike," I said.

Grandpa nodded.

"Go by closer to eight," grandpa advised.

I went upstairs and peeled off my basketball shorts and T-shirt. I went into the bathroom and washed up and brushed my teeth. I slipped on a clean T-shirt, fresh underwear, jeans, and my basketball sneakers and headed downstairs with Bo by my side.

A little before eight I returned the mountain bike Mister Nelson had so generously loaned me back to grandpa's neighbor.

"You know Zee, you can keep it," Mister Nelson said dressed in T-shirt and sweats. "I can't imagine you not needing a bike and I definitely don't need it as much as you do." Mister Nelson smiled. "Have fun with it."

"Thank you, Mister Nelson," I said and rode the bike back to grandpa's house. I put the bike in the back of the U-Haul.

"Mister Nelson told me to keep it," I said to Mom and Bird.

After breakfast I took Bo on another walk. He was jumpy. I figured it was because he knew we were returning to Chicago.

I walked Bo to Banker Street and as I was heading back to grandpa's house found Frankie standing on Eiche looking at the guarded field. I walked over to him.

"Hey," I said.

Frankie looked and gave a nod.

"What you doing?" I asked.

Bo sniffed Frankie. Frankie reached down and patted Bo on the head.

"Just thinking," Frankie said.

I nodded. Bo sat and listened by my side.

"Heard you're leaving," Frankie said.

I raised and lowered my chin.

"You know this ain't over?" Frankie asked. He got silent for a moment., then added. "There's got to be a way to find Solomon."

I again raised and lowered my chin.

Frankie looked to the left and smiled. I turned and was a little surprised to see Donny and Trey on the corner

"What are you doing here?" I asked the two.

"You guys are leaving," Trey said. "We can't just let you leave without a going away party."

A party? I smiled at the idea. In all the time we had been in Effingham we had never had a party of any kind.

"Where's Bird?" Trey asked.

"I'll get her," I said.

I went into the backyard with Bo and up the stairs to get my sister.

A few moments later Bird appeared all smiles.

"What are you guys doing here?" Bird asked, stepping onto the driveway.

"I just told Zee that we can't let you go without a little going away party," Trey said.

Frankie and Donny were smiling from ear-to-ear.

I could not stop smiling as Paris came walking up the driveway with a paper grocery bag.

Frankie and Donny ran and grabbed the paper bag and Paris continued walking toward Bird.

"Bird, no hard feelings," Paris said. She stopped at arm's reach.

"No hard feelings," Bird said.

"You didn't know?" Paris asked, concerned. "Did you?"

"No," Bird said.

Paris nodded and smiled and gave Bird a big embrace. The two hugged for a long moment.

I smiled at the two getting past the betrayal of Amber James.

Frankie and Donny had six individually sliced pieces of cheesecake. They were all different.

Paris had a slice of strawberry cheesecake. Bird had a piece of chocolate-peanut butter cheesecake. Donny had a slice of blueberry cheesecake. Frankie ate New York cheesecake. Trey ate a slice of chocolate-peanut butter cheesecake. Me, I ate a slice of strawberry cheesecake with Bo watching.

I grabbed Frankie and got his attention.

"Frankie," I said. "Can you give this to Zada Gallamore?"

Frankie looked at the sealed letter in my hand.

"You know she works at the mall at the fashion store," I said.

He nodded. Frankie took the letter and weighed it.

"Any money in it?"

"No," I chuckled. "And thanks for everything," I said.

Trey, at first, gave Bird some space. He edged toward her. He was nearly within arm's reach when I walked toward Trey.

Trey watched me cautiously approach.

I looked at Trey and smiled awkwardly. I lifted my hands as I approached, showing Trey I was unarmed.

"What up?"

"Can you do me a favor?"

Trey looked at me unsure.

I gave Trey a letter to be dropped off at the Effingham Police Department.

Trey examined the letter and pointed out that it wasn't sealed.

"It's okay," I said.

"You sure?"

I nodded.

Trey read the Effingham Police Department letter too, standing in the driveway.

The letter to the Effingham Police Department was simple. In the letter I explained that the missing people would not magically end just because it was the fall. I had written that based on my research Effingham had a serial killer. I told them that I believed the killer was snatching a very specific target. As long as that target was available, he would continue to prey on those men. The disappearances had to continue until the killer was captured. I pointed out that whoever was snatching these men had to be big enough to overpower full grown men. I didn't explain my reasoning. Instead, I wrote that my conclusions were not difficult to determine.

Mom and grandpa came out of the house a little before ten o'clock.

"Hey Mister Clark," Donny said with a small smile.

"Donny," Grandpa Clark said with a crooked smile. "How's your family?"

"Good," Donny said.

"Tell them I said, Hey," grandpa said.

While grandpa and Donny said hello to everyone I searched for Paris.

Near mom's Toyota Paris and Bird were saying their goodbyes.

Seeing Paris so close, I walked to her.

"Paris, can you do me a favor?"

"Sure," Paris said.

Bird watched as I gave Paris a letter to give to the Effingham Daily Record. The contents of the letter to the newspaper were identical to the letter I planned on giving to Trey.

"Zee," Bird said, concerned.

"It's okay," I said to Bird.

Lastly, I looked around and found grandpa. He was talking with mom. I walked up and listened.

"Looks like you are packed and ready to go," Grandpa Clark said checking the U-Haul one last time.

Mom seemed more concerned with grandpa.

"This place is so far from us, dad," Mom said. "I would be more comfortable if you considered moving back to Chicago. You can come up for a few months until this whole missing and dead thing is settled."

"I'll be fine," Grandpa Clark said. He turned to me, ending the conversation with mom.

I smiled under the gaze of my grandfather. I smiled awkwardly, looking at mom and waving two letters at grandpa. Grandpa Clark studied the letters in my hand.

"What's this?"

"A couple of letters," I said with a smile. "Can you drop this one in the mail?"

He took the first letter I offered.

"Who is Reita Carr?" Grandpa Clark asked.

"Just someone I met this summer," I said.

Grandpa nodded.

"I'll put it in the mail for you today," Grandpa Clark said with a tiny smile.

I smiled at my grandpa's smile.

"And this?" He asked, after I handed him another letter. Grandpa narrowed his eyes looking at the letter addressed to him.

"It's my letter to you," I said. "Don't open it until we're on the road," I said.

He nodded.

"Thanks."

Grandpa's letter and the letter to the Effingham Police Department were the only letters not sealed. Grandpa was the first to read his letter while we were pulling out of the driveway.

In his letter I thanked him for opening his home to us. I thanked him for a great summer. I also gave a clear step-by-step explanation of what I deduced. I pointed out that the investigation was not over. I wrote:

"Watch your back, grandpa. There is no South-Central Illinois Werewolf but there is a reason there is a 198-foot cross in Effingham."

I signed all the letters, simply, Zee, amateur sleuth.

Of course, as mom's Toyota Rav4 drove away from Eiche Avenue and down South Banker Street and back up I-57 and toward

Chicago I did not believe the police were really looking to solve these missing person cases. It seemed they were more interested in making Effingham a publicity stop on the way to St. Louis.